RIGHT TO DIE

RIGHT TO DIE

DIE

A JOHN CUDDY MYSTERY

Jeremiah Healy

POCKET BOOKS

New York   London   Toronto   Sydney   Tokyo   Singapore

POCKET BOOKS, a division of Simon & Schuster
1230 Avenue of the Americas, New York, NY 10020

Healy, J. F. (Jeremiah F.), 1948–
  Right to die / Jeremiah Healy.
    p.   cm.
  ISBN: 0-671-70809-0 (hardcover) : $18.95
  I. Title.
PS3558.E2347R54   1991
813'.54—dc20   91-8396
                                                            CIP

First Pocket Books hardcover printing July 1991

10 9 8 7 6 5 4 3 2 1

In memory of
Dennis Schuetz

RIGHT TO
DIE

1

PART OF IT STARTED AS A DARE, SORT OF.

I was thinking how Massachusetts is crazy about giving its citizens days off for events it's not really observing. For example, the third Monday in April is known as Patriots' Day. Supposedly, the Commonwealth closes down to honor those who served in war. Actually, it just excuses us from work for the Boston Marathon. I once warned a friend who'd called me from Texas, a diehard Dallas Cowboys fan, that he'd have a tough time arriving here on Patriots' Day. Awed, he said, "Y'all have a holiday for your football team?" In fact, Suffolk County alone sets aside March 17 for the Wearing of the Green. The Irish pols neutrally dubbed that one "Evacuation Day," commemorating the momentous afternoon the colonists kicked the British troops out of Boston harbor. I've never mentioned Evacuation Day to the Texan; I'm afraid of what he'd think we were celebrating.

Nancy Meagher said, "God, it's freezing!"

She was standing in front of me, my arms joined around her. Or, more accurately, around the tan L. L. Bean parka over bulky ski sweater over long johns that she was wearing. On a brutal Saturday evening in early December we were waiting with forty thousand other hardy souls on Boylston Street, across from the elevated patio of the Prudential Center, for the lighting of the Christmas tree. A

1

fifty-foot spruce is given to the city of Boston each year by the province of Nova Scotia. The gift commemorates something else, but without a masking holiday, I can never remember what it is.

A man on an accordion platform was adjusting a camera and klieg lights. Several hundred smarter folks watched from inside the windows of the Pru Tower or the new Hynes Convention Center. The smell of sausage and peppers wafted from somewhere near the Paris Cinema.

Nancy said, "Unconscionable."

"Sorry?"

"It is unconscionable not to start on time when it's this cold."

Hugging Nancy a little tighter, I looked around at our immediate neighbors. High school and college kids, not dressed sufficiently for the temperature, stamping their feet and stringing together ridiculous curses in the camaraderie of youth. Parents more my age, rubbing the mittened hands of their kids or wiping tiny red noses with wads of tissues pulled from pocket or handbag. A couple of cops in earmuffs, standing stoic but watchful. The crowd was well behaved so far, but occasionally you could hear coordinated shouting. If the Japanese restaurant behind and below us could have put up sake to go, they'd have made a fortune.

The weather really afflicted Nancy, but I was wearing just a rugby shirt under my coat and over my corduroy pants. Some Vikings must have come over the wall in my ancestors' part of County Kerry, because I rarely feel the winter.

To take Nancy's mind off it, I said, "You know, this is where the finish line used to be."

"The finish line?"

"Of the marathon."

No response.

I said, "The *Boston* Marathon?"

She cricked her neck to frown at me. Black hair, worn a little longer since autumn, wide blue eyes, a sprinkling of freckles across the nose and onto both cheeks. "Not all of us are day-labor private investigators, John Cuddy."

"Meaning?"

"Meaning I've lived in this city all my life, and I've never once seen the marathon in person."

"You're kidding?"

2

"It's too cold to kid."

"But the marathon's a holiday."

Nancy shrugged off my arms. "When I was little, traffic was too snarled to come over here from South Boston. When I was in law school, I thanked God for the extra day and studied."

"Nance, even the courthouse closes for the marathon. What's your excuse now?"

"I never knew anybody stupid enough to run that far."

"It's not stupid."

"It is."

"Is not."

She almost smiled. " 'Tis."

" 'Tain't."

"I suppose you think you could run it."

"I suppose I could."

"John, you're too big."

"Six two and a little isn't too big."

"I meant you're too heavy. The guys they show on TV are string beans."

"One ninety and a little isn't that heavy. Besides, I'd train down for it."

"John, anyway you're too . . ."

Nancy tried to swallow that last word, but I'd already heard it. I said, "Too what?"

"Never mind."

"Too old, is what you said. You think I'm too old to run the marathon."

There was a feedback noise from an amplifier. Some "older" men were fiddling with a tall microphone on the patio under the tree. Then a male voice came over the public address system. "On behalf of the Prudential Center, I would like to welcome you to—"

The rest of his comments were drowned out by the swelling cheer of the crowd.

Over the roar I said into Nancy's ear, "Now it's down the street a couple of blocks."

"What?"

"I said, now it's down—"

"What is?"

"The finish line of the marathon. It used to be just about where

3

we're standing. But when Prudential decided to scale back its operations here, the John Hancock agreed to sponsor the race and moved the finish line down almost to the Tower." I pointed to the Hancock, a Boston landmark of aquamarine glass now known more for its sky deck than for the four-by-ten windows that kept sproinging out and hurtling earthward just after it was built.

Nancy didn't turn her head. "Fascinating. And still stupid."

At the mike a priest delivered a longish invocation. I let my eyes drift over to the Empire Insurance building. My former employer. I don't think Empire ever sponsored so much as a Little League team.

The priest was followed by our Mayor Flynn, who was blessedly brief in his remarks. Then the premier of Nova Scotia began an interminable speech that I couldn't follow. Nancy huddled back against me.

About ten feet from us, four guys wearing Boston College varsity jackets started a chant. "Light the fuckin' tree, light the fuckin' tree."

I laughed. Nancy muttered, "You're contemptible."

Finally, Harry Ellis Dickson, the conductor emeritus of the Boston Pops Orchestra, had his turn. He introduced Santa to much squealing and wriggling among the kids, many of whom were hoisted by dads and moms onto shoulders. Then Harry led the crowd through several carols. "O Come, All Ye Faithful," "Joy to the World," "Hark, the Herald Angels Sing." Everybody knew the first few lines, most of us dah-dah-ing the rest.

Between carols Nancy sighed. "We've become a one-stanza society."

Two slim figures in oddly modified Santa outfits danced up the steps of the patio.

Nancy said, "Who are they supposed to be?"

"Santa's eunuchs."

Again she shrugged off my arms. "I take it back. You're beneath contempt."

After a few more carols the star on top of the tree was lit, setting off a reaction in the crowd like the first firecracker on the Fourth of July. The long vertical strips of lights came on next. Then, beginning at the top, sequential clumps mixing red, blue, green, and yellow flashed to life, more a shimmer than individual bulbs, until the magic had hopped down the entire tree.

4

We finished with a universal "Silent Night," the crowd breaking up while the last notes echoed off the buildings.

"Maybe a half each left?"

Nancy shook her head as I held the bottle of Petite Sirah poised over her glass. She had traded the sweater and long johns for a puffy print blouse that brought out the color of her eyes. We were sitting at the dining table of the condo I rented from a doctor doing a program in Chicago. Only a couple of blocks north of the Pru, it was a short but cold walk from the tree-lighting ceremony.

Cold in more ways than one.

Nancy said, "I cooked, so you clean."

I corked the wine and cleared the table of the remains of a pretty good meal of lamb chops with mushroom-and-sausage rice. My praising the food, even its color and arrangement on the plate, hadn't done much to warm Nancy up.

From the kitchen I said, "We can talk about it, or we can brood about it."

No reply.

I loaded the dishwasher and sponged down the sink and counter.

Back in the living room, Nancy was sitting stiffly on the burlappy sofa, using her index finger to swipe tears angrily from the sides of her eyes.

"Nancy—"

"Just shut up, okay?"

I stopped dead.

She said, "I hate to cry."

I believed that. As an assistant district attorney, Nancy had seen an awful lot. A person who cried easily wouldn't get through one of her typical days, much less the couple of years she'd put in.

I said, "Is it one of your cases?"

Shake of the head.

"Medical? Physical?"

"No, dammit, it's you."

"Me?"

"Yes."

"My face? My breath? My—"

"Goddammit, John. It's . . ."

I walked toward her. Not told to stop, I sat next to her.

5

Nancy turned sideways to me, took a breath. "Look, it's not easy for me to talk about my emotions. It never has been."

"Hasn't affected—"

"Don't interrupt, okay?"

"Okay."

She took another breath. "My dad died when I was little, John. Three years old. They didn't have a tree-lighting ceremony in Southie, but even if they had, I didn't have him to swing me up onto his shoulders to watch it. I really don't remember him, not from real life. Just his face in photos, the pictures Mom kept. Holidays, especially Christmas, were hard on her because she did remember him from real life."

I thought back to my holidays with Beth, then to the period after I'd lost her to cancer.

"Once Mom died, my last year of law school, I didn't like the holidays anymore. All I'd had of the early ones was Mom, trying her best to be both parents at once. The later ones, I was always kind of propping her up, keeping her in the spirit of the season. When I rented the Lynches' top floor, they tried to include me in their stuff, but it was awkward, you know? I wasn't anybody's niece or girlfriend or anything. I was just the poor tenant with no place else to go."

"And then?"

"I met you. And for the first time, I thought I had somebody to share the holidays with. Really enjoy them, equal to equal, nobody making up for anything. I've been looking forward to the tree-lighting for weeks, then you behave like a freshman on his first trip to the big city."

I thought she was overreacting, but I said, "I'm sorry, Nance."

"No. No, you're not. You don't even understand what I mean, do you?"

"I understand. I guess what happened in my life just turned me a different direction as far as the holidays go."

She sniffled.

I said, "Maybe you just got under my skin a little over the marathon."

A sour face. "You big turd."

"Finally, a term of endearment."

She punched me on the arm. A little hard, but now playfully. "That rugby shirt doesn't even fit anymore."

6

Standing, I pulled it over my head, whirling it by a sleeve and letting it fly across the room.

Nancy looked at my pants. "Never cared much for those corduroys, either."

Leaning forward, I braced my hands on the back of the sofa to either side of her head. "Lady, are you trying to get me into bed?"

"That depends."

"On what?"

"On how much harder I have to try."

Afterward, we lay in the dark under just a sheet. The window was open a crack, the wind whistling through. I was on my back, Nancy on her side, cuddled up against me.

"John, you ever think it's odd, the way we talk about it?"

"Can't be helped. Catholic upbringing."

"No. I don't mean *us* us. I mean people in general. We call it 'making love.' "

"As opposed to . . . ?"

"I mean, it just sounds so mechanical, almost like a label for some manufacturing process."

"It's worse than that, Nance."

"Why?"

"We tend to say, 'I want to make love to you.' "

"Yes?"

"Using 'to you' makes it sound like a one-way street. Provider to customer."

"How does 'I want to make love with you' sound?"

"Pretty good, except we'll have to wait a while."

She snuggled closer. "Why?"

"Well, a man my age takes two, three weeks to recharge."

Another punch to the arm. "You're still sore from the marathon remark."

"I'm still sore from where you punched me before."

"Man your age, decides to run the marathon, he'd better get used to pain."

I shifted my face to Nancy even though I couldn't see her in the dark. "What makes you think I'm going to run the marathon?"

"The look you gave me after I almost kept from saying you were too old for it."

7

"What kind of look was it?"

"A stupid look."

I shifted again, about to talk to the ceiling, when the telephone rang.

That started the rest of it.

2

"JOHN! GEE, HOW LONG'S IT BEEN?"

Tommy Kramer forgot to take the napkin off his lap as he rose to greet me. It fell straight and true to the floor. Only heavy cloth for Sunday brunch at Joe's American Bar & Grill.

"Tommy, good to see you."

He sat back, crushing a filterless cigarette in an ashtray but not noticing the napkin between his penny loafers. Moving upward, the flannel slacks were gray, the oxford shirt pale blue, the tie a Silk Regent with red background, and the blazer navy blue. Dressing down, for Tommy.

I took in the room's detailed ceilings and mahogany wainscoting, pausing for a moment on the bay window overlooking Newbury Street. The shoppers below bustled around half an hour before the boutiques would open for Christmas-season high rollers. We had a corner all to ourselves, the yuppies holding off until after twelve, when the booze could start to flow.

Tommy's rounded face seemed to lift a little, making him look younger. "You know, my old law firm used to own this place."

"I didn't know. The Boston one, you mean?"

"Right, right. Firm got started before the turn of the century, one of the first in the city to decide to make a Jew a partner. When word leaked out about that, the downtown eating clubs very politely told the firm's established partners, 'Well, you understand, of course, that we can't serve him here.' At which point the partners basically looked at each other, said 'fuck you' to the clubs, and bought a restaurant downtown for lunch meetings and this one here in Back Bay for dinner."

"So they could eat where they wanted."

"With whoever they wanted, including the new Jewish partner."

"The firm still run the place?"

"No, no. Sometime after I went out on my own in Dedham, they sold it. Back then, though, it was heady stuff for a young lawyer like me to be able to walk into one of the finest restaurants in Boston and be treated like the king of Siam."

"Your practice going well?"

"The practice? Oh, yeah, yeah. Couldn't be better. We're at eight attorneys now with the associate we brought in last week. Evening grad from New England."

Nancy's alma mater. "Kathy and the kids?"

"Terrific. She's gone and got her real estate ticket. Salesman, not broker yet, but that'll come in time. She's showing real estate all over town and having a ball. Slow market, like everywhere, but she knows the neighborhoods and the schools. Jason's on the wrestling team, Kit's doing indoor—oh, I get it. If everything's okay on the practice and home fronts, how come I drag you in here on ten hours notice?"

"Something like that."

A waitress in a tux came to the table and asked if we'd like to order. Both of us went with orange juice, eggs Benedict, and a basket of muffins.

When she was beyond earshot, Tommy said, "It's not for me. It's for somebody I owe."

Tommy's oblique way of reminding me that I still owed him for a favor.

"I'm listening."

He coaxed another cigarette from the Camel soft pack. "Okay if I . . . ?"

"The smoke doesn't bother me if the surgeon general doesn't bother you."

A match from the little box on the table flared, giving Tommy for an instant the look of a combat soldier, the curly hair still full enough to mimic a helmet. "Who would've thought, twenty, thirty

10

years ago that someday you'd have to ask permission to light up?"

When I didn't say anything, he took a deep draw, then put the cigarette down, using the thumb and forefinger of his other hand to tweezer bits of tobacco from his tongue. "The guy approached me because he's not a lawyer himself, but he wants confidentiality in sounding you out."

"Tommy, the licensing statute requires me to maintain the confidentiality of whatever the client tells me."

"Right, right. And this guy knows that. It's just . . . well, he wouldn't exactly be the client."

"Somebody wants to talk with me—"

"Wants me to talk with you—"

"But this somebody wouldn't be my actual client?"

"Right."

Our orange juice arrived. I sipped it. Fresh-squeezed, not from concentrate. Like the difference between chardonnay and Ripple. "Okay, I'm still listening."

"A friend of this guy is getting threats."

"Threats. Like over the telephone?"

"Like through the mail. Cut-and-paste jobs using words from magazines."

"The friend of the guy been to the police?"

"Not exactly."

"What exactly?"

"The secretary of the friend of the guy tried—"

"Tommy, this is getting a little out of hand. How about some real names."

He turned that over, shook his head. "How about some titles to make it easier?"

"Titles."

"Until you know whether you're interested or not."

"Okay. Titles."

Tommy pulled on the Camel, wisps of smoke wending out of his nostrils. "The guy I owe, let's call him the Activist. His friend who's getting the threats, let's call the friend the Professor. The Professor's secretary—"

"Tried going to the police."

"Right."

"And?"

"And the cops can't do much. I'm not into criminal law, but I'm assuming they checked the notes for fingerprints or postmarks and all, and came up empty."

"So you want me to do what?"

"I want you to talk to the Activist and the Secretary as my agent, if you're willing."

"As your agent."

"Right."

"Talk to them about what, bodyguarding the Professor?"

"No, no. She—they can talk to you more about that."

"Tommy . . ."

"Look, John, I know this sucks a little, but like I said, I owe the guy."

"The Activist."

"Right."

"Can you at least tell me how you owe this guy?"

Tommy took another puff. "When I was with that firm in Boston, they were real civil rights conscious."

"Good thing to be."

"Yeah, well, most of us young associates signed up as volunteers, whatever, for different causes through the BBA."

"Boston Bar Association?"

"Right, right. I drew . . ."

He stopped, took a puff out of sequence. "I drew this activist, and after I helped him out a couple of times, he started throwing a lot of business my way, business I really needed once I broke off on my own."

"Activist, Professor, Secretary."

"Huh?"

"Tommy, these don't sound like people who need the layers of confidentiality you're throwing up around them."

"John, that's kind of their business, don't you think?"

"Tommy, you want me to meet with them, it's kind of my business, don't you think?"

He put a casual look on his face, checking the room. "This activist, John, he's . . . Alec Bacall."

"Rings a bell somewhere."

"He's a gay activist, John."

Bacall. Majored in housing and employment rights, minored in AIDS issues. "Tommy, the professor here. Maisy Andrus?"

He flinched. "Keep your voice down, okay?"

"The right-to-die fanatic."

Tommy reddened. "She's not—" He caught himself speaking too loudly, our waitress thinking he meant her to come over. Tommy shook her off with an apologetic smile.

More quietly, Tommy said to me, "She's not a fanatic, John. She was a professor of mine, back in law school."

"At Boston College?"

"Right, right. Before she went over to Mass Bay."

I waited for Tommy to say something about my year as a student at the Law School of Massachusetts Bay. He didn't.

I said, "So Andrus was a professor of yours."

"And she helped me get that first job, at the law firm. Letter of recommendation, couple of phone calls, I found out later."

"So you owe her too."

"Yeah."

"And now she's being threatened."

Tommy ground out the cigarette. "Right."

"And she turns to you to turn to me."

"No, no, Alec—Bacall—is the one who called me."

I sat back. Watching him.

"What's the matter, John?"

"Quite a coincidence."

"Huh?"

"You contacting me to maybe help these people who preach the quick-and-happy ending."

Tommy looked very uncomfortable. Which was as good an answer as my next question could bring.

"John, look—"

"Tommy. I lost Beth to cancer, slowly. Bacall pushes the right to die for AIDS victims, Andrus casts a wider net. I'm the first one you think of?"

"John, I'm sorry. I should have . . . Look, I owe these people. From a long time ago, but I owe them. I once mentioned to Alec about Beth. Not directly, just that I could understand his position because I had a good friend who became a private investigator partly because his wife died. I never used your name or Beth's, it was just . . ."

"An example."

"Yeah. I'm sorry, but yeah. Then Alec calls me yesterday, and the guy's got a mind like a steel trap. He remembers me mentioning your situation, John. And he asks me to ask you."

Picking up my orange juice, I pictured Tommy dropping everything to help me with Empire and with Beth. To Tommy bailing me out when I was filling a hospital bed, a bullet hole in my shoulder and a skeptical D.A. on my neck.

"I'll talk to them."

"Great, great. Uh, John?"

"Yes."

"Today maybe?"

Nancy was at work, catching up on some research. After one more stop in the neighborhood, I'd be free for the afternoon.

"Two o'clock, Tommy. My office on Tremont Street."

"Alec said he'd be at the professor's house, so I'll call them now. I really appreciate this, John."

Getting up, Tommy got his feet tangled in the napkin and nearly fell into our waitress and eggs Benedict.

3

"JOHN, YOU WORKING OUT FORMAL NOW?"

Gesturing at my coat and tie, Elie put his Dunkin' Donuts coffee on the front desk. His olive skin and blue eyes were twin legacies from the broad gene pool in Lebanon. Maybe twelve people were using the Nautilus machines in the large room behind him, a separate aerobics class thumping in the back studio.

"I was in yesterday, Elie. You got a minute?"

"Sure, sure. How can I help you?"

I waited for a heavyset man in a Shawmut Bank T-shirt to dismount the Lifecycle closest to the desk and head for the showers.

"Not for publication, but I'm thinking about running the marathon."

A look of concern. "Boston?"

"Right."

"You still doing what, three to five miles?"

"Three times a week. Most weeks, anyway."

"John, I'm not a runner, but if I was as big as you, I wouldn't try it."

"Why not?"

"Running is awful tough on the joints over the longer distances. Your size and weight, there's going to be a lot of stress on the knees, hips, even the ankles."

"Can't I train for that?"

"I don't think you can train without that. But like I said, I'm not a runner, and unfortunately, nobody on the staff here is. Biking and rowing, sure. But the marathon? No."

"How can I find somebody?"

"You mean like to train you? That costs a fortune. Tell you what. I can go through some magazines at the library."

"Magazines?"

"Yeah, like *Runner's World,* that kind of thing. They got to have an article on doing your first marathon."

"Elie, I don't want you to go to any trouble."

"No trouble, really. They're all out in the open, second floor."

"Elie, thanks but no. I can check the library on my own. Any other suggestions?"

The concerned look again. "Friend to friend?"

"Yes."

"Don't do it."

"Did Nancy get to you?"

"Nancy who?"

"Never mind."

By the time I left Elie, it was pretty sunny, so I walked downtown along Commonwealth Avenue. Commonwealth begins at the Public Garden and rambles forever westward. Over the first ten blocks, a wide center strip hosts civic statues and grand Dutch elms that so far have survived both the disease and occasional hurricanes. With a dusting of snow, my route would have been a postcard.

Midway through the Public Garden, I stopped on the bridge spanning the Swan Pond. In warmer weather the city raises the water level to provide swan boat rides. In colder weather the city lowers the water level to form a rink. Tourists with cameras, many of them Asian, stood at the edges of the ice, taking pictures of some locals playing pick-up hockey. None of the skaters was very good, but Boston does have the knack of creating photo ops at every time of the year.

Crossing Charles Street, the Common was bleaker, as usual. Centuries ago, the site really was used in common by farmers for grazing their livestock. Now the three-card-monte dealers and souvenir wagons had flown south for the winter, replaced by raggedy runaways hopeful of peddling themselves for a warm bed and manageable abuse. Further on, groups of three or four men stood around benches, glancing in every direction while gloved hands traded glassine envelopes or plastic vials for folded currency.

My office was in a building on Tremont, near the Park Street subway station. Derelicts clustered in irregular patterns around the entrances to the station, grateful for the canned heat from below and the solar variety from above. A few jerked up their heads as they became aware of how close I would come to them. I looked away to calm their fears of being rousted.

There used to be a lot of pigeons on the Common. Now there are a lot of homeless people and not so many pigeons. You figure it out.

I used my key to get into the building, taking the elevator up to my office. On a piece of paper, I wrote "Cuddy, ring bell" and drew an arrow underneath. Back downstairs, I taped the directions to the glass door. Then I returned to the office to kill some time and paperwork, waiting for two o'clock.

They made a striking pair, if not quite a couple.

Alec Bacall ("Call me Alec, please") was as tall as I am but slim, with a ramrod posture and a steel-clamp handshake to go with the steel-trap mind. Pushing forty, his hair was still the color of wheat and probably streaked toward platinum if he spent much time outdoors in the summer. The Prince John beard and mustache were a shade darker, clipped so perfectly that trimming might be a daily exercise. Bacall wore a light gray suit with double-pleated pants. His shirt was a long-point requiring a collar stay. The paisley tie was woven in a pattern that catalogs caption "ancient madder." Bacall sat in one client's chair, or friend of client's chair, and crossed his right leg over the left.

Inés Roja ("I am the secretary of Professor Andrus") wore very little makeup and needed less. Early twenties and perhaps five two in sensible shoes, she had lustrous black hair wound into a bun, high cheekbones, and irises that were almost black. Wearing a simple blue suit with schoolgirl blouse, Roja held a burgundy briefcase on her lap and crossed her ankles as she sat in my other client's chair. Or secretary of client's chair.

Bacall said, "Perhaps it would be easier if you were to tell us what Tommy has already told you. So that we won't bore you with details you already know."

17

"Tommy wants me to keep this as lawyerly as possible, Mr. Bacall—"

"Alec, John."

"Alec, so maybe it would be safer for you to tell me what you think the situation is."

Bacall used his left index finger to touch both lips, then said, "I'll try. Then you can ask anything you want. Inés, please feel free to jump in anytime."

Bacall looked at the woman only as he spoke her name, coming back to me with the rest of the sentence. I got the impression Roja didn't feel all that free to jump in.

"Maisy Andrus is a full professor of law, meaning with tenure, at the Law School of Massachusetts Bay. She's been a controversial figure in legal education for some time, but I'm not versed enough in legal theory to give you all the ins and outs of why. Her stand on the right to die is what draws most of the fire. She's put her money where her mouth is, so to speak."

"How do you mean?"

"Well, Maisy was never a poor woman, but after graduating from law school she made some shrewd investments with family money, and her writing and lectures have pulled in a good deal more. She also was involved in, well, the incident in Spain."

"Somebody in her family, right?"

"Her husband. Or former husband, more precisely. A Spanish doctor named Enrique Cuervo Duran. A virtual Dr. Schweitzer in his own country, but suffering horribly toward the end from a stroke. He was considerably older than Maisy."

"You ever meet him?"

"No. Oh, no, I've known Maisy for only . . . what, eight years now? The tragedy with Dr. Duran was all in the seventies, just after the generalissimo died."

"Who?"

"Franco."

The little I knew about Franco I'd learned from *Saturday Night Live*. "I remember reading an article that claimed Professor Andrus helped—sorry, do you use the word 'euthanasia'?"

"Actually, 'help' is just fine, John. It's both descriptive and down-to-earth. Maisy used humane means at hand to help the doctor end his agony. An injection."

I was thinking, "easy to say," when Roja did jump in.

"Perhaps, Alec, if we could show Mr. Cuddy the letters, he would see the problem we are bringing to him."

She spoke precisely, a Hispanic accent beneath New York–accented English.

Bacall sat back. "Good idea."

Roja unzipped the briefcase and fished out a couple of sheets. "These are Xerox copies of the three letters."

I reached across the desk as she passed them to me. Calling them letters was being generous. In scissored syntax, with words of varying size and background, all were pretty similar.

The first read, "ONLY GOD NOT YOU CU-NT," the "CU" in the last word from a different source than the "NT."

The second read, "THEY DIE YOU DIE BIT-CH," with different sources for the last word again.

The third read, "YOUR TIME COMES SOON SLUT," the letters in the final word all from the same source.

"Any physical contact by the sender?"

They said no together.

"How about the telephone?"

Bacall said, "Not connected to these."

I laid the copies of the letters on the desk as though I were dealing solitaire. "Which arrived first?"

Roja said, "Like this," pointing to each in the order I'd read them.

"How did they arrive?"

She said, "The first two by mail to the professor's office at the law school."

"And the third?"

Bacall said, "By hand. In her mailbox."

"Mailbox? Like a faculty mailbox?"

"No, John. At her home."

I thought about it.

Bacall added, "Maisy has a town house on Beacon Hill. The third note was in with the delivered mail but not stamped."

"Where are the originals?"

Bacall said, "Inés?"

Roja indicated the "ONLY GOD" note. "When I opened the first, I told the professor. She said not to worry, but I kept it anyway.

19

When I opened the second, I called Alec. I told him I wanted to go to the police. He told me just to call them, so I did. But they did not seem very interested, the police."

Bacall said, "When the third one arrived, Inés contacted me again. I told her this time maybe she'd better go to the police with the things."

I said to Roja, "And did you?"

"Yes. I went to the police, and I brought the letters with me. They told me they cannot do much, but they kept the originals and told me to call if we get another one."

"Did you bring them the envelopes too?"

"The first one, no. I tore it up when I was upset about the letter in it. The second one, yes, and the third one too."

"Name and address the same as the notes?"

"I do not understand?"

"On the envelopes. Were there cut-and-paste words like on the letters themselves?"

"Oh. Yes, yes."

"Postmarks?"

"Here in Boston."

"So the police have the originals."

"Yes."

I looked at the sheets on my desk. Bright, clear duplicates. "And they made these copies for you?"

Roja said, "No. I made them. At the law school."

"You made them."

"Yes."

"Why?"

She looked at me as though I were born without a brain. "I am a secretary, sir. I make a copy before I give away the original of the document."

I said to Bacall, "You go with her to the cops?"

"No."

"Why not?"

Bacall smiled, arching an eyebrow. "I don't always bring out the best in peace officers."

I said to Roja, "Where did you go to the police?"

"I called the headquarters on Berkeley Street after the second letter. Then I called them again after the third one, and they told me to go see the police by the Government Center."

Area A station house, the division that encompasses Beacon Hill. A simple complaint about unsubstantiated threats wouldn't be taken too seriously, especially when directed against a lightning rod like Andrus.

"Do you remember who you spoke to there?"

"Detective William K. Neely." Roja dug into the briefcase and produced a business card which she passed across the desk. "He did not want to give me that, but I insisted and so he did."

I handed her back the card. "Does the professor receive a lot of threats?"

Bacall said, "Ten, twelve a week. More after a lecture or TV spot."

"Like these?"

"Oh, worse. Vicious voices on the phone, photos of aborted fetuses, nasty packages through United Parcel with the remains of dead animals laminated inside them. Imagination is one capacity our opponents do not lack."

"Then why are you reacting to these?"

"Because most of the hate mail Maisy gets is signed, you see, names and return addresses. Expecting a direct response, believe me."

"And these are anonymous."

Roja broke in. "And we have never before had one delivered by hand to the professor's home."

I gathered the sheets into a pile. "Does the professor share your concern?"

Bacall and Roja exchanged glances.

He said, "Well, no. It takes rather a lot to get Maisy concerned."

"Then it doesn't exactly sound like she's interested in hiring me as an investigator, and I'm not much for bodyguarding."

Roja said, "The professor does not need a bodyguard."

Bacall caught himself starting to smile. "Maisy doesn't need a bodyguard because she already has one."

I looked from one to the other. "I don't get it."

Bacall said, "A man her former husband befriended and raised in Spain. Manolo's really more of a house servant, but he never strays far from her side."

"You keep saying 'former husband.' She's remarried?"

"Yes. Tucker Hebert."

"The tennis player?"

21

"He'll be pleased to hear you remembered him."

"Please, sir." Roja thrust her head forward, the eyes and mouth set for imploring. "I believe, and Alec believes, that the professor could be in real danger. We need you to help us."

"It sounds more like you need someone to convince Ms. Andrus that she should take this seriously. Without her cooperation, there's not much I can do."

Bacall sat forward. "John, let me be perfectly frank here. Inés and I both have a bad feeling about this. I can't tell you it's completely rational, because feelings aren't rational to start with. But we both believe someone should be looking into this, and I agree that you can't do much without Maisy's cooperation. However, that's why you are the perfect person to help us."

"I don't see it."

"Maisy is terribly concerned about appearing invincible to the public. Hence our concern about confidentiality with Tommy and with you."

Bacall dropped both the tone and the pace of his voice. "And there is another factor too. Some time ago, Tommy told me about your wife, John. It's precisely because of your experience that Maisy might let you look into this for her."

I shifted in my chair. "Spell it out."

As Bacall hesitated, Roja said, "Mr. Cuddy, we respect your decision in your own life. What Alec means is that the professor would not speak to most investigators we could find, but she would be . . . interested in you."

"Because she'd see me as a whipping boy for her own views?"

"No," said Bacall. "Because she'd see you as someone who understood her views but hadn't embraced them. She'd find that . . . interesting, as Inés said."

"And if I don't especially feel like being a convert-in-waiting?"

Bacall sat up straighter. "I imagine that you often have to pose as someone other than who you are. We aren't asking that here. We're simply asking that you be yourself, the man Tommy described to me, so that Maisy will receive the professional help she requires despite herself."

There was a certain dignity in the way Bacall made his argument. He seemed to care as much about stating his position accurately as about ultimately persuading me of it.

22

Roja said, "Please, Mr. Cuddy?"

"Okay, I'll meet with her. Then it's her decision and my decision from there."

Bacall said he'd call me at home that night with details. Roja just said thank you.

4

MONDAY MORNING THE CLOCK RADIO WOKE ME UP AT SIX-THIRTY.
I had stayed at the office for a while Sunday afternoon, then walked
home via Newbury Street to do some window shopping toward
Nancy's Christmas. By the time I'd gotten back to the condo, Alec
Bacall had left a message on my telephone tape machine, telling me
to come to the law school by ten-thirty A.M. Monday and ask the
security guard for Inés Roja. The four hours gave me plenty of time.

After using the bathroom, I heeded the weather forecast by pulling on a T-shirt and Puma shorts under an outer layer of sweatshirt
and sweat pants with elastic cuffs. I laced up the running shoes I'd
broken in over the prior few months and contemplated my first
training run toward the marathon.

The longest distance I'd ever done before was a little under six
miles, but that was in the summer, when I carried less weight. I
figured the seven or so miles to Harvard Square and back would be
just the ticket for burning off the extra pounds from Thanksgiving.

I figured wrong.

The condo I rented was in the rear of a brownstone on the corner
of Beacon and Fairfield. Coming out the front door of my building,
I could just about see the pedestrian ramp rising above Storrow
Drive to the running and biking paths along the Charles River.

The wind was blowing fifteen miles an hour from a northeastern

24

sky that understudied snow, the temperature in the high twenties. As I approached the ramp, a homeless man sat against the foundation of the expensive high-rise catercorner from my brownstone. He was wearing a bunch of tatty sweaters under a brown tweed sport jacket. The jacket's seams burst across the shoulders, a wilted red carnation in the lapel. His soiled Washington Redskins watch cap was pulled over the ears, his eyeglasses taped at the nose and both temples. He waved to me as I passed him on the other side of the street. I waved back, crossed over Storrow on the ramp, and started west.

Halfway to Harvard Square, I'd already perspired through the T-shirt and into the sweats. At the Larz Anderson bridge, I decided to turn around instead of going uphill into the square itself. Even so, as soon as I reversed direction, I was running into the teeth of the wind. Soaking wet.

My hands got cold first.

My feet got cold next.

My legs chimed in third.

By the time I reached the Boston University bridge, maybe a mile and a half to go, my head and chest both hurt. My pace flagged, meaning more steps to finish, but I didn't see that I had much choice.

I wheezed to the Massachusetts Avenue bridge, breaking down to a trot and finally a walk. A fast walk, because as soon as I stopped running, my teeth began to chatter.

There are a few public benches upriver of the Fairfield ramp. The bum in the Redskins hat was sitting on one of them. As I drew even with him, my right calf cramped. I stopped walking to stand still on it, then tried to stretch it, using a tree as support for my palms.

A voice behind me said, "A little of that beforehand'd do you a world of good."

I turned my head. The bum on the bench nodded. Without replying, I turned my head back to the tree.

He said, "Might also run into the wind first. You won't sweat so much, and on the homeward leg, you'll be going with her and feeling cozy."

I gritted my teeth and over my shoulder said, "Right."

"But consider the source, eh?"

This time I turned completely around. The man's voice had the singsong quality of Frank Perdue hucking chickens. The eyes behind the glasses were alert, almost jovial. What hair I could see sticking

25

out from under the hat looked black and gray, the three-day growth on his cheeks and chin grayer still.

I said, "Sorry. Thanks for the advice."

"Another thing?"

"Yeah?"

"You won't ever get to the marathon, much less finish her, without changing your stride some."

Watching him, I put my fists on my hips and tried walking gingerly. The cramp was still there, but not as compelling. "The marathon."

"That's right."

"What makes you think I'm aiming at that?"

"Everything. It's cold enough, the fair-weather folks are on treadmills or stationary bikes somewheres, comparing their portfolios with the person next to them. You're out here, early enough in the morning, but you obviously don't know how far you can go in this weather and that kind of outfit. Or much about your own endurance curve and how to build it. Oh, the shoes are beat up, so you haven't been on your dead ass all year, but basically you don't have a clue how to condition yourself."

"Anything else?"

"Yeah. You're the right age too."

I stared at him. "The right age."

"Yeah. The age where you start wondering, 'Can I really do it?' That wondering, that gives you the look."

"I've got the look too, huh?"

"Like Rocky in that first training scene, where he gets to the monument steps and looks like he's maybe gonna infarct."

I laughed. Which made me shiver and reminded me how cold I was. I shook my head and turned to go.

"One suggestion about that stride?"

I stopped. "Yeah?"

"Man your size has to lengthen his stride a little, cover more ground. Otherwise, you're gonna pound your knees to powder, all the steps you'll be taking in training. Only two ways to lengthen the stride. One's to lunge with the front foot. Bad in more ways than you got time to hear. Other way's to push off with your back foot a little more, use the quads at the front of your thighs to kind of launch that back leg into the next stride. Try that, the longer distances'll come a little easier."

Made sense. "Thanks again."

The man stood up. In a quieter voice he said, "Better get yourself inside and warm now," and began moving upriver, hands in the side pockets of his jacket.

I said, "Hey?"

"Yeah?"

"Why all the free advice?"

The man stopped, turned partway. I didn't think he was going to say anything, then he spoke quickly. "When I was sitting against that skyscraper over there?"

"Yes?"

A shrug and the quieter voice again. "You waved back."

After showering I wolfed down a couple of English muffins and a quart of ice water. I put on a suit and tie, then started walking to the South End.

Boston has law schools like New York has museums, seven all told. Harvard is Harvard. Boston College and Boston University are both solid institutions often confused with each other by people from out of state. The schools with the most interesting histories are New England (founded to give women the opportunity to study law) and Suffolk (founded to give male immigrants the same). Northeastern's co-op program fills the niche for people who want to alternate school and on-the-job training.

Mass Bay thought it could fill a niche too. In the late sixties some entrepreneurs figured they could prosper on the baby boomers' abject horror of graduating college and having nowhere to spend their parents' remaining money. Even though both New England and Suffolk offered long-established evening divisions, Mass Bay felt it also could cash in on full-time employees who wanted part-time law study. After getting back from Vietnam, I was one.

Given that my stipend under the G.I. Bill would cover most of the tuition, a career counselor at Empire allowed as how it wouldn't be a bad idea for me to do one year of law school. I chose Mass Bay because I hadn't been what you'd call a scholar during my undergraduate days at Holy Cross. Also, I did about as well on standardized tests like the LSAT as Ray Charles would shooting skeet. The only standardized number Mass Bay cared about was 98.6, and the school was located within blocks of Empire's office tower. At the end of the year my grades were a little better than average, but I knew the law and I would not enjoy each other over the course of a lifetime. So I simply didn't register the following fall.

Mass Bay's first and only building was a converted armory, the facade of pink granite and turrets still impressive. The security desk was just inside the entrance, only a few students sitting on plastic chairs in a linoleum lobby.

"Help you?" said the guard, a pensioner with a green uniform shirt, khaki pants, and no tie or badge.

The clock on the wall told me I was ten minutes late. "I'm here to see Inés Roja."

The guard moved something around in his mouth. "Good luck to you." He pushed a button on an old-fashioned switchboard and said into the receiver, "Inés, you expecting somebody? . . . Didn't say . . ." He looked up at me. "Yeah, yeah, that's him. . . . Right."

Hanging up, he pointed to the elevator at the back of the lobby. The only elevator. "Take that to three and turn left. Can't miss it."

"Thanks. Kind of quiet, isn't it?"

"Kids are out for Christmas already, you can believe it. We're in special session now." He spoke the phrase the way a prison guard would say "rehabilitation therapy."

When the elevator doors opened on three, Inés Roja didn't give me a chance to turn left.

Pulling back the cuffed sleeve of a copper-colored suit, she checked her watch. "The professor teaches at eleven. I will take you to the classroom. After that you and she can return to the office to talk."

"Wait a minute. I'm going to sit through a whole class hour before I talk with her?"

"It will not be as long as an hour. It is the initial meeting of special session, so it will be short. The professor wants you to see her in the classroom. Please?"

Roja got on the elevator with me, and we rode down to the second floor. She indicated a door marked 205. The room I'd sat in for my first-year courses.

"Please, go in and make yourself comfortable."

From what I remembered about 205, that would be quite a trick.

5

"TAKE YOUR SEATS, PLEASE."

Shuffling mixed with comments and laughter as thirty or so students arranged themselves in the classroom that could hold seventy-five. Unlike my day, the ratio of women to men was now almost fifty-fifty.

The room itself hadn't changed, though. Floor flat rather than pitched, tiled rather than carpeted. Fixed, narrow tables in straight lines. Fixed, narrow benches as well, the backs too low and at right angles to seats too shallow. It was as though an extraterrestrial designer had been told the function of the room without being shown the human bodies that would occupy it for hours at a time.

A slightly raised stage was centered at the front of the room, a blackboard on the wall behind Maisy Andrus. She looked at her notes on the podium, then looked at us and said, "Welcome to the special session course, Ethics and Society."

Andrus came down off the stage and began moving around the room, a trial attorney opening to the jury. She was even more imposing at floor level. Nearly six feet tall in one-inch heels, she had auburn hair swept up from her ears and back behind her neck, sprigs of gray here and there. The face was boxy but attractive, Germanic or Scandinavian in cast.

Andrus wore a yellow sweater-dress gathered loosely by a teal sash at the waist, the hem riding a bit above her knees. She spoke about the required text, office hours, and other housekeeping details of the course. Her manner reminded me of a black Special Forces captain in basic training who ran the TTIS, the Tactical Training of the Individual Soldier, the most miserable obstacle course I ever experienced.

". . . and regarding class hours, your attendance and punctuality are not just expected, they are required. Sufficiently severe absence, especially in a four-week course such as this one, will be grounds for barring you from the examination. Effective class participation can raise your grade. Ineffective, incompetent participation can have the opposite effect. Effective participation requires preparation of the written materials assigned for discussion as though you were the lead counsel litigating that case. You by now have the expectation of being treated like the budding lawyers you are. Appreciate that I will hold you to the standard such professionals are expected to attain and maintain."

Every head, male and female, followed Andrus. Each student had a notebook open and a pen or pencil in hand, but nobody took notes. No one even smiled or jabbed a neighbor in the ribs. All were focused on her.

A blocky man in a continental suit and old-fashioned pompadour had come into 205 with Andrus. Pompadour sat, arms folded and feet flat on the floor, watching her with the rest of us. Just occasionally he glanced over at me, seeming not to care if I noticed him doing it. I bet myself that Pompadour was the house servant Alec Bacall had called Manolo. If so, Manolo was acting very much like a bodyguard.

". . . and now, a little warm-up for tomorrow's session." Andrus swung her head once in an arc of the room, then pointed to a gawky kid with blond hair. "Male student in the maroon shirt. Stand, please."

I'd never seen this before. The kid got to his feet.

"Your name?"

"Uh, Dave."

"Your last name."

"Oh, uh, Zimmer."

"Mr. Zimmer, do you believe in the use of torture to extract information from someone under governmental control?"

30

Zimmer blinked.

"Mr. Zimmer?"

"Could you repeat—"

"It's a rather simple question, Mr. Zimmer. Torture, yes or no?"

"No. Uh, no, I don't believe in that."

"Why not?"

"Why?"

"W-h-y. Why don't you believe in it?"

"Well, because . . . it's not right."

"Why isn't it right?"

Zimmer took a quick look around the room. No volunteer sent up a hand to take the heat off him, and I sensed that none would.

"Mr. Zimmer. Today, please?"

"Because it's an invasion of the right of a citizen."

"The right not to be tortured by one's own government?"

"Yes."

"Why?"

"Why is that an invasion?"

"Yes."

Zimmer seemed to rally a little. "Because the government's supposed to exist to defend a citizen from invasion of his rights, not to do—"

"His or her, Mr. Zimmer."

"Excuse me?"

"In this class, if you refer to a person who hasn't been identified as a man or woman, you will use 'he or she,' 'his or her.' In the real world, you must not run the risk of offending your audience. This is especially important if the 'person' involved is a client or an authority figure in the system, like a judge. Now, Mr. Zimmer, please restate your point."

Zimmer inhaled. "The government's job is to protect a citizen's rights, not to invade his or her rights itself."

"And, ultimately, why is that, Mr. Zimmer?"

"Why . . . ?"

"Why is it that government is to defend its citizens from invasion of their rights?"

"Because everybody has the right to life."

"I see." Andrus turned and pointed to a brunette woman who had squirreled herself in the farthest corner of the room. "Female student, pink blouse. Stand, please."

31

Rising, the woman knocked her notebook askew, the pen rolling off the page and down onto the floor in front of her table.

"Your name, please?"

The woman seemed to speak to her departed pen. "Queenan."

Andrus cupped a hand to her ear and said, "I can't hear you."

The woman lifted her head and boomed a little. "My name is Queenan."

Andrus nodded. "Ms. Queenan, do you agree or disagree with Mr. Zimmer's position?"

Hopelessly, Queenan looked at Zimmer, who had folded his hands in a fig-leaf pose of prayer.

"Ms. Queenan?"

"I agree that a government shouldn't use torture on its citizens."

"Just its 'citizens,' Ms. Queenan?"

"I'm sorry?"

"Your rule of no torture would apply only to protect the citizens of the country involved, not visiting tourists or resident aliens?"

"No. I mean, yes, the government shouldn't use torture on anyone."

"On anyone. Mr. Zimmer, agree or disagree."

"Uh, I agree."

"Because you hold human life of any citizenship sacred, correct?"

"Correct."

"Ms. Queenan?"

"Right. I mean, I agree with that."

"Is that a pretty basic principle for you, Ms. Queenan?"

"Basic?"

"Yes, basic. Bedrock belief. The sanctity of human life above all else."

"Well, yes, I guess so."

"You guess so."

"I mean, yes. Definitely."

"Definitely. Mr. Zimmer, definitely for you also?"

"Yes."

"Very well, then. Mr. Zimmer, a deranged man has kidnapped a four-year-old girl from outside a day care center. He has placed her in a homemade coffin, with only a limited air supply. By great luck, someone saw the man near the center, and the police have arrested him. There is no doubt the man in custody is the kidnapper. He even boasts that the girl has only three hours of air remaining.

You are the highest-ranking police officer available, Mr. Zimmer. Do you authorize torture to extract from the man the location of the girl in the coffin?"

Zimmer looked at Queenan, but she was staring at her notebook as though it were the Holy Grail.

"Mr. Zimmer, yes or no?"

"No. I'd have my cops search his house and all first."

"Excellent idea, Mr. Zimmer. Ms. Queenan, same hypothetical, only now you are the police commander and the search has come up empty. Any other suggestions, or is it torture?"

"No." Queenan seemed to spark a little, even copying the rhythm of Andrus' speech pattern. "No, it's never torture."

"Never."

"That's right."

"You'd never break your rule of no torture."

"That's right."

"And why is that, again?"

"Because human life is sacred."

"All human life."

"Yes."

"Including the little girl's?"

Queenan pondered that.

"Ms. Queenan?"

Zimmer spoke. "That's not fair."

Andrus turned on him, but more excited than angry. "What's not fair, Mr. Zimmer?"

"You're putting her in an impossible position."

"Am I?"

"Yes. You're asking her to sacrifice her principle."

"No, I'm not. I've been asking Ms. Queenan, and you, if you agree with a given rule of society, and then I've been asking you about the ethic you have that drives that rule, that justifies it. Both of you seem to think that the no-torture rule makes sense, and both apparently for the same ethical reason, the sanctity of human life. Now I'm just asking Ms. Queenan a simple question. Ms. Queenan, how about it? Is the kidnapper's life more important than the little girl's?"

"No. I mean, they're equally important."

"Equally," said Andrus. "Let me get this straight. No doubt that the girl will die from lack of air if the police don't find her."

"All right."

"And no doubt that the police have the right man. Both an eyewitness and his own confirming confession."

"Yes."

"But still no torture?"

Queenan looked around the room. For the last few minutes every head had moved to each player in turn, like a tennis audience at match point.

Queenan said, "If I use torture, I save this girl, but I open up a lot of people to torture in the future."

"So you let the girl die."

"I have to. I mean, otherwise I break this rule and everybody might get tortured."

"Mr. Zimmer. Do you let the girl die?"

Zimmer took a very deep breath. "No."

"No?"

"No. I torture the guy to save her."

"You do? Why?"

"Because she's more innocent than he is. Also, if I torture him, maybe nobody dies. If I don't, we know she'll die."

"Ms. Queenan, does Mr. Zimmer's new logic persuade you?"

"No. I mean, no, it's not new logic. Now he's sacrificing his principle."

"Sacrificing his principle. Mr. Zimmer, are you doing that?"

"No. If the principle behind the rule is to have the government protect human life, then torturing him advances that principle."

"How, Mr. Zimmer?"

"Torturing the kidnapper saves her life without killing him."

Andrus said, "Ms. Queenan, if you don't save the girl by torture, haven't you let your rule control the reason or ethic behind the rule instead of the other way around, instead of the ethic or reason controlling the rule?"

Queenan shook her head. "I don't know."

"Not acceptable, Ms. Queenan. That answer is not acceptable in this class. You must always come up with a response to an opponent's argument. Otherwise, the opponent has won. To close this hour, let me make an argument you might have made, an argument I'll be asking several of you to pursue next time. Mr. Zimmer?"

"Yes?"

"Mr. Zimmer, what if he dies?"

"What . . . ?"

"What if, in torturing the kidnapper, he has a heart attack and dies before telling you where the girl is?"

Zimmer opened and closed his mouth twice before saying, "Then I broke the rule and got nothing for it."

For the first time since she'd left the stage at the beginning of the class, Andrus returned to the podium. "Did you? Or did you, and Ms. Queenan, find yourselves in a conflict between rule and purpose, between the rule you use to protect society and the purpose you had in mind in imposing the rule on society to protect it. These conflicts will arise, and you must learn to reason them through even if they present unattractive alternatives for action. We shall see you next time."

Andrus closed her own notes and exited the classroom immediately. Manolo of the Pompadour jumped up and elbowed a male student out of the way to follow her.

A black woman sitting next to Zimmer stood, clapping him on the shoulder. "Hey, Zim. Gonna be a long season, I'm thinking."

With the change of class, more students were milling around in the halls. By the time I found my prospective client's office, Andrus was nowhere in sight. Manolo was sitting in the anteroom, next to a desk with a little brass pup tent on it saying INÉS L. ROJA. Eyes on me and palms on his knees, he pushed himself to a standing position that blocked access to an inner doorway behind him.

Roja came quickly through the inner door, stepping between us. Reluctantly, Manolo's face left me to look at her.

Moving her lips very slowly and using some kind of sign language, Roja said, "He is here to help the professor."

After watching carefully, Manolo moved his head up and down once. More a wrenching than a nod, accompanied by an abrupt hand signal. Simmering, he sat down, again palms to knees.

Roja said to me, "Manolo is very protective of the professor."

"Is he armed?"

"No. But helping her is his purpose in life."

"And every life should have a purpose."

Roja didn't seem sure I wasn't joking. "Yes, I believe that." She reached to her telephone console and pushed a button twice. "You may go in now."

I opened the inner door and entered an office that was awash in papers. Some were stacked haphazardly on tables and chairs. Other piles had slumped against walls and onto windowsills. Trapped in a corner was a computer that seemed accessible only by helicopter. On the desk in front of Maisy Andrus several books peeked out from a mass of yellow legal pads, pink message slips, and dog-eared photocopies.

Andrus stood and smiled in a receiving-line way. "Mr. Cuddy."

"Not 'male detective, gray suit'?"

Shaking hands, the smile went lopsided. "Sit, please."

Back in her chair, Andrus fixed me with an interrogation look. "You don't care for my teaching technique?"

"That depends."

"On what?"

"On what level students you're using it with."

Andrus picked up a pencil. "Would you explain what you mean?"

"It seems to me that what you were doing in there was boot camp. Kind of tear them down before you build them back up."

"Let's assume you're correct. Therefore?"

"Therefore I'd think it was something you'd do with first-year students, not upper-level kids taking a short course on ethics and society."

Andrus tapped the pencil silently on the only corner of her desk blotter visible under the mess. "You attended law school, Mr. Cuddy."

"Yes."

"Where?"

"Here."

"But you never graduated."

"That's right."

"Are you curious how I knew these things?"

"No."

"No?"

"Ms. Andrus, it's your nickel, so we can play around as much as you'd like. I used the expression 'first-year' instead of 'freshman.' I knew Ethics and Society would be an upper-level course. Accordingly, it's a good bet I attended law school. But I went here, and you hadn't heard of me, which probably means I'm not a grad who decided to become a detective, because that's the kind of oddity that would get around the halls. So you could have deduced that I attended but didn't graduate law school, or you could just have asked Tommy Kramer. Either way, I'm not curious about how you know these things."

Andrus appeared pensive. "You're acting out a bit. Could it be because you feel a little uncomfortable being back at your old, almost alma mater?"

She had a point. "Maybe. Sorry."

"Nothing to be sorry about. Tell me, why did you leave law school?"

"I didn't think it had all the answers."

"Is 'it' law school or the law itself?"

"Both."

Andrus shook her head. "Losing faith in law school is all right. We must occasionally lose faith in most means in order to eventually improve both means and end. But the law itself, you must never lose your faith in the law, Mr. Cuddy. The law is what protects us all."

"St. Thomas More?"

The lopsided smile again. "Yes."

"Pre–Henry the Eighth, anyway."

Andrus gave me a real smile, one that made her seem ten years younger with aggressive good looks. "Alec has always had a capacity for finding good people. Tell me truly, what did you think of the class just now?"

Let the games continue. "I've never seen people have to stand before."

"It helps get them over the butterflies of presenting in public. Also, I'm terrible with names, and making them stand helps me to remember them, at least in the short term. But I really meant, what did you think of my hypothetical?"

"The Dirty Harry thing?"

"I can no longer rely on the students having read the classics, Mr. Cuddy. So, I disguise subliminally familiar movies or television shows as my hypos. Again, what did you think of it?"

"I think torture is a serious matter. I think you do your students a disservice by abstracting it and then making it seem they have no way out of an intellectual puzzle."

"Have you ever witnessed torture, Mr. Cuddy?"

I thought back to the basement of a National Police substation in Saigon. Suspected Viet Cong subjected to bamboo switches, lit cigarettes, telephone crank boxes and wires. Walls seeping dampness, the mixed stench of body wastes and disinfectant, the screams—

"Mr. Cuddy?"

"No, Professor, I've never seen torture."

She looked at me more carefully, her lips pursing. "I'm sorry. Truly."

"Like you said before, nothing to be sorry about."

Andrus exhaled once. "The notes I received, Mr. Cuddy. What is your professional opinion of them?"

"I'm no lab technician, and I haven't talked to the police about what they may have found on the originals."

"I meant . . . do you believe I have anything to fear from the author?"

"Nobody could tell you that, even psychiatrists after examining the guy."

"You're assuming it's a man."

"From the words used to describe you, yes."

A nod. "Mr. Cuddy, I have received many threats. Half the unsolicited mail that arrives here disagrees with my position in a way that could be interpreted as threatening."

"But most sign their names, and all are delivered here by mail, not to your house by hand."

Back to tapping the pencil. "That is correct. I would still like to hear whatever analysis you can give me of the notes."

" 'Analysis' may be too scientific a word."

"That's all right."

"Notes don't usually make sense if somebody's rationally trying to kill you. They're just an additional warning and possibly a lead the police can follow back to the killer. Notes do make sense if the guy is just a nut trying to get his jollies from scaring you. Or if he wants to get some publicity from you going to the cops and the notes becoming a media football."

"Which is why I was opposed to Alec and Inés going to the police in the first place."

"Yes, but our guy didn't send the notes to the press or tack them to your office door. As I understand it, two were mailed to you here, and one was in your mailbox on Beacon Hill. For your eyes only, so to speak."

"How do those facts fit your theory?"

"They fit if we have a nut who wants to scare you."

38

"And if we have a 'nut' who wants to scare me and kill me?"

"It's a possibility, but that brings us back to the psychiatrists, Ms. Andrus."

"I wonder, could we drop the 'Ms. Andrus'?" It makes me feel like Our Miss Brooks."

"Professor, then?"

"I call my students by their last names, and I expect the same from them, because I'm preparing them for a world in which formality, especially in the courtroom, is necessary to avoid the appearance of favoritism or sexism. I call my secretary Inés, but even after six months on the job, she can't get over using Professor for me. Something from the respect someone her age in the old Cuba was supposed to show for university teachers. So be it. For us, how about Maisy and John?"

"It's still your nickel."

The face hardened a little. "Yes. Yes, it is. Tell me, John, what do you think of my position?"

"Your position."

Andrus dropped the pencil and all of the smile. "What do you think of my position on the right to die?"

"You think that's relevant to my working for you?"

"No, I don't. But I am curious."

I cleared my throat. "You know about my wife."

"Alec told me that she died of cancer."

"Brain tumor. She lingered for a long time, months. In and out of awareness, a lot of pain. We didn't end it, the doctors and I."

I had the feeling that I'd stopped too soon, that Andrus was hanging on my starting again.

I said, "That's it. We waited, and she died."

"What did you . . . feel about that?"

"About her dying?"

"Yes."

None of your business. "I think I'd still like to keep my own counsel on that."

Andrus smiled sympathetically, but in a practiced way. "Then let me tell you about my spouse, John." She squared the chair around, elbows on the desk.

"Working for a large law firm in Washington, D.C., I represented hospitals, among other clients. I met Enrique at an interdisciplinary conference in London. Medical-legal issues, that sort of thing. Enrique was fifty, a respected doctor in northern Spain. I was barely thirty, only fifteen years older than his son. I had no Spanish, no ear for languages at all. Enrique's English was wonderful, and if I'd still been a virgin, the romance novels would say he carried me away on a wave of passion. But that really was how it felt. I left the firm for a teaching position at a law school in a D.C. suburb, just to have summers off to be with him."

"You and he were married but didn't live together?"

"During the school year. At Christmas and summers I'd fly to him, or he'd somehow make time to fly over to me. Anyway, we'd been married for two years, doing this transatlantic shuttle—money was no object, we were both quite comfortable—when Enrique had a stroke. Now, you have to understand, he had been a saint to the poor people of his area, noblesse oblige, during much of Franco's dictatorship. Manolo is a good example."

"The guy in the anteroom?"

"Yes. Manolo was born deaf. His parents cast him out. Literally. Enrique took him in, taught him rudimentary signing, and made him a sort of houseman/orderly to help with the patients he saw. In any case, Enrique had the stroke. Incapacitating. He was paralyzed, could barely sign to Manolo, seemed to forget his Spanish, and only I could understand him, in terribly garbled English."

"Where was his son?"

A muscle jumped in her jaw. "His son, Ramón, was over here, in the States. Studying. I told him he should come back, it was his duty. But he didn't, not until almost the end. And then . . ."

I gave Andrus time.

"Sorry. Enrique was deteriorating, horribly. Bodily functions . . . as a doctor, he knew exactly what was happening to him. He knew he couldn't get any better, and he had too much pride, too much respect for the human spirit, to drift into getting worse. One night, he asked me, begged me to end it for him. I refused. For weeks I watched him decline, his begging now reduced to a single word, John. 'Needle.' "

The tic again. "Ramón finally arrived. Repelled by his father's condition, he couldn't even sit in the same room with him, his own father. I wasn't getting much sleep, but I was doing a lot of thinking. I decided that what Enrique was asking me to do was illegal but not immoral. Finally, one night, I found a bottle with a label on it that I could read, and I injected him."

Her voice quavered. "Enrique was aware of what I was doing. He smiled at me, John. He slipped away blessing me."

Andrus used the edge of her index finger to wipe her eye. It was so like Nancy's gesture that I started a little in my chair, but the professor didn't notice.

"That should have been the end of it. But I didn't know much about Spanish politics. General Franco had just died, and the leftists were trying to push the Franquistas out of government. The undertaker saw the needle marks, how awkward I must have been when I helped Enrique. There was an autopsy. The prosecutor—Spain has a different system, but what we'd call the prosecutor was a Franquista. Except for Enrique's funeral, I never met him, but apparently my husband had once saved the life of the prosecutor's wife. So the man felt indebted to us and basically sat on the autopsy report. I returned to the States, trying to put my life back together while some Spanish lawyers probated Enrique's estate."

Andrus shook her head. "A journalist, a real left winger, got a whiff of the autopsy results, showing that Enrique died from an overdose of drugs. When it turned out the Franquista had covered it up, there was a scandal. Worse, it was made to look like corruption, as though I had somehow bribed the man. The prosecutor was ruined, and I became a fugitive, though my lawyers here were able to fight the halfhearted extradition effort. I never even lost my holdings as Enrique's widow in Spain."

Andrus came forward in her chair. "That's the perversity of it all, John. I helped a man I loved move through the pain and hopelessness of incurable illness to the peace that follows. Everyone who tried to do the right thing in that direction was vilified by the system, but in the end nothing changed in the society."

"How did the son feel about all this?"

"Ramón? He seemed pretty indifferent. Almost glad that it was over. Enrique's will split the estate between us. I got the house on the ocean in Spain—in Candás, near Gijón—though I just rent it out. Ramón was interested more in the movable assets."

"Movable?"

"Yes. He decided to settle in the States, even shortened his name to just Ray Cuervo."

"Where does he live?"

"I believe somewhere on the north shore. I haven't seen him in

41

years, but . . . Marblehead, perhaps." Andrus altered her expression. "Why do you ask?"

"I might want to talk with him."

"I can't believe Ramón could be involved in this."

"How about Manolo?"

"Manolo doesn't know anything. I've questioned him extensively. Over the years he's become good enough in recognizing English for us to communicate with him on simple things."

"I meant, could Manolo be involved in this?"

"Manolo?" A laugh. "Manolo is like the sun and the moon, John. He was devoted to Enrique, never left his side."

"Manolo watched you inject your husband?"

"Watched me with the needle, yes. Not with the bottle."

"Manolo ever figure out that you killed your husband?"

"John, Manolo is loyal, in the medieval sense of the word. I'm sure that at some point Enrique signed to him that he was always to serve me. After Enrique died, I packed to come back to the States. So did Manolo. In his mind there was no question that where I went, he went. A simple man, but not stupid. For example, if you talk to him, you have to say the words out loud, not just mouth them. Otherwise, Manolo can tell from the way your throat looks that you're not really speaking, and he's hurt."

"How did you ever get him into the country?"

"I was able to work things out with immigration before the dam broke in Spain. Manolo has stayed on with me ever since. I even got him a driver's license, but please don't ask how. He has no place else to go and nothing else to do."

"How does your present husband feel about that?"

"Tuck?" Andrus seemed amused and affected a southern accent. "Tucker Hebert rolls with the punches, John." Resuming her voice, she said, "Nothing bothers him, which is a refreshing attitude to share once in a while. Tuck gets along fine with Manolo. Besides, Manolo was already a part of my household when Tuck met me."

"At a tennis tournament?"

"At . . . ? Oh, no. Well, yes. I guess so. It was at Longwood Cricket Club, where they hold the pro championships out in Brookline? But he wasn't playing actively anymore."

"How does Tucker feel about your position on the right to die?"

Andrus tented her fingers, rested her chin lightly on the fingertips and rocked her head back and forth. "If you'll be working for me, you can ask him."

"You realize that I can't both bodyguard and investigate at the same time."

"Manolo's presence is all the 'bodyguarding' I can tolerate, John. Understand this, please. I didn't like the idea of Inés and Alec going to the police precisely because of my position on the right to die. It cannot look as though I can be bullied by crank notes into playing turtle. I will not dilute one aspect of my approach to the cause, including tonight's debate."

"Debate?"

"At the Boston Public Library. Three of us extremists will go hand to hand in front of a slavering crowd."

"I'd like to see it."

"Fine." She softened a little. "Because of what happened to me with Enrique's death, I will not be stopped until what should happen morally is what can happen legally. However, I think that having you investigate is not inconsistent with that goal. I believe we understand each other, even if we don't agree."

"As long as you understand that if I do my job right, the sender of these notes is going to realize you've hired me to go after him."

"That's fine. Let him think about being the target for a while. And, if you catch him, so much the better."

"I'll want a retainer of twelve hundred against four hundred a day fee, plus expenses."

"Only three days worth up front? You think you're that good?"

"No, but I think you're that rich you're good for it."

"Inés has the checkbook."

"I'd also like to see some of your other hate mail."

"Inés keeps an alphabetized file. Steel yourself."

As I opened the door back into the anteroom, Manolo was already on his feet, but this time facing a man about five feet ten in a three-piece suit with lapels an inch out of fashion. Fortyish, he had brown hair with a very narrow widow's peak and a brown mustache, both hair and sideburns a little too long.

The man held a fat manila folder near Inés Roja's nose as he dripped sarcasm. "With all the world's problems preying on her mind, no doubt Professor Andrus merely forgot that she's a member of the Long-Range Planning Committee."

"As I said, sir, I left a message for you that the professor could not attend the meeting because of an emergency."

The man acknowledged me with a scowl. "A pressing issue no doubt. 'Should we pull the plug on Grandmama now or wait till after she's stood treat for lunch?' "

Roja said, "I will ask the professor to call you as soon as possible."

"Yes, yes, you do that, Inés. I'll no doubt be in the dean's office, discussing nonteaching faculty responsibilities and how to assure them."

He turned and walked away, his toes splayed outward like a duck's.

Manolo sat down.

Roja turned to me and said, "I am sorry."

"Who was that?"

"Professor Walter Strock."

"He usually come on that way?"

"He and the professor do not get along well." More seriously, Roja said, "Is there anything I can do?"

"Write me a check for twelve hundred dollars so I can start looking into the notes."

Her eyes lit up. "I will do it."

"I'd also like to see the other hate mail the professor's gotten. You have a file?"

Roja nodded and moved to a tall metal cabinet. Taking a key from the pocket of her suit jacket, she unlocked the top before sliding out a drawer. "All these, alphabetic by the name of the person or organization writing. Except the last folder, for the unsigned ones."

I whistled through my bottom teeth. "You have a box I could carry those in?"

"I can get a carton from the Xerox room."

"One other thing. This debate tonight?"

"You will attend?"

"What time is it?"

"Eight o'clock. At the Rabb Lecture Hall of the Boston Public Library."

Time for dinner first with Nancy. "I can make it."

"Good. Alec will be there too." She smiled and blushed. "I am really glad now that we asked you to help."

"Don't be too sure, Inés. Your boss seems to put her faith in the law."

"I would rather put my faith in people, John. Meaning no disrespect to the professor."

As Roja said it, I realized that I couldn't seem to call Andrus by her first name either.

6

"YES, WELL, NINA, I'M SURE YOU UNDERSTAND."

"No, Professor Strock, frankly I don't."

I had told Inés Roja I'd be back for the files. Searching for Walter Strock, I'd found him outside his office, confronted by a pudgy, determined woman with a lumpy knapsack on her back.

"Nina, there were many students interested in being my research assistant, and well, there was only one slot open."

"But you announced in class that you'd be weighing our exam grades heavily, and I got the highest grade on the final."

"I certainly did weigh that factor, Nina, but I weighed others as well." He gave her a funeral director's smile. "I'm sorry."

"Yeah. Right. Thanks."

Nina seemed disgusted as she stomped by me, the knapsack bonking the top of her rump.

Strock was entering his office when I said, "Professor?"

He turned. "Yes?"

"I wonder if I could have a word with you?"

"I'm rather busy. Do I know you?"

"It's about Professor Andrus."

"Ah, yes. The man she favored over her institutional obligations."

"That's part of what I'd like to talk with you about."

Strock looked me up and down, tugging on an earlobe. "For that, I always have time. Come in, come in."

His office stood in marked contrast to Andrus's bombsite. A polished wooden desk was the centerpiece of the room, several folders and books on it but not a paper out of place. One wall was covered by plaques and framed documents, a couch like the people eater in my landlord's condo nestling underneath them. The other walls sported lowboy oak filing cabinets, Currier and Ives hunting prints, and bookshelves. On the shelves stood trophies for riflery and a statue of *Star Wars'* C3PO holding a sign saying MAY DIVORCE BE WITH YOU. Two captain's chairs emblazoned with the school's logo were arranged in front of the desk. I took one of them as Strock sank into a judge's large swivel chair, swaying arrogantly.

"And you are?"

"John Cuddy, Professor." I nodded back toward the door. "I sure hope I'm not catching you at a bad time?"

"Bad . . . ? Ah, Nina. No, no, just one of many disappointments she will suffer. In a mediocre career stretching long and lonely in front of her."

A sweetheart, old Walter. "Professor, let me get right to it. My lawyer is thinking of involving Professor Andrus on this case I have, and . . ." I did my best to wring my hands. "Well, I have to keep this confidential."

"As you wish, but . . ."

"I wonder, I couldn't help but overhear you with the professor's secretary—"

"Ah, the lovely Inés. Pity she's a bit frigid. A *Marielito,* something to do with an incident on the boat coming over from Castroland. Tried to help her talk it out once upon a time, but she just won't open up."

I swallowed hard. "I've always believed, you want to know about a person, first talk to somebody who doesn't like them."

"Then you've come to the right place regarding Dame Andrus, sir." Tilting his chair back, Strock entreated the gods. "But where to begin, where to begin?"

"I thought you said something about her missing committee assignments?"

"The tip of the iceberg. Maisy fancies herself a latter-day Joan of Arc, you see. Believes that a faculty appointment here is merely the springboard for her cause, her great crusade."

"Which is?"

"To turn the sick of this planet into creatures with no more rights than an incontinent household pet."

"The right to die, you mean?"

"No, but that's how she'd phrase it for you."

"Aren't there 'living wills' or something now?"

"Yes, yes. The Supreme Court in the *Cruzan* case validated the concept. About forty states have statutes on that, allowing hospitals to withhold or withdraw heroic measures, even food and water. Our own compassionate Commonwealth has no such statute yet, but it doesn't matter much."

"Why not?"

"Because Massachusetts has a lot of case law on termination of treatment, and even in the living-will states, only ten percent of the citizens ever reach the stage of executing one."

"Sounds like you've made quite a study of it yourself."

Strock preened the hair at his temples. "Only to make the point, Mr. . . . ah, sorry?"

"Cuddy."

"Cuddy, yes, Cuddy. You see, Maisy doesn't teach here to improve the hearts and minds of our students. She doesn't give the proverbial rat's ass about whether they're minimally competent to pass the bar examination and actually enter practice. No, our Maisy cares only about her crusade."

"Then why does she bother to teach at all?"

"Not for the money, I assure you. Maisy's in fine shape that way." Strock pitched forward in his chair. "Do you know how she came to have that money?"

I short-circuited a little. "My lawyer said her husband died and left it to her."

Strock laughed meanly. "Ah, very good. I'd have been proud to teach your lawyer, sir. He makes accurate statements without telling the truth. A valued skill in an advocate. Her husband died, all right, but she gave him about ten cc's of propulsion along the way."

"She killed him?"

"The word I've heard her use is 'help.' She helped him find the peace that comes with sleep a tad sooner than his system otherwise dictated. Understand now. We're not talking about pulling the plug on a machine that's maintaining some veggie. We're talking murder."

48

"Like that Michigan doctor and the 'suicide machine'?"

"Not exactly. The doctor merely designed a machine for that unfortunate Alzheimer's patient to use. Aiding and abetting a suicide, so to speak. Maisy went way beyond that. She gave her husband a fatal dose, and still gets to inherit from him. Outrageous, no?"

"My!"

"Yes. And that's not the half of it. There was some incredible scandal in Spain—that's where all this happened. Some prosecutor got bribed, poor bastard blew his head off, I think. But Maisy enjoys the dead don's money, and thanks to our revered dean, she gets to teach the courses she wants at the times she wants to, curriculum and schedule and the rest of us be damned."

"Why is that?"

"Not for the reason you'd think. No, our Maisy is oh-so-happily married to some tennis has-been she wouldn't think of spreading them for anything so crass as professional advancement. You see, the dean is sitting in his chair around the corner because she turned it down."

"Professor Andrus was offered the deanship?"

"And she said, 'Oh, no thanks, I have all these other, more important irons in the fire. I couldn't possibly take on the mundane task of guiding the institution that nurtured me.' My God, can you imagine the regents offering her the job of administering this law school? I mean, forget that Maisy snuffed her own husband, the woman can't even keep up with her committee work!"

"What do the students think of her?"

" 'The Cunt That Belches Fire'?"

I thought about the notes.

Strock continued without prompting. "They love her. There is no justice, is there? Of course, Maisy teaches nonsense subjects like Law and Society or Sociology of Law. All of the touchy-feely stuff is really just a cover for indoctrinating the poor munchkins. The woman treats them like shit, then gives everybody A's and B's, so they figure they learned something. All they ever learn is how to be thankful for being manipulated into agreeing with her theories."

I'd about had my fill of Professor Strock. "Well, thanks for all your help."

He made a dismissive gesture. "Far be it from me to discourage you from retaining Maisy, even indirectly, but you're aware, are you not, that she is leaving us for a while?"

"Leaving?"

"Yes. A visitorship for the coming quarter. Spared of the cruelest months of the winter by venturing to San Diego with Bjorn."

"Bjorn?"

"Or whatever the tennis bum's name is. I've never actually met him, but I hope he bleeds her dry. That would be poetic justice, at least."

I stood up. "Thanks again."

Strock made no effort to rise. "Pleasure."

As I reached the door, he said, "Oh, Mr. Cuddy?"

"Yes?"

"One more thing. Maisy is participating in a debate tonight."

"She mentioned it."

"You really ought to go. Get a sense of how she comes across in a public forum."

"Will you be there, Professor?"

Strock smiled like a man serving his kids roast rabbit for Easter dinner. "Wouldn't miss it for the world."

7

After leaving Walter Strock, I picked up my box of files from Inés Roja. By the time I got outside the school building, I realized the load was going to be too heavy to carry under one arm and too awkward to ferry in front of me under two. Since there were no cabs, it seemed to make more sense to find a place for lunch. Across the street and down from the school was Bandy's, a burger-and-beer dugout owned by another Vietnam vet in my student days.

Sometimes nostalgia is a bad emotion to indulge.

The interior was still dark and just a little dank. The floor was still tacky from spilled beer, the vinyl in the booths still taped at the seats. But instead of the Stones or the Doors, the speakers blared Grace Jones doing a bad Katharine Hepburn imitation as she recited rather than sang some lyric about walking in the rain. The barkeep had a purple Mohawk and more pieces of metal piercing his ears and nose than a shrapnel victim.

The only obvious holdover from the original Bandy was a television monitor above the bar, showing a video of a Celtics-Lakers game. Bird holding the ball on his hip, glaring at an official. Kareem, with shaved head and goggles, a praying mantis seeking just one more grasshopper before calling it a night. The screen jumped to a clip of the Lakers slaughtering some team you never saw play from a city that made you think of rodeos, not hoops.

I'd already lost my appetite when the Mohawk said, "Help you?"

I started to say no, then recognized one of the facial scars the artifacts couldn't quite hide. "Bandy?"

"Yeah. I know you?"

Maybe not from this incarnation. "John Cuddy. I went to Mass Bay a long time ago."

"Cuddy? Cuddy, sure, sure." He stuck out a hand. "Southie by way of Saigon, right?"

I rested the carton on the bar, and we shook. "Good memory."

"Wish I could say the same about business."

I tried to look encouraging as I surveyed the room, seeing only the backs of three other customers, one a woman, scattered over twenty stools. "Lunchtime's bound to be slow."

"Tell me about it. Gave the cook a week off because it just wasn't worth it, with Mass Bay out of regular session." He flung a hand at the nearest stereo speaker. "This punk shit's the only thing brings them in."

"I listen to their songs, but I just can't hear the music "

"Aw, some of it ain't so bad. There's U2, Talking Heads, Fine Young Cannibals. They got something to say."

"Oldies like you used to have just don't cut it?"

"Shit, no. Held on as long as I could, but you gotta be downtown with a big dance floor for the yups or out in the burbs with parking for the young parents. Around here it's new wave or no wave. But kids today, they can't read, we probably shouldn't figure they'll listen too good either. How's about a beer?"

I again started to say no when the female customer turned on her stool. Nina, the student from Strock's office. Lifting the box of files from the bar, I asked Bandy to bring us two drafts and walked over to her.

"Mind if I sit with you?"

She barely looked up. "Sit. Don't talk and don't touch."

I set the carton on the floor as the beers arrived. I paid Bandy and took one, Nina draining the mug she'd had in front of her.

"For you," I said, pointing to the second full one.

She looked at me a little closer. "You're the guy who was waiting to talk with Strock, right?"

"Right."

"I can pay for my own."

"I didn't mean to imply otherwise."

Nina cocked her head. "All right. Why does a man who knows the difference between 'imply' and 'infer' want to buy me a drink?"

I showed her my identification, which she had to hold up to the light as Grace Jones finished on a warbled high note and the radio station's deejay segued into a group called the After-Births.

"I'd like to ask you a few questions about Professor Strock."

Nina closed the ID holder and handed it back to me. "You know a sergeant on the Mets named Nick Russo?"

Anywhere in Boston outside of sports bars and Fenway Park "the Mets" means the Metropolitan District Commission Police, a force that patrols major roads, parks, and waterways.

"Never met him."

"He's my father. Just so we know where we stand."

"Fine."

Nina Russo took a gulp of the beer. "Why are you interested in Strock?"

"I can't tell you."

She considered that, nodded. "Why should I talk to you about him?"

"Because you don't like him, and I won't tell anybody else what you tell me."

A tired smile. "Maybe I ought to cover the beer."

"You don't believe me?"

"Mister, law students get trained not to believe a lot of things. Especially things some stranger promises them in a bar."

"You know Lieutenant Robert Murphy, Boston Homicide?"
Russo perked. "No."

"How about Sergeant Bonnie Cross, also Boston Homicide?"

"No. Why, could they vouch for you?"

"Uh-huh. How about Officer Drew—"

"Enough." She took a little more beer, then rearranged her fanny on the stool. "Let me tell you a few things, okay? Then you can decide if you want to talk to me."

"Okay."

"I'm not the first person in my family to go to college, but a lot of them had to do school off-shift or weekends. I am the first one to go past college, which kind of makes me the center of attention that way. The flag bearer, get it?"

"Yes."

"Well, I want to specialize in Family Law, Domestic Relations. That means mostly divorce, but it also gives you adoptions, appointed work for abused kids, the chance to do some good for people who are in the worst time of their lives and really need the help. Strock teaches Family Law here. Before that, he was this big-time divorce lawyer. Doesn't talk about it, but I think he got tired of the hassle and decided to sort of retire to teaching. He maybe consults for some of the dom/rel firms in town, to keep his hand in, but mostly he's just a teacher and a . . . mentor."

"What kind of mentor?"

"The kind that can make or break your résumé."

"Like by who he chooses for research assistant?"

"And he chooses the assistants with a critical eye."

I was beginning to get it. "As in eye of the beholder?"

"The student who beat me out of the job is named Kimberly. She has long hair that I actually heard her call 'flaxen' once. If Strock's sitting down, she has to tuck some of that hair up and over her ear when she leans forward to look over his shoulder and glance at him sideways."

"Sexual harassment?"

"No. At least not the way you mean it. Kimberly was angling for the job more than Strock was angling for her, I think."

"But on the merits, you should have been picked?"

"Hands down. I know, that doesn't sound real modest, but I got the highest grade in his family law course last quarter and was the best performer in class."

I didn't say "as opposed to after class," but I did picture the couch in Strock's office. "All right, Ms. Russo. I understand the context. What can you tell me about the guy otherwise?"

"Otherwise. Well, he's pretty insecure."

"In what way?"

"He's not a very good teacher—not just my opinion, by the way. Student evaluations as well as anecdotal comments by the other kids. He tries to get by on his reputation, but I don't think he's been inside a courtroom in ten years. He takes the simple law school administrative stuff and kind of blows it out of proportion. Probably makes him feel like a big man."

Something clicked. "Strock ever shoot for the deanship himself?"

"Yeah. At least that's the rumor. But he didn't get it. Don't know why, but maybe that's part of the insecurity."

"Sounds to me as though you shouldn't feel too bad, not having to work closely with the guy."

"Give me a few days."

"How about Strock's relationship with the rest of the faculty?"

"Hard to say. They're all kind of a blank to us about how they feel toward each other, unless one mentions another in class."

"Has Strock ever done that?"

"Once in a while. The only one he seems to have it in for is a woman named Andrus."

No surprise so far. "Maisy Andrus?"

"You've heard of her."

"Some."

"Well, she's got this thing about the right to die, but she also makes her students stand when they participate in class, so Strock always refers to her as She-Who-Makes-You-Stand, like that's the way he believes we think of them all."

"Of the faculty?"

"Yeah. Like He-Who-Has-Dandruff, She-Who-Smokes, like that." Russo drank some beer. "You know, you're right. He really is a dork most ways."

"You said Strock does consulting work?"

"I said maybe he does."

"You think that brings in much money?"

"That's what I meant by maybe."

"Go on."

"Well, just looking at his suits and car and all, I get the impression he might be hurting for cash. He's supposed to have this great house over in Cambridge, but he's sure around the school a lot more than the professors who consult in the corporate and tax areas. Also, I never really see people coming to see him, although I guess he could do a lot of that over the telephone."

"Anything else?"

"About the money thing or Strock in general?"

"Either."

Russo took a little more beer, then pushed it aside. "God, I hate to drink in the afternoon. Makes me worthless for the rest of the day." She shifted around to me. "About the money, I guess all I know is that Professor Andrus is supposed to be really rich, and Strock's jibes at her go beyond the usual joking. Makes you think he really resents something about her."

"What about Strock in general?"

Russo closed her eyes, then opened them. "I don't want you to think I'm fixated on this Kimberly thing."

"But?"

"Well, if somebody like Strock has the eye now, it wouldn't surprise me that he's had it for a while."

"And not for just law students?"

"There are a lot of stories you hear, about how . . . how well a divorce lawyer can do sexually with all the distraught people who come to him, or her, I suppose, as a client."

"And you figure Strock might have been like that?"

"I don't know. But if he was, and he's not getting the opportunities from practice anymore, maybe there've been some other Kimberlys."

I thanked Nina Russo and gathered up my box of files. As I said good-bye to Bandy, the deejay promised his faithful listeners a program entitled "Throbbing Gristle, a Retrospective."

I was able to hail a taxi on Columbus Avenue, giving the driver the address for my condo because it was closer than my office. I made a ham sandwich on rye and washed it down with more ice water as I began reading the Andrus files. I decided to save the anonymous folder for last, focusing first on the letters with identified names and addresses. The tones ranged from fastidious politeness to unintelligible harangue. Doctoral candidates expounding from Ivy League schools to functional illiterates exploding in Walpole State Prison. Every letter containing the buzz word "cunt" or "slut" came from a man. Those using "bitch" were all male except for a woman from Alberta.

It grew redundant quickly, so I started flipping faster, pulling out the ones I wanted to read more carefully, especially any repeat correspondents. Then I turned to the anonymous file. None used snipped-out words or letters. Many of them were block-printed with frequent misspellings.

After sifting and sorting, I was left with three people who had written more than one signed letter, were reasonably local, and had used one or more of the buzz words. The first was named Steven

O'Brien, a rabid pro-lifer from Providence, Rhode Island. O'Brien believed Andrus to be part of an "international atheist plot to overthrow all that is decent." He referred often to the incident in Spain, calling Andrus a "slut" for doing in her own husband.

The second repeater was Louis Doleman, showing an address in West Roxbury. His letters, six over four months, chronicled the decline and "premature" death of his daughter from leukemia. Apparently "Heidi" had taken up the "sudo-religion" that the "Devil's bitch" Andrus "esposed." After reading the professor's "witchery," the daughter had taken her own life.

The third repeater's name was Gunther Yary. His smudgy letterhead proclaimed him Grand Marshal of the American Trust, some kind of skinhead group. The return address sounded like a storefront in a white section of Dorchester. It seemed Gunther and his "folowers" believed strongly in "heterosexuity" and not in the "preverted" hoax of "mercy death" that "Zionists, Faggots, and Niggers" created to wipe out the last "vesttiges" of native Aryan stock. Yary employed all three buzz words and more.

I wedged the correspondence of O'Brien, Doleman, and Yary into a waterproof plastic portfolio and had copies made at one of the Copy Cops on Boylston Street. Then I deposited the Andrus check in my client's account at the Shawmut and continued toward police headquarters on Berkeley.

Even though the door was ajar, I knocked on the frame before looking in. Lieutenant Robert Murphy was cradling the telephone receiver on his left shoulder, signing a series of documents while somebody on the other end of the line talked to him. Murphy motioned me in. His black hand provided a photographer's backdrop for the gold pen he held.

I didn't like it when Murphy smiled at me.

Into the receiver, he said, "No problem . . . happy to help . . . right, right. Bye." As the receiver slid down his chest, Murphy caught it in his left hand. "You must be getting psychic, Cuddy."

"Who was it?"

"Don't suppose you know a Met sergeant named Nick Russo?"

"You're the second person who's asked me that today."

Murphy hung up. "Yeah, well, it seems he got a call from that first person after she talked to you. Seems that first person had second thoughts about your word being your bond."

"I plied her with strong drink."

"I bet you did. Think a cop's kid'd be smarter than to talk with a P.I., even without law school and all."

"She will be next time."

"Suppose that's how everybody learns, all right. You get your permit to carry back yet?"

"August."

"You ever hear the story, about Jesus and the lepermen, and one of them come back to thank him for the cure?"

"I called to thank you. Three different days. Left a message each time."

"Maybe some saviors, they get asked in person, they like to get thanked in person."

"You're right, Lieutenant, and I appreciate what you did for me."

Murphy let his lids get sleepy, showing about as much eye as teeth. "That A.D.A.?"

"Which prosecutor is that?"

"You still seeing her?"

"Yes."

He kept watching me.

"Lieutenant?"

"Just getting into the Christmas spirit, Cuddy. Not trying to pull anything."

"Or suggest anything."

Murphy made a face and shook his head. "Well, it's obvious you got no feeling whatsoever for the holidays. And you're back here in person. That means you'll be wanting another favor, huh?"

"You know a detective over at Area A, William Neely?"

"Neely? Yeah, from a time back. Why?"

"I'm representing somebody in his neighborhood. The client got some threats, and I'd like to talk with him about them. Wondered what kind of guy he is."

Murphy glanced out his window and then back. "This client, he or she?"

"She."

"She go to Neely?"

"Her secretary got referred to him."

"Her tough luck."

"Why?"

"This between you and me, or you going to be explaining it to real folks?"

"You and me."

"Neely, he fancies himself an old-time hard-ass dick. Runs a few informants, reacts when the brass gets edgy. Otherwise, low profile and count the days."

"To retirement time."

"Uh-huh."

"I don't see what I've got jeopardizing his pension."

"What do you got?"

I went through it, without names.

Murphy said, "Neely, he got the complaint to start with, it'll stay with him unless somebody gets nasty enough with a deadly weapon."

"I wasn't trying to go over his head here, Lieutenant."

"Sure you were, Cuddy. And once you meet Neely, you'll realize you were right to try too."

"Any suggestions on how to approach him?"

"Neely ever took a promotion exam, he got stuck on name and address. Play up to the man, let him talk."

"Okay. Thanks."

I was at the door when Murphy said, "Oh, and Cuddy?"

"Yeah."

"Neely's got a nickname. 'Beef.' "

"Beef."

"Yeah. Don't say it to him, but use it, huh?"

"Use it how?"

"Take the man to lunch."

I looked at my watch. "But I thought I'd go over there now."

"Won't matter to old Beef."

"Thanks again, Lieutenant."

"One more thing."

"Yes?"

"You'd best visit a bank somewheres first."

"Pass the Worcestershire, willya?"

"Sure."

"And maybe some more of that A-1 too."

I put both bottles in front of Neely. He spritzed the Worcestershire on his second cut of prime rib. The meat lapped two inches a side over the platter.

59

Victoria Station was done in a railroad car motif. It was the one restaurant Neely had said would have prime rib for sure, that time of afternoon. I had offered to cab it, but he said, "It'll look better, I sign out a unit." We were the only people in the room except for our waitress, and even she left, probably to call Central Supply and tell them to butcher another dozen head for the third course.

"My hand to God, I love this joint."

At least, I think that's what Neely said.

"They got—" The tongue wasn't quite quick enough to catch a dribble of *jus* cascading down his chin and onto his tie. Which was wider than the napkin he'd cornered into his collar.

"They got real food here, you know? The kinda stuff we fought wars to eat."

Neely had stopped the beer after one stein, switching to tonic water. About six feet tall, counting crew cut, I couldn't even guess his weight. The knot of his tie was only an article of faith under the jowls. He rocked his head after every third or fourth bite, as though he were positioning the food to slide down a different chute. Small eyes were squinched up under the brows, a piece of toilet paper on a shaving cut near his right ear.

Neely generously rested his knife to point at my salad bowl. "That all you're eating?"

"Diet," I said.

He nodded like he'd heard the word but never studied the language that spawned it. I waited until he finished the slab and was tricking with the little veins of meat marbled in the fat.

"Neely?"

"Uh-huh."

"About these threats?"

"Yeah, sure. What about them?"

"What do you think?"

"Think." He put down his utensils, rolled his rump as if to fart, then just wallowed deeper into the booth. "I think this broad's asked for it, what I think."

"Can you tell me what you found out on the notes?"

"The notes? Jesus, everybody but Jimmy Hoffa handled the things and the envelopes before the little secretary brought 'em in to me. Even so, I followed routine. Had 'em run through the lab."

"You take elimination prints from Andrus's people?"

"Nah. Just sent the notes on through. They even did that Sherlock thing, the computer search out to 1010 Commonwealth there?"

Neely suddenly straightened a little. "Look, Cuddy, I'm no brain trust, but I know what's what, okay? I keep up with things the best I can. The staties didn't find no match with any of the prints they got on file."

"I give you some names, will you run them through too?"

"See if anybody's got a sheet?"

"Yes."

"Sure, I'll do that. Sure." He rifled his pockets for a pad and pen. I gave him O'Brien, Doleman, and Yary from the threat files, then Walter Strock as well.

Neely scratched his forehead. "Strock?"

"Something?"

"Not sure. I'll run it. You got social security numbers on any of these guys?"

"No."

"How about D.O.B.'s?"

"Just the addresses."

"Even so, gonna get a hell of a list for the O'Brien, although thank Christ it ain't 'John' or 'James,' computer'd be burping all fuckin' night. I'll still give it a try for you."

The waitress came over with a bowl of salted peanuts. Neely thanked her, his fingers plowing through the nuts like the blades of a backhoe.

He said, "Anything else you need?"

I decided to follow Murphy's advice. "You get many of these threat things, Neely?"

"Aw, you know how it is. Runs in cycles. Broad like this Andrus, though, she probably could hire a stevedore, haul them away for her."

I told him about the drawerful of folders.

"That's my point. I get one of these, I end up chasing after scum-bags write the kinda fan mail you wouldn't wish on Geraldo there. Jesus, Cuddy, every day some shithead sees somebody new on the tube, he decides to make the lady his personal project, you know? Guy can barely read the labels in a Seven-Eleven writes a love poem, then jerks off into the envelope before he licks it. Whaddaya gonna do?"

"Okay if I follow up on the names? Go talk to them?"

"Fine. Let me just tell you, think about what you want to have happen here."

"What do you mean?"

"Start with the Secret Service, okay?"

The Secret Service. "Okay."

"Now, they got thousands of guys, no shit, got nothing better to do than guard a couple of big shots like the President and all, maybe total with the Kennedy kids and Truman's widow, total twenny, twenny-five."

The Kennedy children were now over-age, and Mrs. Truman left us in the early eighties, but I didn't want to wreck Neely's train of thought.

"And even the Secret Service can't keep track of all the scumbags writing letters and making phone calls. The calling, I gotta admit, that's gonna slow down some, now they got these computers, you can see the number the guy's at with this little screen thing on your phone there. 'Course, soon's the scumbag union finds out about the screens, they'll just call from some pay phone and a different one every time.

"But your letter-writing scumbags, now, they're different. All's you got is the handwriting and the postmark and maybe, just maybe, the saliva or cum juice or whatever the fuck other fluid they leave on the envelope, right? Only there's got to be enough of that for some other kind of test that even 1010 don't do but has to farm out. So, you see what I'm saying here?"

"Even with better physical evidence, not much chance of actually tracing the sender."

"Right, right. And not only that. What does your client really want?"

"Want?"

"Yeah. She want the scumbag to just stop or she want him hung by the balls too?"

"Probably both."

"Yeah, well, probably the best you're gonna be able to do for her is scare him off. Even if you catch the guy in the act somehow, what's a judge gonna do with him? Twenty days down to Bridge-water for observation in the rooms with the cushy walls? Shit, we're letting real bad dudes walk now, there ain't enough cells in all the slams to hold 'em."

"Good point."

"Yeah. Hey, look, I don't wanna come across like some lug, got no feelings. Jesus, I was the one getting these notes, especially the one by hand in the mailbox there, I'd be jumpy as a pregnant nun too. It's just, even if you do the best you can here, it ain't gonna be that much."

"Listen, Neely, I appreciate your being so open with me on all this."

"Don't mention it." He seemed to sniff something in the air. "Say, you pressed or we got time for dessert?"

8

WHEN WE FINALLY LEFT VICTORIA STATION, I ASKED NEELY TO drop me off in South Boston. The weather was bell clear, and I hadn't made a visit since Thanksgiving.

I bent over stiffly, laying the bunched poinsettias lengthwise to her.

You getting old on me?

"No."

John, you're creaking.

"Finally decided to try the marathon, Beth."

What, the Ironman Triathalon was already booked up?

"You're supposed to be supportive of a poor widower rising to a challenge."

Even when he's being stupid?

I looked down at the shoreline, the chop smacking against the foot of her hillside. Half a mile out, a Coast Guard cutter was knifing its way toward the harbor. During every season, the cod boats have to be watched over and the drug smugglers watched for.

Something besides the marathon's on your mind.

"Tommy Kramer approached me to help a professor who's getting threatened."

And?

64

"The professor is a woman who pushes for the right to die."

A pause. *Why does she bother you?*

"I don't know."

I half expected Beth to say, "That's not an acceptable answer, Mr. Cuddy."

John?

"I guess because when her husband was dying, in a lot of pain and frustration, she helped him to die."

Another pause. *And that makes you feel . . . ?*

"Uncomfortable."

Why?

"I suppose because it makes me think back. To your being in the hospital."

John, we talked about . . . ending things then.

I stood up. "No, we didn't. We talked around it."

And why do you suppose that was?

"Because I saw it as helping the cancer take you away from me."

Instead of helping me get away from the cancer.

"Right."

John, what we decided to do, or not to do, shouldn't cloud you on other people's views.

"Of course it should."

Another pause. *There's something else, too, isn't there?*

I kicked at a gum wrapper that somebody should have picked up. "Nancy."

Trouble?

"It's the holiday business."

In what way?

I told her about Nancy's dad and the blow-up over the tree-lighting.

You remember our first Christmas?

"Yes. You insisted we have a real tree, even though we couldn't afford a stand for it."

So you took that glass jug that held—what was it?

"Grape juice."

So you took that jug and filled it with water and put the tree in it.

"Right."

And what happened?

"I left the window open, and the water froze solid, cracking the glass."

Remember the row we had over your lack of holiday spirit?

I remembered. "But that's the point, Beth. While the holidays didn't ever mean all that much to me, at least I remember them, even the tree and the argument and all, as real life, something I was part of."

What about the holidays since?

"Empty. I don't know, maybe like a foreigner watching a baseball game."

And now?

"Now?"

With Nancy?

I thought about it. "Not completely a stranger, but not completely a participant either."

An invited guest?

"Who's maybe a little afraid to join in."

Given her family situation, don't you think that's what Nancy really needs? Someone to join in with her?

"Maybe."

John, you want to give it a chance with Nancy, don't you?

"Yes."

Then to give it a chance, you might have to take a chance too.

The other pieces of stone and I watched the Coast Guard cutter pass a point of land and snug back into the harbor.

After a purchase at the Christmas Shop on Tremont, I got to the Suffolk County courthouse about four P.M., going through the metal detector on the first floor. In the district attorney's office the receptionist told me where to find Nancy.

I walked into a courtroom on the ninth floor. High ceilings, nondescript carpeting, failing sunlight fuzzing the large windows. There were a few people standing around, but no judge, no jury, and no Nancy.

I saw a court officer I'd met before and went over to him. "Carmine."

"John, how're you doing?"

"Fine, thanks. Where is everybody?"

"Judge excused the jury for the day." Carmine inclined his head toward a door near the bench. "He wanted to see counsel in chambers. Little talking to before the defense starts his case-in-chief."

The defendant, a sullen white male in his thirties, sat at a table, a court officer on each side of the chair. The defendant noticed me eyeing him and tried a hard-con stare. Couldn't quite pull it off.

I said to Carmine, "How's Nancy doing?"

A smile, the head this time inclining toward the defendant. "Lemme put it this way. Our boy was Bob Hope, his theme song'd be 'Walpole by Wednesday.' "

"He'd better work on that look before he hits the yard."

"Or put a case of Vaseline in his letter to Santa."

". . . and then the judge says to my opponent, 'You're going to have your man take the stand, then?' and the defense attorney, who acted like he was on his first heavy case, says, 'Yes, Your Honor.' So then the judge turns to me—a twinkle in his eye, but the court reporter can't dictate that into her machine—and he says, 'Ms. Meagher, if I were fairly certain that perjury had been committed in my courtroom, what do you think I should do?' And I can see the defense attorney losing what little color he has left in his cheeks, and I say, 'Why, inform our office, Your Honor, regarding the perpetrator and accomplices, if any.' And the judge says, like he'd never thought about it before, 'Accomplices? Accomplices, yes, yes. Oh, my, yes.' And the defense attorney coughs and says, 'Uh, Your Honor, might I have a . . . uh . . .' and the judge says, 'A moment to confer with your client?' and the kid says 'Yessir.' So we go back to the courtroom, and the kid pleads the guy out ten minutes later."

"And so here we are."

Nancy and I were finishing dinner at The Last Hurrah, a restaurant in the Omni Parker House on School Street, halfway between the courthouse and the subway. Wearing a soft gray suit and a pearl blouse, she'd been doing most of the talking, embellishing a relatively small victory to fill the air. It felt as though Nancy still wasn't over Saturday night either.

I reached into my coat pocket and said, "Hold out your hand."

She did, and I dropped the two-inch-by-six-inch ribboned package into it.

"What's this?"

"Open it."

Nancy tore off the gift wrap and pried open the box. Lifting the Angel Gabriel from enveloping cotton, she hefted him in her palm. "Kind of light for a paperweight."

"Look under the wings."

"Poor Gabe! He's been disemboweled."

"By design, Ms. Meagher. He's going to be on top of our tree."

Nancy canted her head, the table light dancing on her eyes like sunshine on a lake. "*Our* tree?"

"Our Christmas tree." I reached over and covered the hand that wasn't hefting the angel.

9

THE POSTER AT THE DOORS SAID THE DEBATE WOULD BEGIN promptly at eight P.M. with a book signing to follow at Plato's Bookshop. Two Boston cops routinely assessed me as I walked past them. One black and one white, both male and big. You can specify size if you're expecting trouble.

The Rabb Lecture Hall itself, carved out beneath the new wing of the Boston Public Library, would remind you of a particularly well-kept school auditorium. I wanted to be early enough to see most of the folks as they filed in. The metal chairs, upholstered with black cushions, were bolted onto a steep slope. All the seats faced the stage, someone having sashed off a section of the bottom rows. I sat on the aisle near the back right corner to give me the best scope for faces.

The stage was spartan. A podium under a baby spotlight. To the left of the podium, a grand piano that probably was easier to ignore than to move. Behind the podium, one chair, positioned subserviently in shadow. To the right of the podium, a longish table in medium light with three chairs. On the table, a paper cloth, a pitcher of water, and three glasses.

The hall began to fill up. A lot of academics and professionals. More black faces than you usually see outside the predominantly black neighborhoods. A smattering of students, some vaguely familiar from the class at Mass Bay that morning, others too young to be in law school yet. Concerned women with rosaries, their husbands in poorly tailored sport jackets, index fingers between collars and necks, trying to expand a sixteen to a sixteen and a half. The rest of the crowd looked like the sort of people you wouldn't stop to ask for directions.

I'd just spotted Walter Strock confiding in a cornsilk blonde who had "Kimberly" written all over her when I felt a strong hand on my shoulder.

I looked up the sleeve into the face of Alec Bacall, a slim black man hovering behind him.

"John! Glad you could make it. May we join you?"

"Sure."

I stood to let them go by me, communion style. Bacall was wearing double-pleated trousers again. They billowed as he shuffled his feet.

Bacall sat himself between his companion and me, saying, "John Cuddy, Del Wonsley."

Wonsley leaned across Bacall, extending his hand. His complexion was deep black, looking almost spit-shined under the strong house lights. The nose was aquiline, a pencil mustache under it and a mushroom haircut above it. Wonsley wore a red sweater with maize horizontal stripes over a knit shirt, collar turned up. His slacks were cavalry twills, the creases sharp.

Bacall said, "We could sit closer if you'd like, John. The first few rows are reserved for family and friends."

"Better view from up here."

"Oh. Yes, of course."

Wonsley said, "Alec told me about you. Can you believe the turnout for this?"

He had a flat Chicago A in his voice.

I said, "Do we know who else is on the program?"

Bacall said, "A doctor from Mass General and a minister from a Protestant church."

Wonsley waved to a middle-aged black man in a lower row, who from the expression on his face curdled cream for a living.

Wonsley said, "Oooo-ooh, the look he gave me. For sitting up here in Sodom and Gomorrah country instead of down there with the Children of God."

Bacall patted Wonsley's forearm. "The best is yet to come, Del. The Hitler Youth make their grand entrance."

70

I was turning as Bacall said it, because I could hear the clumping on the floor. Five white kids, heads shaved, were stamping their boots just enough to attract the attention of the cops. The cops couldn't do much when the kids stopped their noise and held up their hands in mock innocence. They took three seats a few rows below us and two more seats immediately in front of the three. All wore brown leather flying jackets over white T-shirts and studded blue jeans, the jeans bloused into the boots like army fatigue pants. Body language suggested that the kid in the middle, a redhead from his eyebrows, was the leader. One of the others called him "Gun."

Maybe short for "Gunther," as in Gunther Yary, the author of the white supremacist hate letters in the Andrus file.

I said to Bacall, "Know them?"

"No."

"See anybody else I ought to worry about?"

Bacall murmured something to Wonsley, and they both craned forward, scanning the room. Each hesitated on a few places as people turned to talk to each other or stood to remove another layer of clothing. Wonsley looked at Bacall, shook his head, and settled back.

Bacall did the same but pointed toward the sashed area. "I can introduce you later, but the striking man sitting next to Manolo and Inés is Tucker Hebert."

Hebert was turned sideways, deep in conversation with his wife's secretary. He had broad shoulders under a dull rose blazer. His hair was dishwater blond, but the cleft in his chin caught you even from the bleachers.

Del Wonsley said, "First time I saw him in tennis shorts, I cried myself to sleep."

The only empty spaces were around the skinheads. A few late arrivals chose to stand rather than sit near them.

Without fanfare, a side door on the stage opened, and the crowd began to applaud. A man and three women, one of them Maisy Andrus in her yellow sweater dress, walked out in a line. The man and one of the other women were white and wore suits. The third woman was black and wore a choir robe.

The skinheads made hooting noises. One of them said, "Christ, Gun, check out old Maisy in the yellow horse blanket."

Gun said, "Fuck all, Rick. She didn't shave her legs, I'da thought she was a Clydesdale."

Rick said, "Maybe the guy drives the Bud wagon knocked off a little early, y'know," then ducked his head and shrank from the look Gun gave him. Like it was one thing to feed Gun a line and another to top his joke.

The white member of the police team came down the aisle. He stopped at Gun's row and leaned in, armpit in a skinhead's eyes. A series of grunts was all you could hear, but when the cop walked back up the aisle, the skinheads were facing front and staying quiet.

Wonsley laid his head lightly on Bacall's shoulder. "Ah, for the paramilitary life."

The white woman on the stage settled the other three into their seats behind the table and moved to the podium.

As the house lights dimmed, she stood in the baby spot and introduced herself as Olivia Jurick, the manager of Plato's Bookshop. Jurick thanked a covey of public and private benefactors for helping to sponsor the event before thanking everybody for coming out on a cold winter night for such an important and stimulating topic of our time.

Then, "Our first speaker will be the Reverend Vonetta Givens. Our second speaker will be Dr. Paul Eisenberg, and our third speaker will be Professor Maisy Andrus. After all have presented prepared remarks, there will be an opportunity for questions from the audience."

Jurick turned a page. "Reverend Vonetta Givens is the pastor of All Hallowed Ground Church of Roxbury. Born in Oklahoma, Reverend Givens is a graduate of Morehouse College in Atlanta and attended several theological seminaries prior to her ordination in 1979. She ministered to congregations in Atlanta, Memphis, and Trenton before assuming her present position in 1984. A charter member of Boston Against Drugs, Reverend Givens leads the African-American community's struggle against the scourge of crack cocaine. She also has been extremely active among the elderly and the infirm."

Olivia Jurick's voice dropped, and I expected to hear Reverend Givens at that point. So, apparently, did Reverend Givens, because she had gathered her papers into a sheaf, almost rising before Jurick continued.

"Our second speaker, Dr. Paul Eisenberg, is a graduate of Cornell University and the Harvard Medical School. Dr. Eisenberg is currently a member of the Department of Internal Medicine at Mas-

72

sachusetts General Hospital and adjunct professor of ethics at the Tufts University School of Medicine. Between college and medical school, Dr. Eisenberg served for two years in the Peace Corps in Brazil, and enjoyed staff privileges at Mount Sinai Hospital in New York and Philadelphia Presbyterian before assuming his present position in 1986." Jurick held up a book. "Dr. Eisenberg is also the author of *The Ethical Physician in the Modern World.*"

Eisenberg, poring over his notes, didn't look up at the audience.

"Our third speaker is Professor Maisy Andrus of the Law School of Massachusetts Bay. A widely known lecturer in the area of legal and societal mores, Professor Andrus is a graduate of Bryn Mawr and the University of Pennsylvania School of Law. Prior to joining the faculty at Mass Bay, she taught at Boston College School of Law and George Mason University. Professor Andrus practiced health and hospital law in Washington, D.C., also serving as a school committee member and a trustee of a battered women's shelter." Jurick held up another book. "Professor Andrus is the author of *Our Right to Die.*"

Jurick lowered the book. "It is now my pleasure to turn the podium over to our first speaker, the Reverend Vonetta Givens. Reverend Givens?"

Steady applause began as Jurick retreated to the shadow chair. Parishioners shouted brief encouragement as Givens moved to the mike. Perhaps five three under a beehive wig, even the robe couldn't conceal the serious tonnage she carried.

Wonsley whispered, "I've heard she's very good."

The mike was on a gooseneck. Givens adjusted it, none too gently, down to mouth level. She spread her notes across the podium, clamped both hands on the sides of the surface, and opened fire.

"You all have been told this is a debate tonight. I suggest to you it is no such thing. I suggest to you that it is a contest, a contest you shall witness between the forces of God and the forces that are not God's."

A few voices said, "That's right," stressing the first word.

"The forces that are not God's are those who would say that life is not for God to take but rather for man. For man to take when man has grown too *tired* of caring for the sick, too *tired* of doing for the elderly, too *tired* of fulfilling the natural and divine duty each and every one of us has to assist his brother and sister in their times of greatest need and weakness."

73

More "That's right" and several "Amens" piped up politely.

"Which of you would cast the first stone by saying, 'It is too much trouble for me to tend my own'? Which of you would sleep better, eat better, *live* better, knowing you had ended a life you knew and loved? A life which God as part of His almighty and miraculous plan had placed before you to nurture. When we wore the chains of the white slave owners, we were forbidden to learn how to read and write. It was a *crime* for anyone to teach us such things. Are we who know the worst of what it is to have decisions made for us and against us and on top of us, are we now to say, 'I know what is best for that life, and what is best is that I should end it?' "

What started as "That's right" and "Amen" became "No! No!"

"Of course we are not to say that. We are not to say that because we are creatures of God and creatures of conscience. Creatures that can love and pray and give thanks for loving and praying both, because those qualities are what truly separate us from the beasts of fang and hoof. If we were to *kill* our brothers and sisters, our fathers and mothers, who gave us life itself, just because it has become more expensive and less efficient to clutch these dear souls to our bosom, then what have we become? We have gone *back* and dropped *down,* we have rejoined the beasts of fang and hoof, tearing at kin and neighbor just to make our own lives easier. And that must never be."

A lot of the black members of the audience leaned forward in their seats, sensing the crescendo before I did. A thin sheen of perspiration above the reverend's eyebrows refracted the baby spot almost mystically.

"That must never be because then who would be safe from the twin swords of expense and efficiency? Who can we *justify* maintaining in our nursing homes as their lives draw to a close in God's unknowable time? Who can we *justify* healing and strengthening at the midpoint of a life so far not productive, so far not in the image that Wall Street and Madison Avenue would have us embrace? And who can we *justify* suckling and warming and bringing forth from the nursery, when we know deep down in our hearts that no one can predict what turn that life might take.

"I suggest to you, to you brother and to you sister, that no one can ap*proach,* that no one can ex*ceed,* that no one can"—Givens fixed Eisenberg and Andrus—"de*bate* the infinite and everlasting judgment of the Lord God and Jesus Christ as to which of the creatures fashioned in Their image is now ready to be returned to Them. Amen."

Givens scooped up her notes and went back to her seat. Most of the blacks and perhaps twenty percent of the whites gave her a standing ovation, stamping their feet harder than they were clapping their hands.

Over the din I heard Rick, the second banana, say to Gun, "We do it, the cops are on us like fucking glue. The niggers do it—"

Gun cut him off by raising his hand in a stop sign.

Jurick waited until the tumult died away before moving to the microphone. "Thank you, Reverend Givens. And now, ladies and gentlemen, Dr. Paul Eisenberg."

Eisenberg, over six feet tall, got up in fits and starts, his chair not gliding back. He was bald, with a full beard and half glasses. His hand shook visibly as he laid his papers on the podium. Eisenberg began to read from them without readjusting the height of the microphone. He stopped and twisted the mike as people in the audience tittered.

Eisenberg started over. "Unlike Reverend Givens before me and Professor Andrus to follow, I am not an accomplished public speaker. Therefore, I have to hope that the logic of what I have to say to you can rise above my awkwardness in saying it. My ultimate message, however, transcends even logic. That message is, 'First, do no harm.'

"That is the cornerstone of all medical training. The physician must first be certain that he does—excuse me, that he *or she*—does no harm to the patient involved. Our entire mission is to save lives, not to contribute, directly or indirectly, to the taking of them. There can be no right to die because there can be no right to kill, not even one's own self, because suicide is an act recognized as a crime by the entirety of the civilized world. To be confronted with a situation in which a patient, or the family of a patient, requests that a physician end life is simply anesthetic—excuse me, is simply *antithetical*—to all we believe in as physicians within a civilized society."

People shifted in their seats, many coughing. One loud sneeze produced a collective low laugh.

"As some of you may know, we have a system in Massachusetts under which the relatives of a terribly sick patient can petition a court of law to rule on the administering or withholding of certain life-sustaining processes. With all respect to the profession of the next speaker, I do not understand how a state like Massachusetts, which has outlawed within its judicial system the death penalty for even the most heinous crime, can then turn to that same judicial system and say 'Please impose the death penalty on a patient whose only transgression is to have fallen sick.' A patient who is typically comatose and who may present"—Eisenberg looked up at us for the first time—"as Reverend Givens so eloquently stated, a, uh . . . excuse me." Eisenberg ran a finger down the page. ". . . a *burden,* may present a burden both financial and emotional, to the family and the treatment delivery system. I am troubled with becoming an advocate and, worse, an instrument for the death of one patient so that another patient, who I believe might benefit more from treatment of a limited availability, could now be accommodated.

"However, I am even more troubled by a system in which such decisions are made secretly, without even benefit of a logically flawed justice system. I am most troubled by the very real possibility of people taking the law into their own hands in a way that is not only illegal but immoral and would undermine the very protections of the individual upon which our society is based. Each of us is only as safe as his or her neighbor. For any of us to be safe, all of us must be safe."

Eisenberg looked up again. "Uh, thank you for your attention."

Strained applause died away before the doctor resumed his seat. Nobody likes to be read to.

Olivia Jurick came to the high mike. On tiptoe she said, "And now, ladies and gentlemen, Professor Maisy Andrus."

Andrus stood smoothly, striding to the podium with no notes. Engaging the audience, she looked from section to section until there was no noise in the lecture hall, not a cough, not a rustle.

Then, "I stand before you tonight for a very simple reason: I killed my husband. Under the laws of most countries, I was guilty of a crime. Under the laws of Spain, where the incident took place, I was guilty of a worse crime: as a wife, I committed parricide, the killing of the male head of the family.

"Well, what I did was no crime in my mind or heart, and I suspect it would be none in yours either. My goal is to have the feelings in those minds and hearts reflected in rational laws which permit society to evolve, as it must, if we are to survive as a species in close contact with each other. Despite Reverend Givens's impassioned presentation, the law is not some capital-letter, quasi-religious absolute. Despite Dr. Eisenberg's dispassionate presentation, the law is not some scientifically logical formula into which factors need merely be inserted to produce uniformly correct answers.

"The doctor alluded to suicide. The original purpose behind the prohibition of suicide was the same as that against male masturbation: to promote the continuation of our species. Given the size of the global population and its rate of reproduction, the rule against suicide is no longer needed to ensure that survival. Indeed, we are now presented with the converse problem.

"In 1988, two-thirds of the doctors polled by the American Medical Association reported being involved in decisions to withhold or withdraw treatment, and the American Hospital Association estimates that seventy percent of hospital deaths now occur because of family and medical termination of treatment. In response to these statistics, courts in twenty states ruled on the right to die, the Supreme Court of the United States recently confirming the constitutional basis of that right.

"The law can, and must, take into account aspects of our changing society. Religion depends on prayer, medicine on technology. But when our religious views become so entrenched and our medicine so sophisticated, we all simply must recognize a basic truth. Each and every one of us has certain rights of person, certain rights of spirit, that neither religion nor medicine nor a government supportive of both should be able to take away. Such is the basis of the right to abortion—"

Hisses and boos jumped out all over the room, vying with applause.

"Such is the right to sexual preference—"

More noise.

"And such is the right to die. To determine for oneself that the time has come when prayer is no longer availing, when the medicine that can prolong life can no longer improve it. I believe it barbaric to force our elderly, our infirm, our comatose and their respective families to continue to suffer when a veterinarian would be reviled for not bestowing a parallel mercy on a similarly situated dog or cat.

"I began tonight by saying that I killed my husband, but there is a difference between cruelly killing someone with kindness and mercifully killing that person kindly. Let me close by describing to you

77

what my husband's life would have been like without my helping him. He was fifty-two years old, he had suffered a stroke. A doctor himself, he knew that the only possible prognosis was irreversible deterioration. His condition cost him his native tongue; cost him the ability to move his limbs, to swallow, to sit up, even to control his bowels. He was no longer a tenth of the vital, loving, caring person he'd been all his life. The alternative to my helping him would have been months of humiliation and pain, both mental and physical, and toward what end? To set some sort of unofficial record for suffering in a sport where everyone insists upon adherence to the rules but no one rewards those who try the hardest. Please, let us reconsider together, unblinded by religion or logic, and simply endorse what is right and fair and appropriate: the ending of life when life has ceased to be what any of us would call living. Thank you."

Sincere applause, growing as Andrus reached her seat. She looked down into the sashed area, smiled, and nodded. I could see Tucker Hebert flash her a thumbs-up.

Olivia Jurick returned to the podium. "Thank you, Professor Andrus. I'd now like to take questions. If you have something to ask, please raise your hand. I believe everyone will be able to hear a bit better if you stand while putting your question. Uh, yes, ma'am, you, please."

An austere woman with straight hair the color of chrome rose and began to speak with Locust Valley lockjaw. "I think it obvious to any rational person that tonight's debate has demonstrated the absolute bankruptcy of the so-called Dukakis 'Massachusetts Miracle' which was always a function of Reagan administration deficit spending on the Commonwealth's defense contractors."

Del Wonsley said, "A wild-card favorite."

As Jurick leaned into the microphone to interrupt, the austere woman said, "That's all I have to say," and dropped back into her seat.

Jurick quickly pointed to an older man with short gray hair. Standing awkwardly and wearing a cardigan sweater, his voice was raspy. "Professor Andrus, my daughter was sick and got ahold of your book." He held up a copy by the binding. "Three weeks later she went and killed herself. How do you feel about that?"

A number of people in the audience gasped. Alec Bacall smiled grimly. "Off to the races."

Jurick didn't seem to know what to do as moderator.

Maisy Andrus never left her chair. "Since I don't believe I knew your daughter, sir, I—"

"Her name was Heidi. Heidi Doleman. Now you know."

I came forward in my seat. I couldn't see any bulges over Louis Doleman's hips, but that didn't mean he wasn't carrying up front for a cross-draw.

"As I was about to say, Mr. Doleman, since I don't believe I knew your daughter, I don't know what to think of her death. If she was suffering, I hope that you and any other loved ones supported her in what she believed to be best."

"Weren't any other loved ones, Professor. Just Heidi and me. But you've said just about what I thought you would."

As Doleman sat back down, Olivia Jurick nearly sighed in relief over the mike. She pointed to a teenage girl directly between us and the stage.

The girl wore a pink beret over sandy hair. "Professor Andrus, do you think it's right for little babies to be taken from the womb and killed before they get asked whether or not they're ready to die?"

Grumbling and shushing in the audience.

Again from her chair, Andrus said, "We're not here tonight to argue for or against abortion, but yes, I think the woman carrying the fetus has such a right, though it is intellectually distinct from the right to die."

The girl raised her voice over more grumbling and less shushing. "I'm not asking you intellectually, Professor. I'm asking you morally. Is it right to kill that baby?"

From the lower left section, a black female voice said, "Answer the child."

Andrus said, "I've already given you my best answer on that."

Reverend Givens cut in. "Child, you want *my* answer on that?"

Reluctantly, I thought, the pink beret said, "Sure."

"Well, my answer is simple. You kill that baby, and you'll never forgive yourself. You'll never in your life forget. You have that baby, and somebody will give it a fine home and a good upbringing."

Gun yelled out, "What if it comes out half black?"

Givens shaded her eyes with her hand, and others in the audience turned to glare at Gun, then turn away as he and his cohort gave them the finger. The salt-and-pepper police team looked at each other and started forward.

Givens said, "I can't see you, but I'm guessing from the tone of your voice you're the type that does better wailing from the darkness than speaking in the light."

A solid round of applause. The cops hesitated, then went back to the wall and crossed their arms.

Givens said to the pink beret, "Child, however that baby comes out, you come see me if you have any troubles about it."

More applause as Olivia Jurick gratefully pointed to a well-dressed older black man.

"Dr. Eisenberg. Can you tell me, Doctor, how all of us are going to be able to afford keeping all these patients alive while you and your friends at the hospital get upward of five hundred dollars a day?"

Eisenberg winced. "That's, uh, more a question for a hospital administrator than a doctor."

"But you're the one's been saying it here."

"Yes, well, you see, it's not really you who pays for all that. The insurance companies do."

"Out of the goodness of their hearts, huh?"

"Well, no, no, of course not. From premiums they collect and investments they make. But—"

"And who be paying those premiums, Jack?"

Del Wonsley said, "Right on."

Jurick said, "I wonder if we could have another question? Yes?"

The black man shook his head in disgust as he sat back down. Jurick's finger pointed to Walter Strock.

Strock rose, Kimberly watching him as if he were the Hope diamond. "Two questions, if I may. First, for Professor Andrus. Professor, earlier you referred to a constitutional 'right to die.' Now, you'll certainly agree that the Supreme Court of the United States in the *Cruzan* case established only that a patient has the right to decline life-*sustaining* medical aid. I wonder, where in the Constitution do you encounter the right to life-*terminating* assisted suicide?"

Andrus spoke very evenly. "Our country was founded on the principles of 'life, liberty, and the pursuit of happiness.' The right to liberty must include a right to die. Otherwise, 'life' and 'the pursuit of happiness' would become inconsistent concepts now that medical technology can, as I said earlier, prolong a painful, hopeless 'life' without any possibility of 'pursuing happiness.' "

"How imaginative of the Founding Fathers to *include* all that."

Over the laughter his sarcasm triggered, Strock said, "And my second question is for Dr. Eisenberg. In your remarks, Doctor, you voiced concern over the situation in which you are asked to terminate a patient who has become a burden on his family?"

"Yes?"

"I wonder, are you more concerned about terminating a patient whose timely death might *benefit* his family?"

Alec Bacall said, "The pompous little shit."

Eisenberg sensed something, but I'm not sure he got Strock's innuendo, because he just said, "Why, yes, of course."

Strock closed with a flourish and a smile. "Thank you, Doctor. That's all I have."

As Olivia Jurick looked over the crowd, Gun got to his feet.

"Hey, I got a question."

Jurick said, "If you could wait—"

"My question is how come you don't have somebody who can talk for real Americans on this panel?"

Jurick said, "Sir, if you—"

The other skinheads prepared for protection as the cops moved toward them.

Gun cranked it up. "How come we got to listen to a shine, a kike, and probably a dyke did her own husband? How come nobody talks about the race criminals in this country trying to strangle it and strangle the people who built it, huh?"

The cops were trying to get to Gun, the rest of the audience trying to retreat, but Rick and the other skinheads had moved toward the aisle to act as a barrier. No weapons I could see.

Jurick said over the microphone, "Officers, if you would please—"

"Fuck all, bitch, you got your goddamn nigger cops and your goddamn kike judges, but you can't silence the real Americans, and we're going to take back what we never should have lost in the first place."

Two skinheads began scuffling with each cop but not throwing any punches. The crowd got really nervous now and started scrambling out of the confining rows and into the surging aisles.

I said to Bacall, "Save my seat, will you?"

Going over the tops of chairs, I grabbed Gun's right ear, my fingers wrapping around the cartilage like a pistol grip. I squeezed until he bent forward at the waist and started squeaking.

I yelled, "Enough."

There was a momentary pause in everything, a video frame of uniforms and skinheads.

"Gun, tell your friends to let go of the cops."

Rick the skinhead said, "Shit, Gun, knock his hand away."

I said, "He knocks my hand away, his ear comes with it."

Gun squeaked some more. "Do it, Rick. . . . Let them go."

Rick released the white cop and said "Shit" again just as he got whirled onto the floor.

Security guards from the library upstairs appeared, and I maneuvered Gun over to the black cop. As I walked back to my seat, Jurick was saying, ". . . and I want to thank our speakers and all of you once more and remind you of the book signing that will . . ."

Alec Bacall said, "And how did you enjoy the debate, John?"

"It was all right. Kind of a cold crowd, though."

Del Wonsley said, "Oh, I don't know. I thought that many were appalled, but few were frozen."

Bacall grinned. "That's why I love him so."

10

Plato's Bookshop occupied a double-wide retail space on Newbury Street, three blocks from the lecture hall. I was delayed at the Rabb, giving the cops and the units that responded to their call the details as I saw them. By the time I got to the store, the signing was in full progress.

The window next to the door held a poster with information about the debate and the signing to follow. Under the poster and inside the shop was a display table. Around an eight-by-ten black and white glossy portrait of Maisy Andrus were maybe a hundred copies of her book. Some lay on their sides in irregular piles while others stood up in little wire holders. A dozen copies of Paul Eisenberg's book were shunted to one corner. There was no photo of Eisenberg and nothing at all about the Reverend Givens.

Two lines of people trailed back from signing tables in the rear of the shop. Eisenberg's line was a lot shorter than the one in front of Andrus, and many of the Eisenberg hopefuls also carried a copy of her book under their arms. I saw Olivia Jurick smiling and shaking hands in a regular-customer way as she moved down the aisle created by the two lines. On side counters were wine and punch, cheese and crackers, grapes and pretzels. I could see Inés Roja standing beside the sitting Andrus, opening the next copy of the book to a given page for the professor to sign. Manolo stood a step behind Andrus, glowering at each fan.

Alec Bacall and Del Wonsley were holding wineglasses and watching Tucker Hebert entertain several fashionable women with what appeared to be hilarious stories. I spotted the blonde I took to be Kimberly and then, when she turned, Walter Strock, which surprised me. He wasn't carrying a copy of Andrus's book, which didn't surprise me. I didn't see the Reverend Givens nor, if skin color was a gauge, many of her flock.

Bacall saw me and beckoned to cut through the Andrus line. Eisenberg was shaking the hand of his last fan and looking around, rather awkwardly, presumably for Olivia Jurick to tell him what to do next. In front of Andrus, a matronly woman had just handed her copy of *Our Right to Die* to Inés for prepping. Roja opened it, turned a page, and then dropped the book like a picnic plate with a bee on it.

I pushed through the line as politely as possible. Andrus had picked up the book and was apologizing to the matron when Andrus saw Roja's facial expression. Manolo saw it, too, and edged forward, eyes mainly on the matron.

I said, "What's the matter?"

Andrus replied, "I don't know."

Inés had one hand to her mouth and the other pointing to the book Andrus was setting on the table.

The matron started to say something about the jacket being damaged and wanting another when I said, "Please?"

Taking out a pen, I prodded the book to a centered position in front of me. Using the pen as a friction finger, I opened the book and turned the leaves until I got to the title page.

There, under "by Maisy Andrus," was a stickum mailing label with the cut-out words: "THIS CLOSE WHO-RE."

"I just couldn't tell you, Mr. Cuddy."

Olivia Jurick was behind her cash register, wagging her head as Maisy Andrus gamely signed the last few books for the faithful who had stayed on line. The offending copy was between Jurick and me in a plastic Plato's Bookshop bag.

I said, "Any way to determine who had access to the books?"

"Not really," said Jurick. "We put the poster up last Monday. Seven days of promotion is about the most our customers can tolerate. But copies of her book have been in the store for at least a month before that. I could check our invoices if you'd like?"

"I don't think that'll make a difference. The woman who brought the book to Inés Roja—"

"Mrs. Thomason."

"Mrs. Thomason said she got the book from the display table."

"Yes, well, I'm fairly certain that all of the books on the table came from the special shipment I ordered for the signing."

"And how long have they been here?"

"On the table, you mean?"

"In the store at all."

"Well, the boxes would have arrived about a week before the poster went up, meaning about two weeks ago."

"And on the display table?"

"We wouldn't have opened the boxes and set up publicly, you know, until the poster notice, so I would say early last week."

"Anyone on your staff mention anything odd about people hanging around the table?"

"No. But then, you must understand, Mr. Cuddy, this is a bookstore. Our customers leaf through books in the process of deciding which to buy. Since that horrible message was already on a mailing label, someone could have stuck it there in five seconds or so. None of my staff would have noticed that."

"Even if the person was wearing gloves at the time?"

Jurick shrugged. "It is December."

I looked over at the display table, nearly emptied of books now. All our boy had to do, any time in the last week, was pick up a copy of *Our Right to Die,* stick the label in it, then bury the copy maybe halfway down one pile. To be sure it wasn't sold pre-signing but would be brought to Andrus during the signing.

Jurick said, "Will the book help at all?"

"Excuse me?"

She stopped just short of touching the plastic bag. "This copy. Will you be able to use it for clues?"

"The guy's been pretty careful so far. I'll take it to the police, but there's not much chance they'll get anything from it."

Jurick shook her head. "Who would do such a thing?"

"You find out, let me know."

11

I said to Alec Bacall, "How is Inés doing?"

He gestured at the massive central staircase. "She went up to her room to lie down."

"Inés lives here too?"

"Oh, yes. Maisy often likes to work at night, and this way Inés can be available for whatever."

Bacall said the last in a matter-of-fact way, no inflection or other indication of double meaning. We were standing alone in a ground floor parlor done in blue pastels. Bacall, Wonsley, and I had taken a taxi together, following another cab with Andrus, Tucker Hebert, Roja, and Manolo to the town house. Once there, Manolo exchanged hand signals with Andrus, then seemed to disappear while Andrus and Hebert climbed the steps to the second floor. Bacall and I had gone with Wonsley into the kitchen before he began opening cabinets and shooed us out the swinging door.

On a mews at the flat of Beacon Hill near Charles, the town house was more truly a mansion. Fifty feet wide at the street, at least seventy feet deep. We were within blocks of the buildings where Daniel Webster, Louisa May Alcott, and Henry James spent their time.

I said, "Just how big is this place?"

"Well," said Bacall, "I haven't seen every nook and cranny, but the design is pretty typical for its vintage. The second floor front has a living room or library, the rear a large study. The master bedroom and bath are on the third floor, with a studio for painting or needlepoint or whatever the hell Mater and Pater did back then. Children's and staff quarters are on the fourth floor, under the eaves, where it's coldest in winter and hottest in summer. The Victorians really knew how to handle that."

Much of Beacon Hill is Federalist red brick, but there wasn't much doubt Bacall was right about the period in which the Andrus home was built. Still, you'd have to be current in the real estate market to know how many millions it would fetch.

When I didn't say anything, Bacall leaned a little closer. "I really don't think you need worry about Inés. She's seen a lot worse than this."

"Coming over from Cuba?"

Just a nod. "She's a strong woman, and a good one too. She used to volunteer at an AIDS clinic Del and I support."

"Used to?"

"Inés found she couldn't stand to see people suffering."

"Not many can."

Another nod.

"Coffee or tea?"

Wonsley was carrying a tray with lots of things on it that I couldn't identify.

"I'll pass, thanks. Can you two give me a while upstairs?"

Bacall said, "Certainly, John."

I climbed to an elliptical landing with double doors on either end. I walked to the front set. Through the narrow slit between the doors came the muted noise of a stadium crowd and the strobing of a video monitor in an otherwise darkened room. I knocked and a southern accent said, "Hold just a second."

Tucker Hebert threw open doors which slid into the walls on either side of the threshold. He'd taken off the jacket, tie, and shoes. His dress shirt was unbuttoned almost to the waist.

I said, "I hope I'm not breaking in on you?"

Hebert grinned. "Just trying to get comfortable. Maisy's in her study. You'd be the detective, right?"

"Private investigator. John Cuddy."

"Tuck Hebert." His grip was almost a vise. "Come on in and set yourself down. Fix you something?"

I could see a crystal tumbler, nearly full of amber liquid and ice cubes, on a cocktail table. "Beer?"

"Easy enough." Hebert went behind a bar of padded leather and brass implates. I heard the noises a miniature refrigerator makes.

The table with his drink squatted close to an Eames chair and ottoman. The chair was positioned in front of a wide-screen television and a console of video equipment. On the screen, two tennis players were moving around, the taller one slowing to serve, the other hopping and snorting to receive. The rest of the room was basically floor-to-ceiling bookshelves. In the flickering light, the only things I could see on the shelves were videocassettes and trophies.

Hebert popped the cap from a bottle of Miller's Genuine Draft with a church key. "I know these fellers are twistoffs, but I cut my racquet hand on one once, and I've been shy ever since."

I took the beer from him, no mention of a glass being made. Hebert picked up a remote-control device, but waited while the point was being played on the screen.

"Watch me crush this one."

I did, realizing the bigger guy was a younger Hebert. He took a ball that bounced near his eyes and swept it away crosscourt, beyond the reach of the opponent with dark hair.

"That was match point against me there. Survived that and went on to take the set seven-six in the tiebreaker. Lordy, old Harold did give me trouble with that moonball of his."

Without looking at the remote device, Hebert hit stop and then off. Pushing a third button caused the recessed lights at the tops of the bookshelves to grow brighter.

He palmed the device lovingly before setting it down. "Little feller does about everything for you except wash the windows. Now, what can I do for you?"

"Maybe answer a few questions?"

"Sure, sure." He curled into the Eames chair and reached for his drink. "Have a seat."

I angled a velvet wingback that probably once felt at home in the room and sat down.

Up close and well lit, Hebert's features were strong but lined, the year-round tan like the patina on the surface of an antique. The ready smile reminded me of locally produced car commercials, the only detraction other than age being a swipe line through his left eyebrow. He took a healthy swig of what looked more and more like Scotch.

"You know I've been asked to look into the threats to your wife."

This time he grinned without showing his teeth and put down the drink. "Tell you what, John."

"What?"

"Let's not dance around too much, okay? I know Alec and Inés went to see you, and I also know that Maisy near pitched a fit over it till she met you. By this afternoon, though, she seemed to think you were an idea whose time had come. I figure that if I was playing in your shoes, I'd wonder how come the younger husband of the older rich lady isn't too concerned about all this. How am I doing so far?"

"Forty-love."

The ready smile again. "You play?"

"Hacked at it when I was in the army."

"Too bad. It was a great game, twenty years ago. Solid American players coming up. Bob Lutz, Roscoe Tanner, Jeff Borowiak. That Borowiak, he had a huge serve, a real stud who could blow you off the court. Smart too. Took the NCAA the year before Connors beat Tanner."

To keep the conversation going, I said, "Wasn't Laver the dominant one in those days?"

"Yeah, but most of the Aussies were good. Laver, Newcombe, Rosewall, Roche. We were all using sixteen-gauge string by then, and some of us even went to double stringing. We called it 'spaghetti,' winding another string around the basic one? Put tremendous spin on the ball before it got banned by WCT and then by individual tournaments too."

Hebert shook his head and laughed inwardly. "Yeah, a great sport, one of the few you can stay with no matter how old you get. And it surely does beat stumbling on gopher holes around eighteen greens just to have an excuse for getting drunk on the nineteenth."

He scoffed a little more Scotch, apparently not feeling the need for an excuse but not really showing any effect from the booze either.

I said, "How long since you retired?"

"Retired? 'Retired,' now, that's a kind word, John, and I thank you for using it. I had to hang up the serious game at thirty-one, which if you're counting was seven years back. But it's not like you work for a corporation and build up a pension and stock plans and all. Nossir, it's get some backers, get in, and get what you can, because the show's over awful fast. Hey, now, I can't really complain, you understand? I had the brass ring for a while there."

Hebert set down the drink to count on his fingers. "One French Open, finalist at Wimbledon, semis three years running at Forest Hills. But what I had was the serve and the crosscourts, like you saw on that tape there. When the old rotator cuff went . . ."

He moved his shoulder in a very slow-motion serve. I could hear a crickling noise that had nothing to do with the starching of his shirt.

Hebert shrugged. "That was all she wrote."

"Can you still play?"

"Lordy, no. That is, not *play* play. You know the difference between, say, a Corvette and a Prelude?"

I didn't know if he was aware I drove a Honda and was toying with me, so I said, "No."

"Well, your Corvette, now, that's a sports car. But your Prelude, now, that's just a spor*ty* car, get me?"

"The difference between an athlete and somebody who's just athletic."

"There you go. Well, I'm a Prelude that knows it used to be a Corvette. Oh, I'm happy to go out and shuck my way through a celebrity tournament for charity and all, but I can't really play no more, no more."

"And this has just what to do with the threats to your wife?"

Hebert finished his drink and got up immediately. "Another?"

I'd barely touched the Miller's. "Not just yet, thanks."

Fridge, rattle of fresh cubes, the neck of bottle clinking against rim of glass. I took in his trophies. Platters, cups, occasionally the racquet and player in metal outlined against a ceramic background.

Hebert returned to his chair. "This all has to do with Maisy like this: I'm her husband. She used to have some doctor from Europe who died, but I'm it now. She's quite a woman, Maisy, but she gets an idea in her head, and it's Katy-Bar-the-Door, you think you're gonna change her mind. Like the players on the tour today."

"I'm sorry?"

"The players today. They verbalize everything. Take 'first serve percentage.' John, do you know I never, ever heard anybody *say* that all the time I played? Nossir, all you'd say to yourself then was 'I hope to Christ I can get this next one in.' Now they actually plan their matches around percentage and tendency and all. I suppose it does make sense. We plan everything else, why not 'first serve percentage'?"

"Or death."

Taking a slug, Hebert said, "Right, right. That's my point. Maisy's got this idea she can save the world by encouraging people to help each other die peaceable. Fine by me. I'm not about to go threatening her about it. I'm happy as can be. You know why?"

"No."

"Take any professional athlete—tennis, football, you name it. Once you've seen Paree, it's tough to give that up. Tougher than kicking drugs, I'm told by those who've known both pretty well. But your body, this thing that's made your fortune, sooner or later it lets you down, John. It goes and gets old on you.

"Now, I never held on to a dime longer than it took to order another round for the house. But it turns out I'm one of the lucky ones. Wasn't a year I was out of the tournaments, with not too many options staring me in the face, when I met up with Maisy. Boy, I was just plain dazzled by her. Don't know what she saw in me other than the usual stuff that the gossips'll spread, and there'd sure be some truth to that."

Hebert grinned. "I learned two things on the tour, John. How to serve and how to bed a woman. You've got to practice both every day, and I can still do the one to beat the band. But Maisy also provides for me."

He waved his hand around the room. "This used to be some kind of library. Well, she let me turn it into a shrine. A place I feel comfortable, like old St. Francis enjoying his sainthood before the pope declared it for him. I get everything I want out of this relationship, and I don't have to speak nice with old fogies that couldn't hit a dead hog with the sweet spot on a windless day. Nossir, I don't have to worry about tips or the IRS or club ladies getting fussy because I haven't made a move to lift their skirts. A lot of players I knew—good ones, too, John. Tough, chew-your-leg-off competitors—they've got to worry about those things. Not me. And if you think I'd piss in the well by threatening Maisy, you've got another think coming."

"Why would I think that?"

Hebert put his drink on the table, nearly sloshing it. "Because I was here when Inés found the threat note in the mailbox."

I thought about it. "You hear or see anything unusual that day?"

"Nothing. Sound asleep for a good part of it. Friend of mine from the *old* old days, he was in town, and we tied one the night before."

"You were sleeping off a drunk."

"Dead to the world till I heard all the commotion downstairs over the note."

"And tonight?"

"What about tonight?"

"You were there, at the auditorium and the bookstore. You see anything?"

"Just what everybody else did. Bunch of neurotics talking to themselves, except for my Maisy. But I was smiling, John. I was smiling because that's my job, and I'm happy to be doing it."

"And you're not taking the threats that seriously."

Hebert retrieved his drink. "You have any notion how many threats Maisy receives in a week?"

"You have any notion who's behind this batch?"

"Sure don't."

"You ever meet the first husband's son?"

"Who?"

"The doctor had a son. You ever meet him?"

"Oh, yeah. Not at the wedding though, I can tell you that. No, there was some kind of business for the estate in Spain. Couple of years ago, still dragging on all that time. Name of . . . just a second . . . Ra-mone was what Maisy called him."

"What was your impression of him?"

A sip. "You ever traveled through Europe, John?"

"No."

"Well, you do, and you get certain vibes from people. Like they know you're richer, maybe more powerful than they are, but they still think they're better?"

"Go on."

"Well, this guy wasn't like that. All-American and pleased as punch about being in the States. Even changed his name to just Ray, I think."

"Anything else?"

Another sip. "Not that I remember. Seems to me Ray signed all the papers he had to, no muss or bother. I don't believe he's been around since."

"So you wouldn't think the son was behind this?"

"No. I'll tell you something, though."

"What's that?"

"I find the feller's been sending these things . . ." Hebert tossed the rest of his drink at the back of his throat and started to get up, then paused halfway. "I'll crush the sumbitch, John. I will, messing with my life support system like he is."

I closed the doors on Hebert and was halfway around the landing when Maisy Andrus stuck her head through the other threshold on the floor.

I said, "How are you doing?"

"All right, I suppose. Do you have a minute?"

"Sure."

I followed her into the study, also lined with floor-to-ceiling bookshelves, these actually containing books. There were law titles, but many seemed to be from other disciplines such as philosophy, sociology, medicine, and history. Andrus settled into a desk chair. Off to one side, computer components ranged over a trilevel table. The monitor was still glowing above one of those backless chairs that resemble a disoriented Catholic kneeler.

I said, "Kind of late to be working, isn't it?"

A tired smile aimed at the computer table. "I sometimes find it easier to write at night. And you're still working, aren't you?"

"Your husband's an interesting man."

Reclining in the chair, Andrus closed her eyes. "Tell me, John. Do you use the word 'interesting' when you're fishing for information about a person?"

"Sometimes."

A laugh with an edge of superiority in it. "Actually, I agree with you about Tuck being interesting. Most people don't adjust well to a fading of the limelight. But Tuck seems to be an exception."

I thought about other people, including me, who'd "adjusted" with alcohol, but I didn't interrupt her.

"You see, John, Tuck truly lived in the fast lane. Money, cars, women. Real glitz, if that's not an oxymoron. But when it was over, he acknowledged the fact, and he's entered a new phase of his life."

"Which is?"

"Being thought of as a 'trophy husband.' "

I remembered the phrase as "trophy wife" from a magazine article on successful male executives. "Meaning you sport Tuck as a trophy husband to show you've made it as a female professional?"

A brighter smile, the eyes opening. "No pun intended?"

"No pun intended."

"My point is, that's how others think of Tuck, as an object of Maisy's overcompensating. But it's not how Maisy thinks of him."

"I see."

"What do you see?"

"I see that you and Wade Boggs are the only people in Boston who refer to themselves in the third person."

Another laugh, but hearty, not superior. "That's what I mean."

"What?"

"My first husband was considerably older than I was. Tuck is somewhat younger than I am. But while that does have its advantages, Tuck is really very smart. Not in a book-learning sense, but like your observation just now. The needle that deflates the balloon, that makes you rethink your own position. From class this morning, recall my insistence that the students use 'he or she' when referring to an unidentified person such as a client or a judge?"

"Yes."

"Well, Tuck once heard me do that, and he remarked that saying it that way took more time. I said that I wanted the students to be comprehensive as well as inoffensive, and he asked me what I did if the client were a corporation or governmental body. I replied that 'he, she, or it' might be appropriate. At that point Tuck gave me that good-ol'-boy grin of his and took out a piece of paper. He wrote 'S/HE/IT' and said 'How about having your students just say it like this?' Well, I pronounced what he'd written, him grinning wider, and it struck me that I had to do a little more justifying with the class on why my approach was important. Tuck wasn't being disrespectful to women. He simply used his wit to make me reexamine my position."

"Can I do the same?"

The tired smile this time. "Go ahead."

"You think your husband is above suspicion?"

Her features distorted. "Certain of it."

"How does he benefit if you die?"

"You call that using your wit?"

"I call that getting you to reexamine your position. How about it?"

Andrus squared her shoulders and sat a little straighter. "He would receive the bulk of my estate, the residue after some charities and public service organizations."

I inclined my head toward the center of the mansion. "Quite a residue. You have everything here but a two-car garage."

She didn't get it. "We keep the Benz around the corner, in the Brimmer Street garage."

A Mercedes in a condo parking space. Add another hundred and a half to the estate. "My point is—"

"I can see your point, John. I just don't think it has any merit. Tuck is many things, but not a killer. Or somebody who'd threaten it by note. He's an in-your-face sort of man. Besides, trite as it may sound, he loves me and we're happy together."

"How about Walter Strock?"

"*Walter?*"

"He was there tonight, both at the lecture and the signing when Inés opened the labeled book."

"Oh, my, John. Perhaps one of us has seen too many movies. Walter Strock is an anachronism. A foolish, petty man whose last refuge from real world inadequacy is a law school faculty where he can play his little mind games. He had to leave practice because the pressure got to him. Anything outside the school itself is now beyond his horizons."

"The Rabb is 'outside the school.' "

"True, but Walter's performance at the library was a real stretch for him. Believe me."

"Strock seems pretty bitter toward you."

"No doubt. Walter thinks I'm somehow the reason he didn't get the deanship, an opportunity to turn Mass Bay into a kind of legal Levittown, his dream of how academia should work."

"How about your stepson?"

"My stepson?"

"Ramón, or Ray?"

Andrus shook her head. "No, no. Ramón and I may not care much for each other, but all that was resolved years ago. Besides, if I were to die, he gets nothing."

"Except the satisfaction that you wouldn't be enjoying all this anymore."

"John, Ramón is just not interested in me now."

Andrus seemed to flush a little.

I said, "Was he ever interested in you?"

"That's not material here. Believe me, Ramón cannot be part of this." She softened a bit. "John, I remember what you said this morning about psychopaths, and I'm not trying to cover old ground. But tell me, this . . . warning in the book tonight. Does it change your view of the situation?"

"According to the bookstore manager, anybody could have doctored that copy anytime in the last week. Whoever did it probably knew you wouldn't be likely to see it until tonight. If you want my opinion, our friend is trying to escalate, to move in closer to you. Maybe a better question would be, does tonight change *your* view of the situation?"

"No. No in the sense that I'm not about to back down from my positions on the issues. But I have to admit I'm taking the possibility of danger more seriously now. And, consequently, I have to admit that I'm also more interested in what you're going to do next."

"I went through the box of letters Inés gave me at the school today, and I talked with the cop on the case. I'm going to approach some people who might know something. You have any objection to my seeing the Reverend Givens and Dr. Eisenberg?"

"Really? They couldn't be involved, John."

"Not directly. But someone who hates you might have sidled up to one of them at some point."

"I suppose that's possible. So you want to know if I object to your telling Givens and Eisenberg about the notes?"

"Yes."

Andrus thought about it. "No, no objection. I've met both of them before, and I know each by reputation. I would trust them to hear what you have to say and to help without publicizing my concern about it."

"In that case, I'll let you get back to work. Or sleep."

I was up and turned when she said, "John?"

"Yes?"

"I must confess. I really asked you to step in here because I'm curious."

"Curious?"

"About what you thought of the debate tonight."

The debate. "First time I ever watched three pep rallies in the same room."

A throaty laugh. "You ought to spend more time with Tuck. You'd like each other."

12

"JOHN?"

I'd almost reached the bottom of the staircase, watching Manolo sitting in a chair near the front door while Manolo watched me descending the steps. When I turned around, Alec Bacall was holding open the swinging door to the kitchen.

"Yes, Alec?"

"Are you on your way out?"

"Uh-huh."

"Let me walk with you."

Bacall got our coats from the entry closet, and we bundled up as Manolo unlocked the front door to let us into the cold.

I said, "Where's Del?"

"I phoned a cab for him. He has an early call tomorrow."

"Early call?"

"Del's an office temp. Knows three word-processing programs by heart. That's how we met, actually, although not really."

"I don't get you."

"Well, I met him when he came for an interview—I'm Bacall Office Help. On Boylston, across from the Common? But I didn't really say anything to him then."

"Why not?"

"Because he was hoping for a job, and I've always thought it a little unseemly to put the move on potential employees."

"Sounds like a good rule for any business."

"It is, believe me. About two months later, though, we ran into each other at a First Night party—last New Year's Eve—and that got us started."

We'd reached the intersection of Beacon. "Well, this is where I turn."

Bacall said, "The meter still running?"

"I charge by the day, not the hour."

"There's something I want to talk over with you. How far is your car?"

I pointed up Beacon. "Six blocks that way."

"A little closer than mine. Can we take a drive?"

"A drive? Where?"

"South Boston?"

"So that's the famous Powerhouse Pub?"

We were passing the gigantic Edison plant on our left, the tavern on the right across Summer Street as it becomes L Street. Bacall was swiveling his head like a kid at the circus.

I said, "You've never been to Southie before?"

"How could you tell?"

"Most people would come by car, and this is the most typical route. You can't miss the Edison, and the pub's pretty obvious."

"Well, you're right. I moved to Boston in 1974. Can you imagine the impression I had of Southie from the bussing controversy?"

In the seventies a series of federal court orders desegregated the Boston public schools. No white kids from South Boston were bussed out, but black kids from other parts of the city were bussed in. The television cameras captured white mothers and fathers throwing curses and rocks at innocent black children, local politicians taking stands that would have made Lester Maddox blanch.

I said, "Not Southie's finest hour."

"No. But it all looks so . . . I'm sorry, but ordinary."

"It is ordinary. Just a stable neighborhood in an era when most people move around a lot. You've still got at least two and sometimes three generations under the same three-decker roof."

"Fascinating."

I didn't think demographics were the reason for the ride, but I gave him time.

Bacall squinted at a street sign. "Broadway. This is where the St. Patrick's Day parade goes?"

"That's right. They march between Broadway station and Andrew Square. Not as big a deal now as when I was little."

"You grew up here?"

"No, but I used to think so."

"Good line to remember. I'm from New Jersey myself, near the George Washington Bridge. When they built the lower level, they called it Martha. That was pretty much the humor when I was little."

When I didn't respond, Bacall said, "John, does my being gay bother you?"

I glanced away from the traffic. He was staring at me.

I said, "It keeps me from being completely at ease."

"How do you mean?"

"Having to be careful what I say."

"In the sense that . . . ?"

"At the Rabb tonight, I enjoyed you and Wonsley joking. But I didn't jump in."

"Why?"

"I was afraid I might say something you'd take the wrong way."

"You don't know many gay men, do you?"

"A few. No real close friends so far as I know."

Turning left onto Day Boulevard, I glanced at Bacall again.

He was smiling, but not in a condescending way. "You put things very well, John."

"Is there a reason you're asking me all this?"

Bacall looked ahead. "Is that Castle Island?"

The old stone fortress loomed out of the moonlit water. "That's it."

"Can you pull in and park?"

"Sure."

We went over the curbstone, the only car in the lot. I killed the engine.

Bacall unfastened his seat belt so he could face me. "I was raised Catholic, John."

"Me too."

"It wasn't till junior high that I realized I was interested in other boys rather than girls. I didn't do anything about it, not even those gross circle jerks that stupid boys do. I went to church a lot, and to confession about the unclean thoughts. I played basketball, a good small forward. I even dated one of the flag twirlers to look right, though I obviously didn't feel right. I came out sophomore year of college, and I haven't regretted it one day since."

Not knowing what I was supposed to say, I didn't say anything.

"It was difficult, but life's difficult. Any life, all life." He lowered his voice. "Have you been following the AIDS epidemic?"

"Just TV reports on the victims."

" 'Victims.' Not a good word, John."

"It isn't?"

"No. Victims shrivel up and die. Persons with AIDS, or PWAs, fight back."

"With these new drugs?"

"There are only a couple of approved ones, like alpha interferon or azidothymidine, which you hear called AZT. Accordingly, most PWAs take other drugs against the opportunistic infections AIDS allows, like pentamidine against pneumonia. I'm not a doctor, John, but we're years away from even a vaccine, much less a cure."

"Which is why you support Maisy Andrus on the right to die."

"Partly. Most of those infected can and will live a long time. Productively too. But for some, there has to be a way out."

Bacall cleared his throat. "In the early eighties, before we knew a great deal about AIDS, a friend of mine contracted it and . . . withered terribly. He begged me to help him end his suffering, but I couldn't . . . see it that way, then. I couldn't do for my friend what Maisy had the courage and compassion to do for her husband in Spain. That's really why I support Maisy, John. She's living proof of the need to convince society that everyone has the right to end the fight mercifully and honestly. Without having to hoard pills from valid prescriptions and before descending into blindness and madness and . . . diapers, goddammit."

Bacall lowered his voice again. "Tommy—Tommy Kramer—told me you served in Vietnam?"

"That's right."

"I have a reason for asking this, John. In the war, how many friends did you lose?"

I looked away. "You didn't . . . When you were over there, you didn't keep some kind of tally."

"Between five and ten?"

I whoofed out a breath. "Ten, twelve. Around there."

"John?"

I looked back at Bacall.

His eyes were wet and glowy, but he wasn't crying, just twitching a little. "John, in the last twenty-four months I've buried twenty-eight friends."

"Jesus."

"They were older, younger, every color. They were the best people and the worst, the most fun and the least. But they were friends, and no matter how careful they thought they'd been before they even knew they needed to be careful, they got taken. Opportunistically, horribly, slowly."

I thought back to being in-country, mostly as a street MP, once in a while in the bush. The way people died, the randomness of it.

Bacall cleared his throat again, then shook his head like a fighter who'd had his bell rung. "Maisy is trying to help us her way. In helping her, you're helping us your way. And if there is anything I can do, you've got it."

"Understood."

Bacall's twitches became spasms.

"Alec, are you all right?"

"No, but I will be." He dug through his overcoat to the side pocket of his suit jacket. "Sorry about this."

"What's wrong?"

"I'm diabetic, John. More a nuisance than anything else, but the last few . . . with all the excitement, I'm a little off my insulin schedule, I guess."

Bacall drew out a leather case. He opened it to reveal an ampule of liquid and a hypodermic needle. Reaching down to his sock, he pulled up his trouser leg past mid-thigh. Even in the faint light I could see the track marks on his skin.

"You want the courtesy light?"

"No. Believe me, I can do this with my eyes closed. The double pleats keep me from having to drop my pants." He took out the syringe and, after two false starts, filled it from the ampule.

I turned away to see a cruiser stopping, the uniforms inside readying themselves to step out and over to us.

Bacall sighed. "There. Be all right in a minute."

I left my hands on the wheel, where the cops could see them. The one approaching me was female, the one coming around to the rear of the passenger side a male. Bacall, eyes closed, was breathing deeply. The leather case lay open on the dashboard.

"Alec?"

"Yes?"

"No sudden movements. We've got company. Leave the works where they are."

Bacall opened his eyes but didn't turn his head.

The woman had her right hand on the butt of her holstered weapon, using the left index knuckle to rap on my window. I rolled it down slowly.

She had close-set eyes and the cratered cheeks bad acne leaves behind. "What's the problem, boys?"

Her eyes left my face to see the paraphernalia on the dash and Bacall's exposed left leg.

I said, "This man's a diabetic. He wasn't feeling too well, so we pulled in and he took a shot."

Bacall said, "Of insulin."

"Want to step out of the car, please."

Bacall started to say something as I said, "We'll step out of the car."

I came out slowly. Bacall fumbled with the unfamiliar door handle. He locked himself in before floundering out to be caught and steadied by the male partner.

I said, "I'm carrying a Chief's Special over my right hip. I have some ID in my inside jacket pocket."

She motioned for the ID.

I took it out. Reading it, she said, "Heard of you. Nancy Meagher, right?"

"I'm seeing her."

"Nance and I went to school together." She arched her nose over a shoulder. "Gate of Heaven. Tell her Sheilah Boyle, she'll remember."

"I will."

Boyle handed me back the ID. "They're okay, Conn."

The male partner said, "Thank Christ, it's like Siberia out here." Then to Bacall, "You gonna be all right there, pal?"

"Yes. Yes, fine. Thank you."

"Have a good night," said Boyle as she and Conn trotted to their unit.

Back in my Prelude, Bacall had gotten his pant leg down and was stowing the hypo case. "Thank you, John."

"For what?"

"This happened to me once before. The police . . . well, as I said back in your office, I don't always bring out the best in them."

I started the car and drove Bacall to his house in Bay Village. On the way back to the condo I tried to convince myself that things would have gone just as smoothly with Sheilah Boyle and Conn if Bacall had spoken first.

13

I WOKE UP TUESDAY RELATIVELY FREE OF STIFFNESS DESPITE THE punishing run the previous morning. The sky outside my window was overcast, the radio quoting a temperature in the high forties. I dressed for running and went downstairs.

No sign of the derelict, but I remembered his advice. Some stretching exercises for the calves and hamstrings, not quite breaking a sweat. I started out slowly, going over the ramp to the river path in a gentle second gear. Then I began pushing off more, using the thighs and the ball of the rear foot, gradually lengthening my stride as he'd predicted. The pace didn't feel faster, but my whole body seemed in tune with the rhythm my legs were setting. I turned around at the Boston University bridge so the run would be just about three miles.

As I approached the Fairfield Street ramp again, the bum was sitting on the bench, a couple of layers of sweater off his torso and knotted around his waist like a backward apron. Nodding and smiling.

I slowed to a walk in front of him. "Didn't see you this morning."

"Saw you."

"You did."

"Uh-huh. Wanted to check first."

"Check? On what?"

"On whether you were one of those know-it-alls, couldn't take any coaching. There're a lot like that."

"And?"

"And you did just fine. The stretching, the pushing off, cutting your distance back after a tough one the day before."

I kept walking, my lungs settling down. "The run yesterday took a lot out of me."

The derelict shrugged, glasses slipping down his nose. "Wouldn't have known it. You looked pretty limber today."

"Thanks."

He thumbed the glasses back up. "Got to get some new tape for the bridge here. They been sliding on me."

I extended my right hand. "John Cuddy."

"John." He shook, but tentatively, almost mechanically, as though he hadn't done it for a while. "Just call me Bo."

"Bo." I used the sleeve near my bicep to blot some sweat off my forehead. "Bo, you really know anything about this coaching stuff?"

A glitter behind the lenses. "I do."

"Feel like training me?"

The lids lowered, and I thought he was going to get up and leave when he fixed back onto me. "Two conditions."

"What are they?"

"First, don't want no money from you."

"That doesn't seem fair."

"I decide what's fair here. I got my life, you got yours. I don't want no money."

"Okay. What's the other condition?"

"I don't want you turning me into some kind of project."

"Project?"

"Rehabilitation. Or pity. Like bringing a soldier home for Christmas dinner. Just me coaching, you listening and doing."

"You've got a deal. Shake on it?"

"We already shook. You ready for some more advice?"

"You bet."

"First thing, lose the sweat clothes and buy one of those fancy Gore-Tex suits. I know, I know, you figure you'll feel like some kind of dilettante. But you'll be able to wear just a cotton turtleneck and shorts under it, and the fabric wicks the sweat right off so you won't get chilled when the real weather comes in. January, February, you'll be running far enough we can't always start you into the wind.

You sweat down into your jock, and penile frostbite gets to be a real possibility, eh?"

"I understand."

"Second thing, go easy on the booze. Beer's okay because it's got plenty of carbohydrates. But lay off the hard stuff, dehydrates you too much."

"Right."

"Third thing, you got to drink water. Lots of water. Half gallon a day isn't out of the question. Also, get used to sugar-electrolyte drinks like Gatorade or Exceed. They'll have that stuff along the course, and you don't want the tummy getting its first taste of it at mile fourteen the day she counts."

"Anything else?"

"We have to put you on a program. You do any lifting now?"

"Nautilus."

"Fine. Stick with that, but drop the weight on your leg machines and increase the repetitions at the lower weight. Want to build that redundant function endurance."

"Okay."

"Now, for the running itself, we'll do six days on, one day off. Your body's all wrong for serious training, but we got better than four months yet. You'll train at the pace you'll maintain during the race. We'll do low mileage five days and give you a long run the sixth day for your confidence."

"I think I can handle that."

"You won't ever do more than a twenty-miler before the race herself."

"Why is that?"

"It's best to leave the last six or so as unexplored territory till you have the crowd to help you through."

"Makes sense."

Bo thumbed his glasses again. "Mornings all right?"

"That's what I'm used to anyway."

"See you here, then. Tomorrow, seven in the A.M."

"Thanks again, Bo."

"Give it a couple months." He rose and began walking upriver as he had the day before. "Then thank me, you still feel like it."

After showering I made some phone calls while my hair dried. A receptionist at Mass General told me Dr. Paul Eisenberg would be unavailable all morning, but could squeeze me in that afternoon if I promised not to take more than fifteen minutes. I promised.

I reached the Reverend Vonetta Givens directly. Nudging the truth a little, I said I'd covered the debate the previous night and wanted to ask some follow-up questions. Givens said she'd be happy to see me at her church and gave crisp directions to it.

Directory assistance had Louis Doleman's number in West Roxbury. He answered on the third ring. Without saying anything, I cut the connection, an odd noise in the background just as I depressed the plunger. It sounded like the birds from jungle movies of the forties.

I shook my head and got dressed.

"I'm here to see the Reverend Givens?"

A black kid sat behind a table inside the entrance of All Hallowed Ground Church. He had a nose that almost touched both ears and a haircut like the front view of an aircraft carrier.

"Your name, please?"

"John Cuddy."

"Just a minute."

The kid dialed two digits. He was probably a football lineman in high school, going to fat at twenty.

Into the receiver he said, "Reverend, you expecting John Cuddy?"

He nodded at the phone and replaced the receiver. "Through the door behind me."

"Thanks."

Someone on the other side of the door threw some bolts, and a near twin of the kid at the desk pulled it open, gesturing with his head that I should enter. He wore a Boston Against Drugs, or B.A.D., T-shirt and brushed against me as I went by him. Then he caught my left wrist deftly, twisted it, and wedged me up against the wall. The desk kid came up and patted me down, finding the revolver and wrenching it from the holster.

The hammerlock was good, immobilizing me just at the edge of pain. I didn't try to resist.

Desk said to Door, "Let's take him in."

Door kept the hold on me as I was ushered before the reverend. She was already on her feet, one hand inside the center drawer of the old desk between us. There were diplomas and prints and photos

framed on the walls, but no windows whatsoever. Door's grip kept
me from appreciating the ceiling, if any.

Givens looked past me, I assumed to Desk palming my gun. She
seemed to notice that I wasn't struggling. "Arthur, you may release
the man."

My arm came free.

She kept her hand in the drawer. "And who are you, really, sir?"

"John Cuddy, like I told you on the phone."

"I made some calls. Brothers and sisters in the media, print and
broad*cast*. They never heard of you."

"I have some identification in my left breast pocket."

"You may reach for it."

I opened my jacket and took out the ID, holding it up for Arthur
or his pal to take from behind me.

A voice that didn't belong to Desk said, "Private investigator,
Reverend. Want me to call 'round on him?"

"No, thank you, Arthur." She withdrew her hand from inside the
drawer. "Please return Mr. Cuddy's identification but not his gun
and leave us. Thanks to you both, again."

I got back my ID, heard two "Yes, Reverends" and a closing
door.

Givens was in a raglan-sleeved sweater and bulging jeans that I
thought might have had to be hand cut and resewn. She pointed to
a chair. "Please."

We sat simultaneously as I said, "Arthur's the guy on the door?"

"That is right."

"Not just another noseguard."

"No. Lionel—the boy at the desk—started three years for Boston
Latin, leading them in tackles. Arthur just returned to us from two
years in the military police."

I felt a little better. "They did a nice job, suckering me in."

Givens seemed to relax a bit, dropping the formal manner. "The
folks they been facing up to for me, they learned some."

"Security out front, some kind of piece in the drawer, no windows.
Who're you expecting?"

"The first drug pusher decides it's time to cross the line, kill him
a preacher. So far the real bad ones just been making fun of us,
telling the kids, 'What makes you feel better, what the fat woman
say or what we sell you?' Sealed up the windows account of that's
the way we built the storm cellars back home."

"Oklahoma."

"That's right. You ever been there?"

"Uh-uh."

"Know much about it?"

"Enough. I'm allergic to tornadoes."

"The twisters, they ain't so bad once you get used to seeing them coming. The whole sky goes green and yellow, and the clouds start moving too fast. Then there's this little band of blue sky at the horizon, and the funnel like to spinning along it, a ballerina toe-dancing her own sweet way toward you.

"I remember one day, I couldn't get home in time. So I jump into this ditch, alongside the road? Got to get yourself below ground level. Well, I feel it coming, the twister, but I don't have enough sense not to look up, and this *apart*ment house, the top two floors, anyway, be flying over my head. I could see the plumbing pipes, even the clothes a-hanging on the bedroom doorknobs. Then dead still, like the Almighty decided against wind as one of His elements, and that big house just dropped like a stone, smashed all to pieces about a hundred feet away from me. How did you know I was from Oklahoma originally?"

Nice change of pace. "Your introduction at the debate."

"You really there?"

"That's right."

"Doing what?"

"Protecting my client's interests."

Givens thrust her head forward to get a better look at me. "That Nazi honkie. You the one took him out."

"Just kind of laid hands on him, really."

She smiled a little. "Who's your client?"

"I'm happy to tell you, but my client would like it to remain in confidence."

Givens waved her hand to say "of course."

"I'm working for Maisy Andrus."

The eyebrows rose, but the hairdo didn't budge. "What's the problem?"

I took out the Xerox copies of the threats from my other pocket and handed them to her. She read one, tsked, and glanced at the others before handing them back.

"Anybody tries to tell people they ain't doing what they should gets these."

"Not in their mailbox at home, hand delivered."

"Oh."

I put the notes away. "There a reason why you didn't go to the bookstore after the debate?"

"There is. You want to hear it?"

"I would."

Givens set her expression for drudgery. "I don't have no book out, Mr. Cuddy. My people are poor, but they are behind me. I go to that store, they go with me. They see other folks, white folks, buying those books, they feel they got to buy some too, support me. They can't afford that."

"One of those notes was inside a book Andrus was given to sign."

The reverend shook her head slowly. "What do you figure you got here, big-time crazy?"

"Daring. Clever. Maybe crazy, maybe not."

Givens looked skeptical. "Why you coming to me with all this?"

"You oppose Andrus on the right to die. I'm trying to talk with anybody that a real crazy might see as a kindred spirit against her."

Emphatic shake of the head this time, almost dislodging the hairdo. "No. No, sir. My people, they are strong and they are tough, but they are good. They vote against what she says and march against what she says, but . . ." She waved her hand at my pocket. "Not anything like that. Not ever."

"Nobody comes to mind?"

"None of my own."

"Meaning somebody else?"

"You already got to be counting those skinhead fools you tussled with."

"I am."

"And the police, they must have some kind of files on this like they do on everything else."

"Not much help there."

Givens looked around the room, as if reminding herself of her own jeopardy. "All right. There's this right-to-lifer. White dude in Providence, name of Steven O'Brien."

Mr. O'Brien, one of the repeaters from the threat folders.

"I believe he is just plain around the bend, but . . . maybe."

I waited. She looked up at me.

"That's all I know."

I stood. "Thanks. By the way, why'd you leave?"

"Leave what?"

"Oklahoma."

A laugh and the gentler shake of the head. "Had me a husband, thought his thing was a battering ram and mine was a door. Knew I had to get out or I'd like to kill him."

Givens became determined, the sermon tone creeping back into her voice. "Before I turned to the Lord, I was turned on to the demon drug too. That's why I know we're going to beat cocaine and crack and what they're doing to our kids. Beat it without Professor Andrus and her just-go-to-sleep-now ideas that pretty soon catch on and seem like a perfect solution to all our ills. And we can't waste an entire generation of Arthurs and Lionels while we're doing it."

"Good luck."

"Luck, as the Lord would say, don't got nothing to do with it."

On the way out I retrieved my gun, asking Arthur and Lionel if they knew anyplace nearby that sold Gatorade by the case.

14

LOUIS DOLEMAN LIVED IN WEST ROXBURY, THE SOUTHWEST corner of Boston's Suffolk County. Predominantly white, West Rox is a mixture of magnificent homes on wide parkways and smallish ranches on narrow streets. From Reverend Givens's church, I took Washington Street to Belgrade Ave, then fiddled around for eight or ten blocks until I found Doleman's address just off Centre Street.

It was a dwarf red-brick ranch among many stunted cousins. From the curb it appeared oddly kept. The lawn, despite the season, was maintained, but the hedges, huddled against latent snow the sun never touched, were untrimmed. The brickwork looked recently repointed, but the concrete stoop was crumbling.

All the window shades were drawn. I pushed the bell next to the front door, heard no chimes, and was about to knock when I heard what sounded like an inner door open and close. Then the front door opened, and Louis Doleman peered out at me.

Standing in front of a closed inner door, he wore heavy glasses and the same cardigan sweater. Liver-spotted skin hung loosely from the neck cords. His short gray hair seemed curiously soft, like the acrylic fur on a stuffed animal. In his right hand, a book, the index finger keeping his place in *Our Right to Die* by Maisy Andrus.

"Mr. Doleman, my name's John Cuddy." I showed him my identification. "I wonder if I could talk with you."

"Sure." He turned his head to look at the inner door. The soft hair radiated from a whorl on the top of his skull.

Doleman turned again to me. "Just step inside here so my space-lock'll work."

Spacelock. I thought, Scotty, beam me up.

"Got to have the spacelock, otherwise Marpessa here would be on her way back to Brazil."

Doleman was sitting in an old print chair, a faded towel protecting the upholstery a bit late in its life. He placed the book on a TV tray to his right, next to some cellophaned cupcakes that should have been labeled less by expiration date and more by half-life.

However, they weren't the main attraction. A bird like a giant parrot perched on his left shoulder. Most of its feathers were shocking blue or canary yellow, but the curved beak was black and the face was white, with long, squiggly lines under the eyes, like a child practicing with makeup.

I said, "Marpessa."

"Marpessa, right. Named her after this Brazilian actress I heard of. Only Brazilian actress I ever heard of, tell you the truth. Marpessa is a macaw. To keep them from flying off, most folks clip the primary feathers on the wing there. All but the last one, cosmetic purposes, you see. You do that, alternating wings each time the feathers grow back, you can let them out in the yard or whatever, because they can't fly. Be like a helio-copter with a bum tail rotor, just spiral down to the ground. But I couldn't bring myself to do that to her, seems like mutilation to me. So I just make sure to keep her in the house with the spacelock. Put that up myself."

To be polite, I turned in my chair to admire the patchwork job Doleman had done in framing a second, inner door at the entrance to form his spacelock.

Turning back, I said, "Sensible. Mr. Doleman—"

"Be crazy to have her outside anyway. With a bum wing, she'd be a sitting duck for cats, dogs, what have you. Used to hunt every chance I'd get, deer in the fall, waterfowl in the spring. Never would take a stationary bird, but I can't say that about a lot of fellows I met. No sense of sport in them. The hell good is it to hunt, you don't do it for the sport?"

"Not much."

"You bet not much. Marpessa here is friendly as a spaniel pup.

113

Comes when she's called, doesn't crap the furniture or rug, just does this little sideways dance, lets me know it's time for her to go."

I could hardly wait.

" 'Course, she's got her dark side too. Costs an arm and a leg this far north to keep her warm enough. And she gets real jealous if there are any kids . . . around . . ."

Doleman seemed to stall, like a motor that was doing fine until someone shifted to drive. His lips moved convulsively, as though he were practicing puckering.

"Mr. Doleman?"

He revived. "She'll talk your ear off too. Even think she understands some of it. She'll hang upside down from a rope I got in the kitchen there, and she'll say, 'Look, look,' like a little kid . . ."

Again the stalling effect.

I repeated his name.

This time Doleman barely came out of the daydream. "What was it you wanted?"

"I'm doing some work on the debate at the Rabb the other night."

"The Rabb?"

"The library. When you asked that professor a question?"

"Oh." Doleman lowered his head, shaking it. Marpessa transferred all her weight to the left foot, using her beak to pick at the claws on the right one. In a clearer tone of voice he said, "Well, go ahead."

"I got the impression from what you said to Professor Andrus that you felt she was involved in your daughter's death."

"Not involved. Responsible. There's a difference."

Now he was more the man I'd seen rise from his seat at the debate. Staunch, certain.

"Mr. Doleman, can you tell me what happened?"

"I can. You have time to hear it?"

"Yes."

Doleman moved his hands as though lathering them with soap. "Heidi was my daughter. Wasn't the name I would have picked out for her, but she was an orphan, war orphan out of Germany. The wife and I couldn't have children ourselves, so we jumped at the chance to raise her."

As Doleman talked, I did some arithmetic. "What happened to your daughter?"

"Once we got her over here—stateside, I mean—she was fine.

114

Oh, some nightmares sure, and she couldn't abide loud noises, probably reminded her of the bombs. And she was shy around strangers, just like Marpessa here." Doleman ruffled the bird's feathers, and Marpessa pecked him lightly on the left cheek. "But she did just great in school, lost most of the accent, went on to be a secretary downtown."

"When was this, Mr. Doleman?"

"When was what?"

"When she became a secretary."

"Oh. Just after they shot Jack Kennedy. She had to start back a couple of grades in school, on account of having no schooling, much less any English, back in the old country. But she was a good girl, no trouble with boys or anything. Then—"

He stopped again, but I didn't prompt him.

"Then the wife—Florence—had the heart attack. It just come on her one night, no warning at all. Heidi was a godsend, taking care of the house for me while I finished up at the MTA—I was a motorman, Arborway line mostly. They call it the MBTA now, but not me. After I retired, Heidi and me were going to sell this place, move somewheres warm, but we never got around to it."

"How old was Heidi when your wife died, Mr. Doleman?"

"How old?"

"Yes."

"Oh, out of her teens for sure. Hard to say. See, she didn't give us any trouble like most kids do, so you didn't pay that much attention to how old she was. She always seemed older, what she'd been through in the war and all."

"What year did your wife pass away?"

"Year?"

"Year."

"Watergate. Was Watergate on the TV when we got back from the funeral."

So call it seventy-three or so. To have been a war orphan, his Heidi had to have been in her early thirties by then. Not much of a life for her, but then, maybe a lot better than she remembered from childhood.

"What happened to your daughter after your wife died?"

"Oh, she—like I said, she took care of the house and all. Was just the two of us, but it was a good life. Good as could be without Florence. But then Heidi . . ."

115

Doleman squirmed in his seat. Marpessa became agitated and flapped her wings, making the cry I'd heard over the telephone and thundering, in that small, quiet room, over to a windowsill near the inner door of the spacelock.

Doleman gave no indication that he noticed the bird. "Heidi took sick. Doctors said they didn't know what, but they did. They just didn't want to tell me. Didn't want me to know what they told Heidi. She was a brave girl, none braver. She never wanted me to worry. But you could just see it in her. The way she didn't have any get-up-and-go. Didn't want to eat, losing weight." Doleman rested his forehead in an upturned palm. "Was the leukemia."

I said gently, "And when was that, Mr. Doleman?"

"Started a year ago, a year ago this month. They took her to the hospital, then she'd be home, then in again. The MTA and the folks at her job, they took care of most of the bills. The doctors said there wasn't anything to be done. But they was wrong!"

Doleman seemed to come back to life, fill himself with a past energy. "Heidi was a strong girl. She'd survived before, in Germany, when everybody around her was dying. Strong and brave. She could have beaten it, weren't for her."

The way Doleman pronounced the last word, there was no question who he meant.

"She wrote this!" He stabbed the book with his index finger so hard I was afraid he'd jammed the knuckle. "This piece of deviltry. Of despair. Don't fight, she says in here. Don't resist the Reaper. And don't just give in. Help him along. Take your own life because it belongs to you, not to anybody else, like your family who loves you and depends on you. Oh, no. It's okay to be selfish, see? It's okay to give up."

"Your daughter read the professor's book."

"She did. I didn't know a thing about it. Can you believe that? Me, her own father, Heidi never told me. Just let on how she was a burden, how it was hard for her to do things anymore. But not a word, not one word about suiciding herself."

I thought back to Beth. The conversations we had, the idea just below the surface. I had the feeling Heidi told her father as best she could, but that he just hadn't been listening.

"One morning in August I got up, didn't smell the coffee. Heidi always brewed the coffee, strong enough to knock you over. Well,

I got up that day and didn't smell it. Didn't know what was wrong at first, because it was something that wasn't there instead of something that shouldn't have been there, like a noise. Then I realized I couldn't hear her either. I went to her door, knocked like I always did since she was old enough to . . . old enough anyway, and I didn't hear her and I knocked louder. Still nothing, so I opened it. And there she was, in her bed, covers up over a nightgown I never saw before. Her hands were folded on top of her chest, and her mouth was open a little, nothing coming out. I touched . . ."

Doleman's Adam's apple rode hard at his collar. "I touched her hands and I knew . . . knew she was gone. Then I saw the little pill thing next to her, vial or whatever you call it, clear so you could tell it was empty. Sleeping pills. And the book. The goddamn book with her note sticking out of it. The note said, 'Papa, please forgive me. Please read this and maybe you'll understand. I'm sure I'm going to be with Mama, and we'll look after you always. Heidi.' "

I changed positions in my chair, Marpessa making a clucking noise behind me.

Doleman fixed me with his eyes. "Well, mister, I started reading this book. Chapter a night, every night. Still read it. Still trying to figure out what the devil's bitch could have said to make a fine girl like Heidi turn her back on her family and take her life like that. But I can't. And that bitch can't either. Never answered my letters, never even answered my question at the library the other night."

"How old was Heidi when she died?"

"How old?"

"Yes."

"Just forty-eight."

"Mr. Doleman, I'm sorry."

"Sorry? Don't be sorry. I've gotten even."

I felt a little queasy. "Even?"

"You betcha. Marpessa there. I've got me somebody now that bitch can't take away." Doleman stabbed the book again. "Marpessa can talk but she can't *read,* see? Great company, and better than a watchdog at knowing when there are people coming round. Why, I was to say the magic word, she'd fly in your face right now, rip your eyes out."

I was trying not to take that seriously when he said, "Macaws, they live to be eighty, a hundred years old. Marpessa'll be here long after I'm gone, mister." His voice dropped to a whisper. "I'll never have another thing in this house that I'll outlive, see?"

I thanked Doleman for his time and moved slowly to the inner door. As I opened it, Marpessa looked at me sideways and squawked, "Bye-bye."

15

I DROVE BACK INTO DOWNTOWN AND FOUND A PARKING SPACE
on Charles near Cambridge Street. Stopping in a bookstore, I bought
the latest Robert Randisi paperback to see how private investigators
in the Big Apple were doing. A couple of chapters went down over
lunch at the Sevens, a great neighborhood bar that's still what the
Bull & Finch used to be before the latter went television as *Cheers*.
I tried to wash the taste of Doleman's bitterness from my mouth
with a pub sandwich and draft ale, but they didn't help much.

Leaving my car where it was, I walked to Massachusetts General
Hospital. Inside the imposing white granite facade, an information
volunteer with the demeanor of a kindergarten teacher explained
the color-coded lines on the floors of the corridors. Following the
path for Internal Medicine, I eventually reached Paul Eisenberg's
office. Or at least the suite that included his office. The waiting area
was crowded, some people obviously in serious if not emergent
difficulty even just sitting, others at attention, as if to advertise that
they were only companions, not sick themselves.

I went to the reception counter, a harried Hispanic woman looking
up from one of twenty or so files teetering next to her elbow.

"Yes?"

"Dr. Eisenberg, please."

"You have your hospital card?"

119

"No, but—"

"You need to go around the corner, with your Blue Cross/Blue Shield, and get a hospital card. Then come back."

"I'm not a patient. I'm just here to see Dr. Eisenberg."

"Oh." She was confused, as though she couldn't process what I'd said. "Uh, what's your name?"

"Cuddy. John Cuddy. I have an appointment."

That she could process. "Have a seat. The doctor will see you as soon as possible."

I was glad I'd brought a book.

"Mr. Curry, is it?"

"Cuddy, Doctor. John Cuddy."

Eisenberg looked at me over the half-glasses. "What seems to be the problem?"

I showed him my ID. Up close, his immaculate hands were steady. The stage fright he'd exhibited at the debate seemed gone.

Eisenberg closed the holder and handed it back to me. "It's hospital policy not to discuss cases without our lawyers present."

"I'm not here about one of your cases. I'm working for Maisy Andrus on a problem she has."

"What problem is that?"

"She's been receiving threats."

Eisenberg sighed, rolling his shoulders like a weary starter in the eighth inning. "Mr. Cuddy, I really don't see how I can help with that, and I have an arkful of patients out there that I might be able to help. So, if you'll excuse me."

I held out the copies of the threats. "These are what she's been getting. It won't take long to read them."

Eisenberg sighed again, but accepted the pages. After the first one, the skin on his forehead wrinkled, flexing the bald scalp above it.

When he got to the fourth one, I said, "That was in one of the books she was given to sign at Plato's after the debate."

"I'm sorry. I can see how she'd be . . . how anybody would be upset over this kind of thing. I noticed there was something wrong at the signing." Eisenberg changed tone. "But I still don't see where I'd come in."

"You're pretty well known for your stands on patients' rights. I

120

thought you might know of somebody who could have written these."

"Hmmm." He brought the right hand up, combing his beard with the fingers. "I think you'd be better off with a psychiatrist."

"I'm not looking for a profile, Doctor. I'd like names, if you have them."

"Toward what end?"

"Toward the end of finding out who's sending these."

Eisenberg combed some more. "Mr. Cuddy, I don't know anyone who would do something like this."

"Has anybody approached you about their opposition to what Andrus is doing?"

He hesitated. "No personal approaches, outside of professional circles, of course, but none of them could possibly be involved in this."

"How about letters or phone calls?"

"I do get correspondence from time to time. From nonprofessionals, I mean. Mainly older persons who don't have much . . . who have the time to read books and articles like mine. The closer we get to the end, Mr. Cuddy, the more the end intrigues us."

"The name Louis Doleman sound familiar?"

"The man at the debate. Who asked the question about his daughter, you mean?"

"Right."

"Well, yes. At the time it did sound familiar, but I was too . . . it wasn't until I was home that I remembered who he was. He'd written me, even made a small splash in the newspapers after his daughter committed suicide. Tragic situation. I believe she was a spinster who cared for him."

"You wouldn't by any chance have a copy of his letter?"

"A copy? No, all I would have is the original. But that sort of thing would just go into the daily file."

"Daily file?"

"Yes. My daily correspondence file for the day it was received. We date and time-stamp each communication. It's simply easier for the lawyers to be able to read everything that arrives on a given day rather than rely on our . . . uncertain filing system for the case folders themselves."

"By 'the lawyers,' you mean for malpractice?"

"Yes. It's eating us up, you know. The insurance rates are soaring, and the state won't let us balance-bill the patients to keep up with it. On top of that, most of us are scared blind of AIDS and can't even test for it without the patient's permission. Crazy."

"Was there any malpractice involved with Doleman's daughter?"

Eisenberg's forehead wrinkled again. "What?"

"Doleman's daughter died of leukemia. Was there any malpractice?"

"What difference would that make?"

"I don't know."

"Well, I don't know either, Mr. Cuddy. I don't even recall where she was treated."

I was starting to tick Eisenberg off, and I didn't want to do that. "Anybody else?"

"Anybody else?"

"Besides Doleman, anybody else contact you about Andrus and mercy-killing?"

"Oh. No, but you have to understand, I wouldn't be thinking of it that way."

"If mercy-killing is the wrong phrase, I—"

"No, no. What I mean is, I wouldn't get a letter and say to myself, 'Aha, another Andrus-hater.' My mind wouldn't have been alert to that kind of thing."

"The name Steven O'Brien mean anything to you?"

Eisenberg laughed. "Poor man. He lives in Rhode Island, comes up to lectures. I'm afraid he's a bit too . . . concentrated in his view."

"Which is?"

"The right to life, but the sort of person who makes debates like the other night a debacle. He talked to me after a presentation I made at one of the local colleges. Nearly ranting, though in a strange way."

"Strange how?"

"Well, he has this little voice, and he speaks very quietly. But he still gives the impression of fanaticism. You'd have to see him to know what I mean."

"You said before that nobody had approached you."

"Approached me?"

"About Maisy Andrus."

"Oh. Oh, I'm sorry. I must have misunderstood your question.

I meant to say that the only people who've approached me about her were professional colleagues, in the circle of physicians or professors of philosophy who are interested in the area of euthanasia and patients' rights. We would talk about many things, Maisy and her writings included. But not in any . . . vindictive way."

"And O'Brien?"

"He may be aware of Maisy's works. In fact, I can't imagine he isn't. But I don't recall his ever saying her name, and that's why I suppose I didn't think of Steven as *approaching* me until you mentioned him by name."

Steven. "Any other characters like O'Brien floating around?"

"Probably. I'm sure I don't know them all."

"How about Gunther Yary?"

"Never heard of him."

"At the debate, he was the skinhead who incited the riot."

Eisenberg didn't laugh this time. "I've read about the skinheads, Mr. Cuddy. Have you?"

"Not extensively."

"They're neo-Nazis. Oh, they come on like states' righters without southern accents, but you heard the words he used for us. 'Nigger,' 'kike.' People like that—like Yary, you say his name is?"

"Yes."

"People like this Yary are very dangerous. They can do anything, as history proves."

"Do you know Alec Bacall?"

"Quite well. If you are active in the area, you come to know most of the others. Alec is a good man, and of all of them—the advocates of euthanasia, I mean—he's the one I could come closest to agreeing with. However, the development of AZT and DDI and the drugs they might inspire merely make my point more strongly."

"Which is?"

"That no patient should be taken from us because medical technology may yet improve to the point that he or she could be saved." Eisenberg consulted his watch. "Look, Mr. Cuddy, I really have to insist."

"I understand. I'd appreciate your keeping our talk confidential."

"I will."

Eisenberg gathered the threat notes but paused before handing them back to me. "One more thing, though."

"Yes?"

"I know you said you weren't looking for a profile, but I can't help but notice something in these notes."

"Which is?"

"The use of words. I think only a male would use . . . those words to describe a female."

"That's how I see them too."

"Foul, but evasive as well. 'THEY DIE,' and so on. As though it were a cause involving a lot of people."

"Why is that evasive?"

"It's hard to work up to violence for a cause, Mr. Cuddy. I think it's more personal."

"Personal."

"Yes. Somebody who lost a loved one to something he blames on Maisy Andrus."

"Like Louis Doleman."

"Like *a* Louis Doleman. Good luck."

"Thanks."

16

"AREA A, DETECTIVES, NEELY."

"Neely, this is John Cuddy."

"Cuddy, how ya doin'?"

"Doing fine. You have a chance to run those names for me?"

"Names? Oh, yeah, just a second, got them here . . . somewheres.
. . . Hold on, okay?"

"Right." Through the phone I heard him tear off part of a sandwich and chew.

"Cubdy?"

"Still here."

"Ga wha chu wan."

"Go ahead."

Neely swallowed. "Okay. We got Yary, Gunther W. You want
just his sheet or D.O.B. and that shit too?"

"Start with his sheet."

"Got a commitment to DYS—that's Division of Youth Services?"

"I know."

"Commitment in seventy-eight on his first juvie. Must have been
a pisser, send him in as a first-timer. After that we got A&B as an
adult, then disorderly . . . disorderly . . . another A&B. Obstructing
a public way, probably some kind of demonstration thing. That's it.
Nothing heavy, no hard time, just your run-of-the-mill asshole."

"Schooling?"

"Hyde Park High, no college here."

"Employment?"

"Delivery service over in Dorchester." He gave me the name and address.

"All right. Who else do you have?"

"On Doleman, Louis R. Just a flag. Seems his daughter was dying from something or other, and he made some phone calls to the doctors, the hospital about it."

"What kind of calls?"

"Says here 'harassing.' "

"You figure that means 'threatening'?"

"Don't know. Ask Mass General."

"Mass General?"

"Yeah. That's where she was at."

Odd that Eisenberg didn't recall the treating hospital. "Anything else on Doleman?"

"Yeah. Gun permit."

"To carry?"

"Sporting. Just rifle and shotgun, not concealed."

"How recent?"

"Last renewal two years three months ago. Probably means the calls to the medics weren't too serious."

"Or he wouldn't have gotten his renewal."

"Right."

At least you'd like to think so. "How about Strock?"

Neely chuckled. "You're gonna love this."

"What?"

"I told you I thought I heard the name, right?"

"Right."

"Well, turns out I caught the call. Seems this guy Strock's a professor. Of law, yet. Also seems he kinda had the hots for one of his students coupla years back. You with me?"

"Go ahead."

"Well, this student has an apartment on the Hill, backside down near Cambridge Street. Old Strock follows her from some kind of student party over there at the school, and tries to slap the make on her."

"Christ. Rape?"

"Uh-uh. But this was four, five years ago, when the heat was on for those kinda things, so I get sent with the uniforms. When she opens the door for us, here's this Strock guy, half into his pants."

"He was in her apartment?"

"Yeah. Seems he gave her a song and dance about feeling sick or something, and she bought it. Anyway, here's this guy, and he's drunk, weaving and stumbling with the pants and the belt coming through the loops and all, trying to make like everything was okay. Kinda pathetic."

"What happened?"

"Oh, nothing. What do you think? Nobody decided to press nothing. Wouldn't even have remembered the guy, but you asked me and the sheet registered, that's all."

"Anything on O'Brien?"

"Not yet. Be a day or two. Call me."

"I will."

"For lunch."

My turn to swallow. "Looking forward to it."

Providence lies about forty-five minutes south of Boston. There's a point, a few miles north of the city, where I-95 hooks just right near the top of a hill, and you catch an imposing view of the state house. Huge white dome like the Capitol in Washington, a pillared mini-temple at each point of the compass.

Downtown Providence is stolid rather than showy but has probably the best indoor athletic facility in New England, the Providence Civic Center. I stopped to check in at police headquarters across from the center. It was change of shifts, a lot of brown and beige uniforms heading out, like United Parcel drivers wearing sidearms. I'm not licensed in Rhode Island, but usually nobody would question that. If they do, it's a good idea to have checked in first with the local department. A real good idea.

The desk sergeant also gave me impeccable directions to the address I wanted.

There was no answer when I pushed the button in the vestibule of Steven O'Brien's apartment building. There were sixteen mailboxes, a glimpse of at least one envelope through the slot with his name on it. I went back out to the Prelude to wait.

For the second time that day, I was glad to have a book with me.

About an hour later a man came walking down the street, taking out a snap-case and carefully shaking free a mailbox key. Roly-poly, he wore a blue insulated Windbreaker, the bottom of a light green tie trailing almost past the fly in his dark green pants. I got out of my car as he turned and pulled open the glass entrance door. He had just put his key into the right mailbox lock when I slipped through the door behind him.

O'Brien looked up suspiciously. Doe eyes, thinning black hair, the first person in years I'd seen with dandruff flakes on his shoulders. When he was young, I bet the other kids called him "Stevie," stretching the first syllable.

"Who are you?"

Paul Eisenberg was right about O'Brien's voice. Like an altar boy on Palm Sunday. "John Cuddy."

I flashed my ID, but he never even glanced at it.

"What do you want this time?"

I ran with it. "Same as last time. Upstairs or a ride?"

O'Brien sighed resignedly. "Upstairs, I guess."

Ascending two flights, I followed him partway down one dim and scuffed corridor. Using three different keys on the locks to his apartment door, O'Brien nearly put his shoulder through it to overcome some warping.

We entered on the living room. There was an old cloth couch outclassed by a leather chair that would have been a showpiece in 1945. A twelve-inch black and white stood on a trestle table that was too big for the television.

O'Brien took off his Windbreaker, having to shrug and tug to clear his elbows. Underneath, he wore a V-neck sweater vest, the shirt badly discolored under the arms. He walked toward the chair, motioning me toward the couch.

I said, "I'll take the chair instead."

With a sour look, O'Brien moved to the couch. Sitting, he said, "You know, I have a First Amendment right to send those letters."

In an even voice I said, "Tell me about it."

"What do you care?"

"Try anyway."

"The bishop isn't doing a thing, not a solitary thing, about the abortion issue. How can he expect me to sit still while God's children are being murdered?"

O'Brien threw me. "Does that mean you had to send the letters?"

"Of course it does. How can I get noticed otherwise? I'm a bookkeeper, for heaven's sake. *I* don't have brazen anchorwomen wanting to interview me. I don't have any access, even to my own church's newspapers. They refuse to print my letters anymore, and the bishop told them not to."

"How do you know that?"

"How do I know? How do I know? You think you people are a hierarchy, with chiefs and captains and sergeants, you should deal with the Church for a while. *I* did. For thirteen years I was in Fiscal, the assistant bookkeeper for the Diocese. Well, for a lot of the diocesan activities, anyway. In all that time, do you think the Church encouraged me? It did not. Instead of taking the time, the effort to bring me into the fray, on the side of God and Life, they pushed me out of a job. Pushed me to go outside the Church to bring my message to the people."

"And just what's that?"

"What's that? I'll tell you what's that. They want to kill us all."

"Who?"

"The atheists. Like the pagans of old, they believe in human sacrifice. The sacrifice of the unborn and the undead. That's where they start, that's where they always start, down through history. They kill the babies and they kill the elderly, and that's how they get everyone used to the idea."

Playing the card, I said, "I don't get you."

"The atheists have taken over our government. They've maneuvered their people to the point of being in power everywhere. The legislatures, the courts, even the Supreme Court of the land, where they said it's acceptable, it's a woman's *right,* to kill her *own baby.* Now they're trying it with the elderly too."

"Explain it to me."

"Look." O'Brien leaned forward, warming up. "We're in a hospital, and someone's Aunt Emma is on the kidney machine. She's basically just being maintained, with some pain, because there is no cure right now for what's wrong with her. Well, Aunt Emma has put aside some money by working hard over her long life, and the only heirs are a couple of nephews. Do you follow me?"

"Yes."

"Now, Emma's doctor is getting a little tired of seeing her on that machine. Oh, Emma can afford it, although she is starting to eat into that money she's saved. But the doctor has in mind this younger patient, who's not on a machine because the hospital doesn't have enough machines to go around. The medical insurance companies would pay for this younger patient to be on a machine if one was available. The nephews see their money, their inheritance, shrinking, so they decide to use her pain. One says, 'Aunt Em, it's so bad to see you hurting like this.' And the other says, 'Aunt Em, I don't know why you've got to go through all this.' And then the first one says, 'Aunt Em, let us talk to the doctor, see if something can be done.' Et cetera, et cetera."

O'Brien's parable sounded like something he'd once heard someone else present. "So?"

"So? So the atheist nephews and the atheist doctors, with maybe some help from the atheist lawyers, get the atheist judge to let them turn off the machine on Aunt Emma. Pull the plug so the patient the doctor wants on the machine can have it."

"Pretty farfetched, isn't it?"

"Read the papers. They do it all the time in Massachusetts and New York. All the time."

"Yeah, I was at a debate up in Boston last night about it."

O'Brien withdrew a little. "Debate?"

"Yeah. That's what they were talking about. This doctor, Eisenberg, I think it was, and—"

"Eisenberg! One of the worst."

"How do you mean?"

"Come on. He's supposed to be this big-time defender of the right to life? Writes books and papers and gives these courses in the med school and speeches all over. But he's in with them."

"With the atheists."

A vigorous nod. "I went to see him a couple of times. At these speeches. And I hung around afterward, to talk to him. I thought, after what his people had been through, over in Germany with Hitler and all, Eisenberg would understand. He'd see what's happening in this country."

"But he didn't."

"He's in bed with them! He gets up and talks about this stuff on the same stage with these people, even has *dinner* with them. For him it's like this intellectual exercise, like he's just talking about something that's not real instead of fighting something that is real, that's horrible and threatening us all."

"Eisenberg's not fighting like you are."

"Of course not! The things he writes, he told me himself, they get edited by the people at the magazines—or journals, whatever they call them—that print his stuff. And who do you think the editors are?"

"More atheists."

"Finally. They're everywhere, like I said."

"Another speaker at this debate last night. Ever heard of Maisy Andrus?"

"That slut! She killed her own husband! I don't even mean pulling the plug and just letting him die. She took a needle and shot him up with poison. It was all over the papers. She's this big-time law professor, marries a tennis player, thinks people forget. Well, I saved every article about her. She thinks people forget? I'll never forget."

"You feel this strongly, how come you weren't at the debate too?"

O'Brien hunkered down. "I was thinking about it, but I couldn't. Had to work. Our fiscal year ends in a couple of weeks. They need me to check things. All kinds of things."

"Who at work can I call about that?"

His head whipped up. "Why?"

"Because I'm asking you politely, that's why."

"I mean, what does this have to do with my letters to the bishop?"

"Maybe I can just call the personnel manager."

O'Brien cowered. "No. No, call . . . call Carla Curzone. She's my . . . our head bookkeeper."

"Give me the number I should use."

He rattled it off, adding the extension as I wrote it down.

"Only . . ."

I said, "Only what?"

"Do me a favor, okay?"

"What?"

"Don't tell Carla you're from the police."

"Don't worry. I won't."

"Bad pizza?"

Nancy watched me carefully from across the glass coffee table in her apartment. On her haunches, she wore a New England School of Law sweatshirt over denim shorts and grasped a beer mug by its handle. Renfield, Nancy's cat, watched me expectantly from under the table as I picked at the slice on my plate.

I said, "No, the pizza's fine. Just a lousy day."

"How so?"

I summarized it for her, starring Louis Doleman and Steven O'Brien.

Nancy said, "It's no fun to be that close to crazies."

It bothered me that I was probably bumming her out, since she had to deal with crazies a lot more often than I did.

"John?"

"Yes?"

"I found a surefire way to get over that."

"Over what?"

"Over being around crazies too much." Nancy took a mouthful of beer.

"What is it?"

"You seek out a no-nonsense, normal person and get deeply involved in an absolutely rational discussion."

"The cure sounds worse than the disease."

"No, really. Logic, deduction, P implies Q. It's the secret."

I tossed a piece of sausage to Renfield, who played croquet with it until he realized the ball was edible. "Okay. How do we start?"

Nancy set down the mug and made her eyelids flutter. "I'll show you mine if you'll show me yours."

17

"Now, John, the race itself is twenty-six miles, three hundred eighty-five yards. You can't think of her as one distance, though. Nobody can really handle that. You got to break the course down into chunks. Think of her as four six-mile runs with kind of a victory lap at the end. That should be manageable.

"Another thing. Talk to yourself when you train, eh? Tell yourself what you want to do and why it's important for you to do it. Concentrate and reinforce those goals and reasons. During the race you're going to be doing the same thing. Don't worry about what people think. Sometimes talking to yourself is the best conversation around.

"One more thing for today. You're aiming at your first marathon, lots of people'll say, 'Don't make it Boston. Because it's in April, you'll have to train all winter, and the course isn't flat enough.' Well, I say bullshit to that. The beauty of Boston is the crowd. All along the route you've got folks two, even three deep, clapping and cheering. Little kids with card tables, handing out cups of water and orange sections. No, Boston's as good a first marathon as any, and better than most. Drink it all in, John. Remember, you'll never run your first marathon again."

Directory assistance had a phone number for Ray Cuervo in Marblehead, a harbor town about twelve miles north of Boston. Trying it, I got Cuervo's tape message. A silky, sales-pitch voice, the Spanish accent coming across only on certain words, the English idioms perfect. It told me that if I needed to reach him, he'd be at the Sarrey Co-op plant, giving a 603 area code. I took out a map of New Hampshire and found Sarrey just about where I remembered it, a little north of the Massachusetts border. It turned out to be only an hour and ten minutes from Boston up Interstate 93 and a couple of scenic country roads that hadn't yet yielded to suburbia's manifest destiny.

The plant itself was three stories high and roughly square. The tall windows were recessed into an old facade of gray brick, giving the impression of a structure that had been built for one purpose and converted to another. I drove a circuit around the plant. On one side was a receiving dock, a Mack tractor-trailer just pulling away. On the second side, facing west, the windows were boarded up. On the third side of the building was another dock, this one with men loading boxes into the back of another trailer. The fourth side fronted a parking lot for a hundred cars, maybe fifty vehicles in it on a Wednesday morning. I left the Prelude next to a large sign saying SARREY CO-OP PACKING—BEST VEAL IN THE EAST.

Inside the main door was a staircase and a blank concrete block wall. The stairs seemed more inviting. At the top was a door standing ajar and a catwalk. The catwalk curved out of sight toward sounds like a carpentry shop in high gear.

The doorway led to a minimalist office, a young woman in a lumberjack shirt and jeans behind an old partners' desk. She was drowning in a sea of multipart invoices and order forms. As the woman flailed through the paperwork, the bangs of her hair fell to her eyes.

I said, "Excuse me?"

She looked up through the bangs like a sheepdog. "Help you?"

"I'm looking for Ray Cuervo."

"He's down on the kill floor with the rabbi."

"How can I find it?"

"If you're not in the business, mister, maybe you don't want to know."

"Please?"

The woman blew out a breath, more to clear her hair than to show exasperation, I thought. "You're not dressed for it." She pointed to the catwalk and said, "Follow the walk around. You'll

134

know it when you see it. Might want to stay on the walk for a while, get used to things.''

I thanked her and moved around the walk.

Below me, about forty men and women were wearing white butchers' outfits, yellow aprons, and black hip boots. At one end of the huge room, a worker prodded a calf from a wooden corral down a concrete ramp. Another worker affixed shackles, trailing chains from the ceiling, to the animal's hind legs. As soon as he was finished, a woman touched a long wand to the calf's temple. It jerked spasmodically and went down like a sack of potatoes. The shackler cranked something, and the calf rose by the shackles, hanging upside down.

The chains moved the calf forward to a burly man in a full beard with ringlets of sideburns. He was dressed like the other workers except for a yarmulke on his head. With one clean slash of a big knife, the man cut the calf's throat. He stepped away from the torrent, joining another man who was holding a clipboard. As the man in the yarmulke sharpened the knife, the man with the clipboard talked with him. I pegged Clipboard to be in his early thirties, about six feet tall and slim, with wavy black hair and a black mustache.

The calf began to move slowly along the line, workers gutting the animal and sorting the organs. Next, two women and a man skinned the calf with hand-held rotary saws like a pathologist would use on the skull during an autopsy. After they finished, one of them brought the hide to a washing machine, taking other hides out and heaving them down something like a laundry chute. At the next station for the carcass, the head was taken off and put on a rack next to twenty or so others, the tongues protruding. Then the rest of the animal, still hanging from the shackles, went off to a room from which I could hear water jets like a car wash. All in all, the process seemed pretty humane, kind of a reverse assembly line in which each part seemed destined for further use.

The only problem was the blood smell. A warm, steamy thickness to the air, like being in a kitchen when someone was steeping the wrong kind of soup.

''Hey?''

I turned around.

Clipboard, stripped to a dress shirt, tie, and slacks, was standing on the catwalk ten feet from me, grinning. ''Ray Cuervo.''

135

"John Cuddy."

"Come on into my office. We can talk."

"Sure you don't want some coffee?"

"No, thanks."

Cuervo sipped from his paper cup. We occupied two metal chairs in a cramped room. The shelves above and behind his desk held some looseleaf binders and a couple of photos in frames. One photo showed a house with beige stone walls and an orange tile roof, the walls bordered by small trees, kinds I was pretty sure I'd never seen before. In another photo, an adolescent Cuervo was standing near a man who resembled a dark-haired Cesar Romero, both wearing hunting gear. An elaborate telephone and a fax machine took up most of the desk.

Cuervo hadn't asked me for any identification, so I hadn't yet brought up why I was there.

"This your first time at the co-op, John?"

"It is."

"We've got a great operation here. Only the second true growers' co-op in this part of the country. We patterned ourselves after Penn Quality out past Albany. Veau Blanc?"

I nodded as though I knew what he meant.

"Toughest part was coming up with the financing. The growers around here, like everywhere else, would just sell their calves to the packing house, never had much idea about the business side of running a plant themselves. But once we got them to see the advantages of fair price and fair grading for their product, they came up with their share of the front money, and we're in business. Doing eight hundred calves a week most weeks now, and that's not bad. Penn's a shade ahead of us, but they started before we did, and they've got this all-star named Azzone selling for them. It'll take us a while, but we'll catch them."

To keep him going, I said, "Where are you concentrating?"

He set down the cup. "Boston, for now. With veal, you know, you're pretty much selling to the supermarket chains and the restaurant distributors. And you pretty much have to hit the ethnics, your Italians, your Jews. I was lucky to get into the business, since it's mostly a family trade. But I'm from Spain originally, and a lot of the Hispanics in the New York/Boston corridor like their veal."

"You ever visit the restaurants on Newbury Street?"

"Newbury? You mean, like in Boston?"

"Yes."

I seemed to put him off track. "Once in a while. Couple of small accounts there. That where you are?"

"A few blocks away."

Cuervo came back on track. "So, what do you think of our operation?"

"Impressive."

"Damned right. State-of-the-art equipment and sanitary standards. You saw the *schochet* down there?"

"The what?"

"The rabbi, like."

"Oh, yes, I did."

"You don't run a clean plant, you don't have to worry about the government inspectors. The rabbis, they'll close you down first. Only use the front quarter of the animal, but you got to have them."

"Even so, it didn't look like you waste anything."

"Right again, John. The heads we send to Mexico—they go for the brains and the cheek meat down there. The hearts, the Italians, they stuff them. Kidneys to the fancy French bistros. The rest of the dropped meat we send off to Europe. The hides to Japan for tanning, then to Italy for gloves and shoes."

"You get a lot of heat from the animal protection people?"

"Pickets once in a while. They'd have us all living on bean sprouts and Velveeta, they had their way. But, hey, there wouldn't be any veal calves if it weren't for the dairy herds, right?"

"Right."

"I mean, what's a dairy farmer supposed to do? He needs the bull to knock up the cows so they'll give milk. But when he gets a boy calf instead of a girl that can grow up to give more milk, he doesn't have too many choices. One, he can let the calf roam with the mother and suckle, which cuts down on her milk production. Two, the farmer can let the calf loose in the fields to feed on grass and become a beefer. Three, he can sell the calf to a Bob-packer who whacks the animal at all of one or two weeks of life and maybe eighty pounds of weight. Four is us. The dairy farmer, if he's smart, can auction the calf to a fancy veal grower like the ones who own this plant. The grower's going to raise that calf for sixteen weeks and come in here at four hundred pounds, giving us maybe two hundred sixty pounds of meat. Now, those are the choices, right?

You want milk, you're going to have male calves and you got to do something with them." He picked up the cup again. "And it seems to me that our way is the best way."

I didn't say anything as he sipped.

Cuervo blinked a few times and then said, "What outfit are you with, anyway?"

"I'm not in the veal business."

He rotated the cup in his hands. "I started to get that idea. What are you doing here?"

"I'm a private investigator from Boston."

Cuervo frowned. "What do you want from me?"

I had decided on the drive up that there was no way around telling him the truth. But maybe not all the truth. "Your stepmother, Maisy Andrus. She's been getting threats."

He laughed, shaking his head. "What's the matter, she flunk the wrong student?"

"How's that?"

"She's a teacher, right? Who's going to get mad at her except the students?"

"I don't think it's like that, Mr. Cuervo."

"Hey, call me Ray, okay?"

"Not Ramón?"

Cuervo took a big slug of coffee. "Look, I know it's not too cool to turn your back on your heritage and all, but it would be kind of tough to go through life over here as Ramón Cuervo Gallego, you know?"

"Your last name isn't Cuervo either?"

"In Spain they do names differently. My middle name comes from my father's family, the very last name, Gallego, from my mother's. So, my father was Enrique Cuervo Duran and my mother was Noelí Gallego de la Cruz, and I'm Ramón Cuervo Gallego. Understand?"

"I think so."

"Besides, I'm not exactly Spanish."

"Now I don't follow you."

"My father, the late great *el Señor Doctor,* had this thing about American stuff, okay? Everything from America was better: cinema, appliances, sporting arms, cars. When we went hunting, it was Remingtons all the way, and we were the only family in Candás, maybe in all of Asturias, that had a Cadillac. Yeah, he had a hell of a time getting that boat through the streets."

138

Cuervo made a hitchhiking gesture behind him at the photo of the house. "Even had to widen the driveway, keep from scratching the paint off. If we ever got snow—which thank Christ we never did, it's more like London weather there—he'd have wrecked it first time out, the way he drove. And when it broke? Good luck getting it fixed. But that didn't matter, right? My father wanted the best of everything, and the best was American, so I got sent off to school over here, and after my mother died he married the showiest American woman he could find."

"How old were you when your father married Maisy Andrus?"

"I don't know. I didn't even go to the wedding. What the hell does it matter?"

"Why didn't you attend the wedding?"

A smirk. "I think I had a track meet that weekend. Yeah, yeah, that was it. The team couldn't spare me."

"You get along all right with Andrus?"

"Get along? I barely ever saw her. You got to remember, I was in school over here. And Maisy went to live in Spain with my father only part of the year. I sure as hell wasn't interested in seeing Maisy over here, and I'll bet Maisy spent more time in old *España* during those years than I did."

"You have a falling out with your father over Maisy?"

"Falling . . . you got a hell of a nerve, interrogating me like this."

I just waited.

"What right do you have, coming into my place of business and asking me all these questions?"

I hadn't checked in with the Sarrey police. "Only trying to do my job."

"Which is?"

"To eliminate as many people as possible from the list, and then focus on the ones who could be threatening her."

Cuervo started rotating the cup again. "Look, I don't have any bone to pick with Maisy anymore."

"Anymore?"

"My father . . . when he died, she got some things, I got some things."

I inclined my head toward the house photo. "She got the homestead."

"Yeah, which if she was able to use it would be a nice place. It sits on this bluff, kind of overlooking the bullring in Candás, near

Gijón. When I was a kid, the family'd sit on the lawn, swilling *sidra*—new cider, sweet, a little alcoholic—and we'd watch the *corridas*—the bullfights. The bullring is built right along the beach, so when the tide goes out, they can have the *corridas* right there. Of course, sometimes the bulls, they notice the hole in the wall and they swim for it, but . . . look, what I'm trying to say here is, by the time it came to dividing things up between her and me, I did fine. I got everything I needed to come back here, go to college, buy a place on the water in Marblehead. My father was right about one thing. American is the best, and I got all I needed from him to have it."

"How did you feel about your father dying the way he did?"

"My father got sick. He was a doctor. I never thought much about him getting sick. When I was young, still living in Spain before he sent me . . . before I came over here for school, I thought he was like Superman, you know?"

"Invulnerable?"

"Right, right. Like God didn't let the doctors catch any diseases. That they always had to stay healthy to keep other people alive."

"And therefore?"

"When I heard about him . . . about him being sick, I mean, I didn't take it seriously. I couldn't even remember *seeing* him sick. When I finally realized how bad it was, I got upset, sure. But there wasn't anything anybody could do about it, so . . . ." Cuervo shrugged.

"How did you feel about your stepmother helping him?"

A quick breath, then he leaned back in the chair and got casual. "I don't think Maisy is my stepmother anymore. I mean, she got to be that because she married my father, but now she's married to somebody else, right?"

"Andrus injected your father with an overdose."

A philosophical smile. "Maybe what she did was the right thing. He was going to die anyway. Maybe Maisy was just making it easier for him, like we do with the stunner on the calves downstairs before they can see the knife."

"You get involved in any of the legal wrangle over your father's death?"

"No. Maisy got charged and I was supposed to testify, but they never—what do you call it?"

"Indicted her?"

"No, like when they . . . extradited her. They never extradited Maisy. This was all after Loredo Mendez—the prosecutor that let

140

her get off to start with—killed himself. Barely remember old Luis now, but he was a friend of my father's from the university and had this young wife my father saved from dying during childbirth." The smirk again. "Younger wives were real popular in my father's crowd."

"You ever go back to Spain?"

"Me? No way. That's a part of the world I've already seen."

"Never get homesick?"

"For what? Candás hasn't been home since I was fourteen."

"What can you tell me about Manolo?"

"Manolo. He still around?"

"Yes."

"Well, I guess he would be. My father was a soft touch, John, a real soft touch. One day he comes home, I'm maybe eight or nine, and he's got this big, scared kid with him. Manolo's family was kind of poor, and his father was a drunk. You don't see much of that in Spain. The people learn to drink *sidra* and sherry young enough to handle it. But Manolo's father was the exception, and with Manolo not being able to talk or anything, I guess it got him frustrated, so he beat the kid. But *el Señor Doctor* took him in. Taught him sign language and turned him into a helper around the dispensary. Kind of a trained bear, if you ask me. But he was like my father's shadow. Wherever *el Señor Doctor* Enrique went, Manolo would be there too."

"How did Manolo take your father's death?"

"I wasn't paying much attention. But I'm guessing that my father must have made him understand that it was okay."

"Why do you say that?"

"Because I know Manolo. If he thought Maisy had killed my father? Hah, he'd kill her. No question. But then, Manolo's not your man."

"Why?"

"Well, he can't talk, can he? How's he going to make threatening calls?"

"I didn't say the threats came by phone."

"Oh," said Cuervo, shrugging again. "I thought you did."

18

I DROVE BACK INTO BOSTON, PUTTING THE CAR IN THE TRASH-strewn alley behind my office building and grabbing a beer and burger at Friar Tuck's Pub. After lunch I called my answering service as I sorted through the mail. Four messages, one of which was from Inés Roja, asking me to reach her at the school by two.

My watch said two-fifteen. I tried anyway.

"Maisy Andrus."

"I didn't expect to get you directly."

"Who . . . oh, John." Her voice darkened. "Is something wrong?"

"Not that I know of. Inés left word for me to call."

"You just missed her. I can give you the number at the clinic?"

"Clinic?"

"Yes, she volunteers an afternoon a week, sometimes more."

"I thought Alec said Inés had to leave that?"

"This is a different clinic."

Recognizing the 269 exchange as South Boston, I did some paperwork first, then drove to it. The small parking area had one slot open, but there were plenty of spaces on the street as well.

Just inside the door was a waiting area. An elderly woman had a wire carrying cage in her lap, a Siamese hunched down on its forepaws and looking out warily. Across from the cat lady was a fat

142

man with a matched set of Airedales, straining at their leashes and licking their chops. The Siamese seemed pleased that the woman had remembered the cage.

I walked to the counter. A high school girl in a faded green smock and moussed hair asked if she could help me.

"I'm looking for Inés Roja?"

"She expecting you?"

"She called me."

The teenager sized me up, then nodded and beckoned. I followed her through one door and immediately another. I thought of Louis Doleman's spacelock as my guide opened the second door.

Containing cages stacked from floor to ceiling, the room sounded and smelled like a menagerie. The crying of birds, the mewling of cats, the staccato barks and mournful howls of dogs. But also the chattering of monkeys, raccoons, and a few other mammals I couldn't place even by continent.

The teenager spoke in a command voice over the din. "Inés?"

"Right here, Deb." Roja stood up from behind an examining table of some kind, cradling a gaunt monkey and holding a baby bottle that the monkey eyed eagerly. Roja wore a green smock, too, which was covered with stains old and new. She seemed surprised to see me as she brought the monkey toward us.

"John, I did not want to drag you all the way over here."

"It was on my way. Don't worry about it."

Deb said, "I've got to go back out front, Inés. Let me know if you need anything."

"Right."

The monkey began making "eek" noises, so Roja moved the bottle to its mouth. The creature began sucking, almost shyly.

Roja said, "You got my message, then."

"I did. Another note?"

"No. No, it is probably nothing really. That is why I just wanted you to call me."

I rested my rump against one of the tables. "Well, I'm here. Tell me."

Roja shifted the monkey to the other arm like an awkward bag of groceries. "The professor and Tucker are going on a vacation."

"I thought she had some kind of visitor thing already lined up?"

"She does. In San Diego. This vacation is to Sint Maarten."

"The Caribbean?"

"Yes. Tucker was invited long ago to participate in a masters-of-the-game tournament there."

"And she's going with him?"

"Yes. The tournament is in January, so they will vacation first, then be together while Tucker plays."

"First I've heard of it."

"I believe she decided to go only last night."

"I just talked to her an hour ago. She didn't even mention it."

Shifting the monkey again, Roja held it on her hip, an inter-species Madonna and Child. "You must not be harsh with her, John. Her mind is . . . different. She can concentrate on something and not think to say something else to you."

"What made her decide to join Tuck on this trip?"

"I think the pressure of the notes and all. But I am concerned about her being . . . vulnerable outside the United States."

"So am I. Are you going too?"

"No."

"How about Manolo?"

"He is to stay here as well."

"How's he going to take that?"

"I am . . ." Roja looked down, but not at the monkey. "I am feeling disloyal telling this to you."

"I can't help you much with that, Inés. Is it important for me to know?"

"The professor told me I am to tell Manolo after they are gone that they have left."

"So Manolo sees them get into a cab, and . . ."

"And he thinks they are going out to dinner instead of to the airport."

"What about luggage?"

"They are not to pack much, and I am supposed to occupy Manolo with some task as they leave."

"I don't like this, Inés."

Roja looked back up. "I am sorry to have to tell you, but I thought you should know."

"When do they leave?"

"Tonight. Their plane departs at eight-thirty, and they said they would be taking the taxi about seven."

"I'll be there by six."

Roja smiled. "Thank you."

"How do you get here?"

"How? By the subway."

The Red Line would take her only to within eight blocks or so of the clinic. "Still a long walk. Why do you volunteer?"

"The animals, they do not know how sick they are. They know only the kindness you show to them." She nuzzled the baby monkey. "And many will get better."

As opposed to the last clinic Roja had seen.

Deb let me use the phone at the counter. I called the D.A.'s office, leaving a message for Nancy that I'd still see her that night, just after eight o'clock. I figured by that time, either I'd have persuaded Maisy Andrus not to go with Hebert to the Caribbean or they'd be on their way.

I sat around the reception area, eavesdropping on Deb and the girl who came to relieve her at five. They gossiped about one of the vets, but I had the feeling that they were more interested in his "totally" blue eyes than in his "radical" rabies research. When Inés Roja came out, I insisted on driving her to the Andrus house with me. At first she declined, saying that the professor would realize that she had told me about the trip. I replied that I'd tell the boss I'd forced it out of her. That brought a feeble smile and a nod.

Outside, the wind was shrieking. I opened the passenger door of the Prelude for Roja, and she scooted in, flipping her coat away from the door that closed a little too quickly from the gale.

Once I got behind the wheel, Inés said, "This is a very nice car."

"It's old, but well maintained."

"Like . . ."

"Like what?"

Roja shook her head as I started the car. "Nothing." She gathered the coat around her neck.

"We'll have heat as soon as the engine warms up a bit."

"I am all right."

To make conversation, I said, "It ever get this cold in Cuba?"

She started to look at me, then turned away. "No. But there are worse things than cold, John."

We drove in silence for half a mile through Broadway traffic, crossing the overpass for the train yards that anticipate South Station.

Roja finally said, "I am sorry."

"Nothing to be sorry about."

"In Cuba, my father did not support Castro. He was in prison. When your President Carter dared Castro to free those who would come to the United States, my father was one. He was too weak from the prison, but they said if we did not go then, perhaps there would be no time to go later, no boat to carry us. So we left Cuba, and my father got sick. He could not breathe. . . . It was only ninety miles to Florida, but the other men would not keep his body on the boat with us. They simply threw him off, like he was . . . not a human being. Into the sea. Then my mother could not . . . Many of the men on the boat were prisoners too, but not political. Criminals, *degenerados,* do you understand?"

"I think so. You don't have to—"

"My mother tried. She screamed and she tried, but she could not . . . keep them from me."

More silence. No tears, just nothing.

"In the United States everyone tried to help us. My mother had relatives in New York, so we went there. We were poor but we were free. And the professor, she has been everything to me since I began to work for her."

I'd been keeping my right hand on the stick shift in the stop-and-go traffic. Roja placed her left over mine. Cool and dry, a hand that was washed a lot but never grew warm.

I looked at her.

She said, "Please keep the professor safe."

Roja withdrew her hand and buried it in the side pocket of her coat.

"If I didn't like you so much, John, I'd swear you were suggesting I can't protect my own wife."

Tucker Hebert was smiling at me, but just barely. He wore a long-sleeved Georgia Bulldog jersey and sweat pants, no socks, and had just turned away from the closet.

Maisy Andrus pushed the open duffel bag toward the pillows and sat heavily on the bed. "John, let's resolve this. First, just what is your objection to my accompanying Tuck on this trip?"

I leaned back against a highboy and crossed my arms. "I don't like the idea of you traveling outside the country, even with Tuck as protection."

"But why?"

146

"Whoever our note writer is, he might know that things are a lot looser in other countries."

Hebert said, "Sint Maarten is a pretty damned sophisticated island, my friend."

"Where an accident happening to a tourist might not be the most desirable subject for publicity or embarrassing investigation."

Andrus said, "Do you really believe that whoever is sending these notes would follow me to a Caribbean island rather than wait for my return?"

"It's possible. If he knows much about police work outside the States, he might know his chances of getting away with it are a little better down there."

Hebert said, "What if he doesn't care about getting away with it?"

Andrus and I both looked at him.

Hebert reddened a little under the perpetual tan. "Lordy, what I mean to say is, this boy's a nut. If he doesn't much care about getting caught, he sure isn't thinking about picking some spot where the cops aren't as sharp as you're used to."

"Given the way he's sent the notes so far, I don't think he wants to get caught."

"John," said Andrus in a soothing tone I hadn't heard from her before. "Isn't it at least as likely that this person doesn't have a passport or the means necessary for a trip like this on short notice? It is the beginning of the high season down there. In order for Tuck and me to vacation before the tournament, we even have to stay over in New York tonight to get a plane out tomorrow."

"You can travel most places on just a birth certificate. Plus, charters fly half full to the Caribbean all the time. He could probably go for a third of the price if he just hangs around a travel agency long enough and is willing to leave on two hours notice. They've already paid for the aircraft, so every seat is a lost margin of profit."

Hebert turned his back to us and began rummaging in the closet, talking into the clothes. "Okay. Okay, let's say this boy could follow us down if he wants to. Problem is, he doesn't even know we're going. Maisy just decided at the last minute to come with me. At most this boy thinks *I'm* going, and that'd mean he'd think he could get to her easier back here, alone and all."

"Except for Manolo."

"Manolo. Manolo, Manolo." Hebert turned back around, a scuba fin in his hand that seemed to match the one sticking out of the duffel bag. "Let me tell you something, John. In a street fight Manolo would be a mountain. He'd take a knife or a bullet, ten bullets, for Maisy, and maybe even a few to save my butt, knowing how she feels about me. But he's deaf, John. Stone cold deaf. A school kid could take him from behind. He wants to play loyal retainer, that's fine with me. But down-home protection? Get real, huh?"

Andrus said, "John, I'm tired. A little frazzled, okay? I've spoken to my dean, and under the circumstances he's agreed to cancel the special session seminar you saw. I think Tuck's right about my being safer on Sint Maarten, though perhaps for a different reason. I don't see my tormentor as a world traveler. I see him as a small, wretched little soul trapped in some way that makes him do this. If I am at any risk, that risk is higher here, where he has already acted, than fifteen hundred or so air miles from Boston. Furthermore, in less than a month I start a visitorship three thousand miles away. I'm not about to sacrifice that, and if I'm not, there is no logical reason I shouldn't enjoy a spur-of-the-moment vacation with my husband beforehand."

I certainly couldn't say I had proof she was wrong. "Tell you what?"

"What?" said Hebert.

"At least let me drive you to the airport."

Andrus said, "Tuck, are you sure you're all right back there?"

"Fine," said his voice from near my left ear.

We were in the Callahan Tunnel, the only functional way to Logan Airport. There are two parallel tunnels actually. The one leaving the city is called Callahan and one approaching the city is called Sumner. Tourists who know they went through one go crazy when from the other side all they can find is the other.

I said, "It won't be too much longer."

Maisy Andrus conformed to the front bucket, sinking into vacation mode. Hebert was sardined into the optimistic "seating for two" in the back, but hadn't complained once. Their luggage, both soft-sided pieces of it, didn't fill even my trunk.

Andrus said, "What will you do while we're gone?"

"I still have a few more people to see or see again."

"Have you come to any conclusions?"

"I don't have enough information yet."

Andrus nodded, as though that was a good answer for the occasion. She inhaled and exhaled deeply. "I'm feeling better already."

Hebert said, "Wait'll we hit this hotel, Maise. It's got everything you could want. Even a few things you'd never think of."

"When will you be back?"

Hebert said, "Tournament's over January sixteenth. We're booked on a return flight the next day."

"Afternoon or evening arrival here?"

"Evening."

"Call me when you get back, will you?"

Andrus said, "Certainly."

"How can I reach you down there?"

Hebert said, "Try Jupiter 8-5000."

Andrus giggled. "Inés has all our itinerary and numbers for both the hotel and the tournament people. She can reach us if you need me."

I'd just opened my mouth when Andrus said, "But John, please try not to call. I'd like a real vacation, if possible."

"All right."

Hebert sighed. "Amen."

I dropped them at Pan Am's domestic terminal for the flight to Kennedy. Andrus flagged a skycap as I opened the trunk. Hebert unfolded himself from the backseat and came around to me, people already honking at us and a state trooper windmilling his arm to keep moving.

"John?"

"Yes?"

"Sorry about riding over you on this, but I think it really is best for Maisy."

"I know."

"She's worn out. More than I've ever seen before from anything. Believe me, this is the best thing for her."

"I hope you're right."

"Besides," he said, yanking the bags out, one in each hand, "we haven't seen a note since Monday. I'll bet all your poking around's scared the sumbitch clear out of the valley."

I watched Hebert reach the skycap, drop off the bags, and hold out his arm for Maisy Andrus to take as they disappeared into the terminal.

19

"I know it's still only December, John, but you've got to think ahead. You see, the marathon's like Good Friday: you'll be on the cross from twelve noon to three. Only for you she'll be more like four, four and a half hours. Of steady pounding and chafing.

"Think about what to wear. You have to dress warm to go out to Hopkinton, on account of you'll be standing around for hours till the race starts. Maybe layers of old clothes that you can just take off and throw away on the street. If it's raining, get yourself a trash bag, one of those big green ones. Cut a head hole in it so you can use it like a poncho, then tear it off with the clothes when you hear the gun. For the running itself, just shoes, socks, jock, shorts, and a T-shirt. If it's below fifty degrees, wear a long-sleeved cotton turtleneck under the T. Remember, usually you dress warm to keep your heat in against the cold. Over twenty-six miles, you'll be wanting to let the heat out. Hell, your whole innards'll be producing heat like a blast furnace. Vent it out through sweat, and the wind'll wick it off, keep you cooler.

"Another thing. Before you put the socks on, turn them inside out and slap them a few times against your thigh. Got to get rid of all the sand or dirt particles. Over the miles, one piece of grit can cut through your toes like a hacksaw.

"Spread some Vaseline around your body. Don't be stingy, eh?

Really slather it on your feet and crotch, and don't forget your nipples. I've seen men finish a marathon bleeding like they'd got arrows in their chest.

"Finally, don't wear nothing next to the skin that you haven't been wearing during training. Something old, soft, and comfortable is what you want. Don't worry about how you'll look for the camera, neither. No matter what you do, two hours into the race you're going to look like shit warmed over."

Turning at the Western Avenue bridge after two miles, I felt the wind billow at my back. My joints were a little rusty, the leg muscles a little stiff. Not from age, I was sure, as much from running each morning instead of every other. It was hard to think about a race four months away, but picturing the details of what I'd be wearing was helping me focus on the early stages of the training program.

Passing Boston University's law school tower, my mind clicked over to Maisy Andrus. Two nights before, I'd driven the professor and her husband to the airport. I'd checked in with Inés Roja the next day, she telling me there was no word from Andrus or Hebert. Roja had called the airline in New York, however. Their flight had departed for Sint Maarten on schedule.

In the car I'd told Andrus I didn't have enough information yet to form any conclusions. I was no further along now. Neely reported no unexpected prints on the note or the book from Plato's.

Four untraceable notes, and a rogue's gallery of people Andrus had offended. Walter Strock, from her politics at the law school; Manolo and stepson Ray Cuervo, from her actions in Spain; Louis Doleman, from losing his daughter; Steven O'Brien, from her stand on the right to die. Even Tucker Hebert, if you didn't believe he enjoyed being a trophy husband.

Which left Gunther Yary and his skinheads. I hadn't talked with them after the scuffle at the library. Back from the river and doing my stretching in the condo, I was thinking about driving to their "clubhouse" in Dorchester, when the phone rang.

"John Cuddy."

"John, it is Inés Roja. Can you come to the law school?"

"What happened?"

"There is another note."

"What does it say?"

151

"I—please, can you come to look at it?"

"Twenty minutes."

Roja was sitting rigidly behind her desk, hands antsy on the blotter. Seeing me, she opened the center drawer, taking out a plastic Baggie as though it held a snake.

I took it from her and turned it over to read.

"YOU CAN RUN CU-NT BUT YOU CAN'T HIDE"

When I looked back at Roja, she was dipping into a tissue box from another drawer.

After she'd blown her nose and wiped some tears, I said, "When did you get this?"

"I came in as always by eight-thirty. It was not here then. I went down to the Xerox room, and it was here when I returned."

"How long were you gone?"

"Fifteen minutes, perhaps more. I had a lot of copying to do for things I need to send out for the professor."

"These trips to the Xerox machine. You do it regularly?"

"I do not understand?"

"Do you usually do the copying first thing in the morning? Predictably?"

"Oh. Oh, I see. No, but the man did not deliver the note."

"How do you know?"

"It was in this." Roja reached down and came up with a manila interoffice envelope, about twelve of the thirty To and From lines already used. The last entry was just a To Maisy Andrus.

"Could you set it on the blotter?"

"I'm sorry." She complied. "I saw nothing wrong with the envelope when I opened it. It was in with the mail and five others of the same kind of envelope."

"Who else would have handled it?"

Roja just resisted touching it again. "All the people who used it before. And Larry."

"Larry?"

"The mail clerk. But he gets many of these. It is easier sometimes just to drop off the interoffice mail in his room on the second floor."

I took out a pencil and tickled the envelope over to where I could read the earlier names. I recognized only one. Walter Strock.

"Can we use your phone to call Sint Maarten?"

Roja had the card with telephone numbers already on it. Within minutes we had a connection and a hotel operator with a lilting voice who would be pleased to ring Mr. Hebert's room.

There was a metallic buzzing, once, twice, three times. "Tuck Hebert."

"Tuck, this is John Cuddy."

"Shee-it, John! The hell can be so important, you got to bother us on our first morning here?"

"I'm sorry, Tuck, but I'd like to speak with your wife."

"Try me first. What's the problem?"

I didn't see that insisting was going to be much help. "There's been another note."

"Well, he's still sending them, he still thinks we're up there."

"That's not the point, Tuck. From the note, he knows about you two taking a trip."

"Read it to me."

I did.

"Lordy, John, all that means is he saw us going with you and some luggage. We already knew he's found out where we live, what with that note in the mailbox and all. Now it seems like he's staking us out. I don't like it much, but I don't see where we're any worse off than before."

"Tuck. Listen to me, will you? Within about thirty-six hours of your taking off, he knew you two were gone and got a note to circulate through the law school's interoffice routing system. I want to talk with your wife and with the tournament and hotel security people."

"No go, John. Folks down here were nice enough to think of inviting an old has-been like me. I'm not about to get everybody into an uproar over a few nut notes."

"Tuck—"

"I'll tell Maisy about it when I figure she's rested up enough to hear it. I'll be with her until the tournament starts, and then I'll tip a guy I know can watch over her when I'm out on the court. Now, that's it."

"You realize—"

"Signing off, partner. Just remember, sticks and stones can break my bones . . ."

I heard a click and static.

Roja took the phone receiver back from me and replaced it very carefully, as though the console might explode.

Then she looked up at me. "What can we do?"

I was thinking about that when a familiar, if not particularly friendly, voice said, "Now that the scintillating Professor Andrus has flown the coop, I wonder if you could come see me about a complaint I'm composing for the Board of Registration of Private Investigators?"

When I followed Walter Strock into his office, the blonde from the library debate was sitting in one of the visitor's chairs. She wore a one-piece wool dress, robin's-egg blue, with a sash.

Strock said, "John Cuddy, this is Kimberly Weymond."

Weymond took about a minute getting to her feet. I was noticing her moist lipstick and heavy eye shadow before it struck me that her dress was a twin for the outfits Maisy Andrus wore.

"Kimberly is my research assistant. She will stay as fair witness to what you and I discuss."

Weymond's hand felt more manicured than callused. "Mr. Cuddy." She smiled in a your-place-or-mine way.

"It seems you misrepresented yourself to me on Monday, sir."

I turned from Kimberly to Strock, who was dropping into his big swivel chair. Weymond resumed her seat. I took the other captain's chair, arranging it so I could watch both of them.

"Tell me, Professor, just how fair a witness is your research assistant likely to make?"

"I rather think I'm a better judge of that than you, sir. Now, more to the point, I believe that when you were here on Monday, the specific false pretenses you asserted consisted of—"

"Why don't we cut the shit and call the cops, Strock."

Weymond just aborted a laugh. Strock stared at me as though he were wondering what I could have said that would have sounded like "cut the shit and call the cops."

"I beg your—"

"Try Area A. Ask for Detective William Neely. He'll remember you, I think."

Whatever words were climbing up Strock's throat lost their footing before reaching his mouth. I had the impression that he was desperately flicking through his data banks, trying to find the incident I was talking about.

"Let me refresh your recollection, Professor. It was the time you got sick after that school party, and you had that difficulty on Beacon

Hill. Down toward Cambridge Street? An apartment, I think—"

"Kimberly!"

His voice was so shrill, she jumped a little.

"Yes, Walter?"

"You're excused."

"But—"

"Please."

Weymond looked from him to me just once. Standing again, her panty hose rustled. She left the room without another word, probably trying to play back and file away what I'd already said.

When the door closed behind her, Strock said, "How dare you! I can have your license—"

"Strock, I can have yours too."

He shuddered once, and suddenly the acerbic academic devolved into someone a lot older and grayer. "What do you mean?"

"I know all about you and the student that called the cops. Now, you're going to answer every question I ask, and politely. Otherwise, the student newspaper gets to play *Washington Post* to your Dick Nixon. We understand each other?"

His lids lowered halfway. "Yes."

"How did you find out that I wasn't straight with you on Monday?"

"The girl that I didn't pick as my research assistant."

"Nina Russo?"

"Yes."

I started to get up. "Sorry, Strock."

"No! Wait, it's true. She was pissed off royally that I picked Kimberly over her. The stupid cu—Russo should have been amazed that she was even in the running, with her looks. She—Russo—was in a bar near here, complaining about me. When Russo said you talked to her about it, one of the male students overheard and later told Kimberly."

That seemed reasonable. It didn't take much to picture male students trying to play up to Kimberly.

"How did you know about Maisy Andrus being away?"

"The dean."

"Fill in the blanks, Strock."

A deep breath. "Maisy told him about some threats or whatever she'd been getting. Said she needed some time off. He told her he understood, even told her she could cancel her special session course. Then he became concerned as he always does about how that might play with the rest of the faculty. So he came to me for counsel." Strock mustered a wan smile. "He may be weak, but he is politic."

"When did he come to you?"

"When? Yesterday sometime. Yes, yesterday evening, just before my seven o'clock. I prefer my classes start on time, you see, and I recall being a bit testy that he was staying so long."

"What do you know about the threats?"

"Only what he told me."

"Which was?"

"Just that Maisy had received them. For God's sake, man, the positions and people she associates herself with, I'm not surprised."

I got all the way up this time. "All right, Strock. Let's leave things at that for now. But keep it zipped, okay."

"You have no right—"

"I meant your mouth."

20

I HADN'T MUCH ENJOYED THE SESSION WITH WALTER STROCK. I figured to enjoy the next one even less.

Most of Dorchester has never been upscale. The streets have terrific names; just the A's include Armandine, Aspinwall, and Athewold. The structures, however, reflect the culture a little more exactly. Peeling three-deckers with decayed porches, burned-out storefronts boarded over with warping plywood, vacant lots full of rubble but free of hope. Working class launching welfare class, generations of experience greasing the skids.

The clubhouse for the American Trust was just off Gallivan Boulevard. From the outside it looked like it might once have been a laundry. Now there were reinforced metal shutters instead of plate glass and professional signs. The two hand-lettered messages on the shutters read: ATTACK DOGS ON PREMMISES and DONT FUCK WITH US.

I got out of the Prelude and locked it. Approaching the door, I could hear the rumble of a loud stereo. I knocked politely twice. Then I banged on the door until I heard the music stop.

A "Joe-sent-me" slot opened on the other side of the door and one of the kids from the library looked out. "Yeah?"

His eyes were bleary from being high, and he didn't place me. "I'd like to talk to Gunther Yary."

"Ain't here." The slot closed with authority.

I started banging again. The music came back on. I kept hammering away until it stopped.

The slot reopened. The same kid said, "Get the fuck out of my face, awright?"

"I want to talk with somebody about Yary."

"I said he ain't here. You deaf or what?"

"You can let me in, or I can camp out here and talk to the first one of you leaves or comes. Your choice."

"Aw, fuck. Just a second."

The slot closed again. I waited. The music didn't come back on. Then the sounds of bolts and maybe a crossbar from the other side of the door before it swung open. A bit too inviting to be credible.

The kid I'd been talking with was smiling. "Come on in, man."

I took a step with my right foot, then drove off it to the left, barging my left shoulder as hard as I could into the door. The metal hit something that gave, then crunched a little as the door wouldn't go any farther.

I jumped to the right as my greeter came at me. I grabbed him by the left arm and spun him around and over my outstretched left leg.

Something sagged behind the door. Something else heavy and metallic clattered to the floor as the door itself swung back. I drew the Chief's Special from the holster over my right hip.

Rick, the guy who'd been feeding Yary set-up lines at the library, slumped forward, scrabbling for the Colt .45 Automatic that was between his legs. Blood was flowing pretty freely from his nose and maybe a lip too. There was enough blood that it was tough to tell.

"Don't," I said.

Rick didn't look up at me. He moved his hand toward where he thought the gun would be.

I cocked mine. At the sound, the guy stopped, weighing things. He wasn't deciding for peace yet.

I said, "This thing makes only one more noise."

Convinced, Rick sat back.

I moved toward him and edged the automatic away. My greeter was just about to his elbows on the floor. I slid the Colt into the pocket of my raincoat. Then I went back to the door, slamming it shut, but using only one dead bolt to secure it.

Rick was gingerly touching his nose and cringing. My greeter was up to his knees, but wobbly.

I took in the room. Hung ceiling with some panels missing, the rest stained. Posters on the walls of scabrous guys with long hair or no hair, done up in leather and gripping heavy-metal guitars like tommy guns. Two flags, a small Confederate war banner, and an even smaller Nazi swastika. The stereo system on sturdy plastic milk crates, incongruously scrubbed-looking in red, white, and blue. A blue crate held stacks of audiocassette tapes. The ones with printed labels were mostly Def Leppard, Motley Crüe, and Aerosmith. The knockoffs were Skrewdriver, No Remorse, and Immoral Discipline.

The floor, once nicely carpeted, was now burned and torn, smelling like stale beer. There were enough cans of Coors around the base of the walls to build an Airstream trailer. Two sets of bunk beds met head to toe at one corner, a cluttered desk to one side.

I said, "The photo team from *Better Homes and Gardens* been here yet?"

"Fuck you," said Rick, burbling a little through the blood.

I moved to the desk and started rooting around.

"Hey," said my greeter, "you can't do that."

"Constitution's suspended for a while, boys."

Most of the paperwork was in the form of leaflets, newsletters, and requests for contributions. White Aryan Resistance and some kind of affiliated group called the Aryan Youth Movement, both from Southern California; The American Front from Northern California; White Heritage from the Midwest. Some newspaper and magazine clippings, but of whole articles. About white supremacy groups like the Klan, the Order, and the Posse Comitatus. One long story from the *Boston Globe* on skinheads in New England. A poor Xerox copy of a report from the Antidefamation League of the B'nai B'rith, defaced with predictable remarks. Even an ad from a British magazine for steel-toed Dr Martens workboots, which seemed to match what the skinheads were wearing.

No mutilated headlines, though.

I walked over to my greeter. "Let me explain the drill."

He looked at me sideways, the way you might watch a kid who steals ice cream from your cafeteria tray.

I patted the pocket with the automatic. "I'm betting this isn't registered, at least not to you clowns. I'm also betting I can get one of you a year the hard way for having it. Who wants to cover my bet?''

Rick said, "Don't say nothing, Tone."

"Tone? Tony, right?''

Greeter who might be Tony didn't say anything.

I said, "Tony, let me spell it out for you, no big words. You guys were stupid, going hand to hand with the cops back at the library."

Tony looked me in the eye now, memory dawning.

"But the piece, the piece is beyond stupid. The piece is getting to play drop the soap in a communal shower. Am I getting through to you?''

Tony was definitely sensing the drift of the conversation. "I wasn't anywheres near the gun."

"You fucking shithead."

I ignored Rick and said, "Where's Gunther Yary?"

Tony worked his mouth.

I said, "Twelve months is fifty-two weeks, three hundred sixty-five—"

Tony said, "He's out on the bridge."

"You yellow fucking—"

"What bridge?''

"The Granite Ave bridge. The judge, the judge gave him public service."

"You're a fuckhead, Tone."

I pointed to Rick. "The guy with the broken nose thinks you're a yellow fuckhead, Tony. The guy who's supposed to be standing next to you, standing up for you. Think about that."

I left the place. In the car I unloaded the automatic. Two blocks later I dumped the gun down one storm drain and the bullets down another.

There were four men working on the surface of the bridge, a couple of orange barrels and a bunch of orange traffic cones keeping the passing cars at least three inches away from arms, hips, and legs. I walked up to the closest man, the only guy who didn't have a tarbrush in his hands.

He was wearing an orange safety vest with yellow X's front and back. Below the vest, patched corduroy pants and sneakers. Above the vest, a green, battered hardhat. He held a filterless cigarette between a thumb and forefinger, the thumb missing its nail.

I said, "John Cuddy. I'd like to talk with one of your men there."

"What's it about?"

"Case I'm working on." I showed him my ID.

"Lemme guess. The Nazi."

"Gifted, isn't he."

"Sonofabitch. Fucking judge don't got the balls to put a guy away so close to Christmas, that I can understand. But putting him on my gang, for chrissakes, don't they even think about that? Judge's got a criminal, what does he do, he sends him out to do my job. How do you figure that makes me feel?"

"Yary been any trouble?"

"Nothing but. Guy opened his mouth about the Jews and the— look, I'm not carrying the torch for anybody, get me? But I had to send this guy, Roosevelt Barnes, off with another crew. My best worker, and I had to send him off. You know why?"

"Yary?"

"Called Rosey a nigger. To his face. I mean, forget Rosey's about three hundred pounds, you don't say that to a black guy, not any- more. Took two a us to hold Rosey back. I'm not about to let a good guy like Rosey, got seventeen fucking years in, get bounced for dropping a piece a Nazi shit off a bridge abutment just because some fucking judge's got his head up his ass. So I send Rosey off for a few days while I get squat outta the Nazi. Go figure."

"I can't. Mind if I talk to him?"

He lowered his voice. "You gonna rough him up any?"

"Not planning to."

He shook his head, disappointed. "Hey, Yary. *Yary!*"

One of the orange vests looked over at us as the other two stopped with their brushes.

My friend motioned him over with two jerks of his cupped hand. To me, he said, "Stay here and talk to him. I wanna spend some time with my guys."

"Right. Thanks."

Yary drew even with the foreman about forty feet from me and tried to ask him a question. The foreman just stayed in stride and walked on by.

Yary continued to me, the hardhat jiggling askew on the shaved head. He slowed before stopping about five feet away and reflexively touched a hand to his ear. "I don't have to talk to you."

"Monday night you sounded like all you wanted to do is talk."

161

"I would have. Till you and the nigger cops and kike money-changers—"

"Tell you what, Yary. You stop the slurs, and I won't fracture your skull. What do you say?"

He kept his distance. "Go ahead."

"What brought you to the library?"

"A bus. It was real big, see? With seats and windows and everything."

I shook my head and sighed. "The foreman said he'd look the other way if I needed to get rough with you."

"You can't do that. You'd lose your license or whatever."

I sidled a little closer to Yary. He thought about backing off before deciding he couldn't and keep face.

"Just had a talk with a couple of the boys at the clubhouse."

Yary didn't reply.

"You know, Gun. Rick and Tone? They said to give you their best."

"How do you . . ." Yary squinted, then jammed his hands in his pockets, suddenly looking very young.

"They told me where you were, Gun. After a while."

"Look, I don't want no trouble from you."

"Little late for that."

"You don't understand. None of you understand us, the Trust, the Movement. We're just trying to get back what's ours, that's all. What the race mixers . . . what the government's let the others take away. One thing I learned from that, from Martin Luther King and Jesse Jackson and their kind. You can win in this country if you just keep talking, just keep in people's faces so they can't believe that you're still around, bothering them, making them face what the truth is. About how everything's been taken away from people who earned it by people who didn't. Once I chased this big nig— once I purified the crew here, one of them started listening to me. Hearing what I was saying."

"Why did you go to the debate?"

"To get some publicity, man. Free publicity. But even the TV and radio don't care about Andrus and her 'friends.' They're shoveling all this shit about the right to die. That's not the point, don't you see it? It ain't the right to die we got to worry about. It's the right to live, to take back what's ours from them that took it from us."

162

"You don't see Andrus and her crowd as a threat, then."

"Threat? Threat, shit no. Those assholes are just a distraction, get it? They're just being used to get attention for issues that don't mean shit so the real issues, the raping of our people by the others, don't get settled."

Watching Yary talk, become animated and sincere, I decided he scared me more than Rick with his automatic.

Finally, Yary said, "So what do you think?"

"What do I think?"

"Yeah. About the Trust, the Movement."

"I think from your rap sheet that you're not as nonviolent as you make out."

"That was then, man. This is now, you know? I learned my lesson, learned it real good. Now I'm into friendly persuasion."

"I think Rick and the others are thinking about taking the Trust in a different direction."

Yary clouded over. "The fuck you telling me?"

"When I visited the old clubhouse today, I got an armed response."

"Armed? With what?"

"A Colt forty-five."

"I don't believe it. I don't fucking believe it."

"Yes you do. You just don't want to admit it."

"They wouldn't do that. They're not that stupid."

"They're that stupid, Gun. Stupid and impatient. Not everybody's interested in waiting out the revolution."

Yary started to tell me how it wasn't a revolution, but just the people taking back what was theirs. I cut him off by walking over to the foreman, who had started toward us.

The foreman said hopefully, "He giving you any trouble?"

"Sorry. Model prisoner."

"Shit."

"Thanks for letting me take him for a while."

"Take him forever, you want to."

Yary walked by us, eyes straight ahead. As he rejoined the crew, he said something and laughed. One guy paid no attention, but the other laughed too. With Yary, not at him.

The foreman said to me, "Fucking judges, make me feel like shit," and spat over the railing.

21

"MERRY CHRISTMAS, JOHN."

Nancy had put on a fuzzy mauve robe before she'd gone into her kitchen. Now she was at the side of the bed, holding a carrying tray in front of her, steam rising from coffee cake and ceramic mugs.

"What's in the mugs?"

"Your leftover cider concoction. Waste not, want not."

I'd mulled the cider, with cinnamon sticks and orange sections, the night before as Nancy made popcorn and strung the product on threads like a rosary, whole cranberries playing the Our Fathers. After lacing the cider with bourbon, we'd looped the strings of popcorn and cranberries over lights and ornaments on the short, full spruce tree we'd spent a cold hour selecting at a Lions' Club lot in Brighton. Shopping for the tree reminded me that I had to act on Bo's advice regarding a Gore-Tex running suit. Late December was feeling more and more like the tundra time of February.

I hadn't seen Bo for a week or so, but I'd been training religiously without him. Following my talk with Gunther Yary, the case for Maisy Andrus had slowed down, as some cases will. After checking to make sure all the people she'd offended were staying home for the holidays, I'd contracted out to another investigator who needed someone to spell his people on an extended surveillance. I did stay in touch with Inés Roja by telephone, me confirming there were no further notes, she advising that the professor and Tucker Hebert sounded happy and relaxed on Sint Maarten the two times she'd heard from them. Andrus wanted to meet with me when they got back, Inés and I agreeing on a breakfast conference for January 18.

Around bites, Nancy said, "You realize this is the best Christmas I can remember?"

She snuggled close enough for me to inhale the herbal shampoo still clinging to the roots of her hair. After decorating the tree, we'd agreed to exchange gifts in the morning and slipped into bed, making slow, drowsy love as the lights twinkled five colors in computer-chip sequence.

"Where are my presents?"

Nancy took another gulp of cider. "Under the tree, junior."

"I want my presents."

"And here I thought you were finally showing the patience maturity is supposed to bring."

"I want my presents now."

"Okay, okay. Smallest to largest?"

"The only way."

We traded gifts, one at a time. Silly ones, thoughtful ones, middling-expensive ones. A Garfield the Cat calendar for her, a T-shirt with the legend BODY BY NAUTILUS, BRAIN BY MATTEL for me; a video of *Adam's Rib* for her, a video of *The Maltese Falcon* for me; a leather briefcase with shoulder strap for her, a teak desk set for me. And so on.

Finally, Nancy said, "Time for the big ones?"

"Uh-huh."

The boxes were remarkably similar in size, about right for a man's suit.

Nancy opened her present, a geometric sweater in five colors from an exotic store on Newbury Street. She held it up, arms stretching arms, chin pressing down on crew neck. "It's beautiful, John."

"Genuine yak fur from the Himalayas."

"Your turn."

My box came open. It contained a man's suit, all right. Ebony Gore-Tex, drawstrings on the jacket and Velcro cuffs on wrists and ankles.

I looked up at her.

Nancy said, "One of the guys in the office runs. He helped me pick it out. If the size is wrong—"

165

"It's perfect, Nance. Does this mean you've decided I'm not so stupid about wanting to run the marathon?"

"No. It means I don't want you getting what my friend calls 'penile frostbite.' Do you know what that is?"

We showed each other there was nothing to worry about.

The week between Christmas and New Year's was miserable weatherwise: temperature in the high thirties with frequent if not constant rain. The Gore-Tex kept me both dry and ventilated, but there was still no sign of Bo, which worried me a little.

Fortunately, December thirty-first turned bright and sunny. Everything dried out toward a crisp, low-forties First Night.

First Night has really caught on in Boston. Originally designed as a way to discourage drinking on New Year's Eve by offering performing arts alternatives, the idea has blossomed into an annual festival of ice sculptures, fireworks, and general revelry. Just strict enough to discourage public carousing, just tolerant enough for hip flasks discreetly tupped.

Nancy had bought us each a button, a blue bird on a black background. The button allowed the wearer to attend almost all the holiday entertainment. We cooked an early dinner at my place, planning over dessert the events we'd visit. Most were repeated on a staggered schedule during the evening.

Out on the streets, the crowds, all ages and sizes, jostled happily. Cloth coats to fur wraps to ski outfits. Mardi Gras costumes, glow-worm necklaces, tinsel tiaras. Women with painted faces, guys with long plastic trumpets. Nancy wore her Himalayan yak fur sweater, which pleased me. I didn't wear my rapidly ripening Gore-Tex suit, which pleased her and everyone around us.

We began at the First Baptist Church on Commonwealth. Minimalist decorations hung beneath conservative rosette windows and dark joists and trusses. There were no kneelers in the pews, and only the barest of cushions on the benches. I browsed through a red-bound hymnal on the rack in front of me as we waited in the swish of people seating themselves.

The four performers were the Mystic Consort. Renaissance music from soprano and bass singers, a right-angled lute, and a harpsichord the size of a hippo. Most of the twelve works involved all four, some a single singer with accompanist or an instrumental solo. A perfect, gentle kickoff.

Our second stop was the Old South Church on Boylston Street. We joined a thick line of nine hundred people moving slowly past port-a-potties. At the doorway we were among the last folks ushered politely into the sanctuary to hear the Old South Brass, Timpani & Organ. The sanctuary walls were done in rose and lavender, an opening-flower motif that was repeated in the carpet. Ornate detail work crept over ivory marble facades. Lustrous beams arched upward, like the ribs of a great sailing ship capsized overhead, just below a center cupola and skylight. Curled chandeliers were attached to the ceiling by brass balls and chains. Overall, I had the feeling of being in Constantinople.

The musicians played trumpets, trombones, and tuba in addition to the timpani and organ, the last a 1921 dinosaur of nearly eight thousand pipes. The conductor moved the crowd without manipulating it, starting with a rousing National Anthem and progressing through various pieces I didn't know to one I did. An arrangement for organ of Barber's *Adagio for Strings,* the signature theme of Oliver Stone's Vietnam movie, *Platoon.*

The Barber music took me back, back two decades to a New Year's Eve in Saigon, a turn of the calendar a month before the lunar new year, a month before Tet, when most of us still thought we were winning.

"John?"

I looked down into Nancy's eyes, suddenly aware she'd been tugging on my sleeve and whispering to me.

"John, are you all right?"

"Yes. Why?"

"I thought you were zoning out on me. You were moving your lips and had this glassy look in your eyes."

I closed my hand around hers. "I'm fine." And I was.

Our third stop was the Arlington Street Church, the one that most reminded me of a Catholic cathedral. All white, elaborate barrel vaults, fluted granite pillars, stained-glass windows with interior shutters. A massive walnut pulpit enclosed in riddled wooden gates dominated the altar. Undecorated pine trees contrasted with garlands and floppy red velvet bows. The pews had café doors and miniature kneelers like shoeshine boxes.

The performing group was the Muir String Quartet. About halfway through the first entry, which sounded a hell of a lot like "Baubles, Bangles, and Beads," I noticed someone familiar on the far side of the church. He was partly in the shadow of a pillar, but I was pretty sure it was Del Wonsley, Alec Bacall's companion, sitting next to a man a little shorter and more stooped than Bacall.

Nancy played finger games with my hand through the remainder of the program, a nice mix of the poignant themes a string quartet can evoke. As we were shuffling out, the stream from the other side of the church merged into ours, and I was startled. I recognized Del Wonsley for sure, but that wasn't what startled me.

The stooped, older man next to Wonsley was Alec Bacall. There was a hollowness in the pouches above and below his cheekbones, as though someone had let the air out of his face. It had been only three weeks since I'd driven Bacall to South Boston after the library debate.

Wonsley said, "Oh. John, right?" The brown eyes were soft but a little unsure of what to say next.

I introduced Nancy while Bacall bundled up, a heavy scarf over his throat and mouth like a Berber tribesman.

Bacall said, "Got a bit of a cold, I'm afraid."

I nodded, and Nancy preempted an awkward silence by taking Bacall's arm and leading him into the foyer, leaving me with Wonsley several steps, and intervening people, behind.

I said, "Is Alec all right?"

Wonsley's expression didn't change. "He's having problems with his insulin dosage. It's not working right sometimes. In fact, this is the first time since before Christmas we've been out. Alec wanted to . . . we met, sort of, on First Night, last year."

"Has he been to see a doctor?"

"Yes. At the . . . a clinic. He recommended Alec have some tests."

Wonsley's expression still didn't change, but the eyes got softer. He didn't say what the tests would be for, and I didn't ask.

We said good-bye briskly on the sidewalk. As Wonsley and Bacall moved away, I asked Nancy if she'd mind cutting our celebration a little short.

22

IT WAS A MILD MORNING SEVERAL WEEKS INTO THE NEW YEAR, temperature in the mid-fifties, Boston nearly basking in the January thaw. I chanced wearing just a sweatshirt and shorts.

I spotted him from the Fairfield footbridge to the river. Sitting on his bench, legs crossed, left arm draped over the backrest, right hand on the bench seat. From a distance he looked the same as before. Up close, the tweed jacket had been mended, the glasses newly taped, and the hair freshly cut.

"John." Neutral tone, a substitute for hello.

"Bo. I missed you."

He glanced away, toward the MIT dome. "Been traveling."

The first time Bo had opened up at all. I didn't want to crowd him. "Whereabouts?"

"D.C. area." His eyes rolled up toward the emblem on his Redskins cap. "I used to teach there, John. And coach. Private school."

I leaned against a tree, keeping my shoes on the macadam and out of the mud. "Get tired of it?"

"No."

Bo moved his left hand over to his right wrist, and I was afraid I'd pushed too far. Then he said, "You ever been married, John?"

"Once."

The voice lowered. "Me too. Even had two little daughters, just

169

toddlers then. But things weren't going so good between Adele and me—Adele was my wife. And the school, it was running low on money and had to let go a lot of people with less seniority than I had. The pressure started to mount because the rest of us were expected to take on extra duties for less pay. John, the pressure, all these expectations, at home and at school, started building inside me. It was like living in a double boiler, and it soured me. I lost interest in my teaching, my family, everything but the coaching. I started to fixate on it, truth be told. Then the school dropped the other shoe. Said they just couldn't see their way clear to keep me on. I'd become 'marginal.' "

"They fired you?"

"They didn't renew my contract. Discreet way to fire a guy, eh? But it wasn't just the job. We lived free on campus, nice little house, John. Nicest little house you'd ever want to see. All brick and ivy, with hedges and flowers. But when I wasn't renewed, all that was gone. I didn't have a job or a roof over my family's head, not even the coaching anymore. I just plain broke down. I was in an . . . institution for a time after that."

"For depression?"

"Oh, they had a dozen different names for it, John. From a dozen different doctors pushing a dozen different drugs. And none of them knew jackshit. I finally broke out of the blues some, but only when I realized that it was the pressure of the family as much as the job that did me in."

"Your family."

"Yeah. Adele could see it, too, last few visits to the hospital. Came time to be discharged, like a year later, I didn't have a job, and after what I'd been through, I couldn't exactly see getting another one. Adele had already set herself and the girls up separately, telling them their father was . . . dead."

"Bo, I'm sorry."

"Hey, it's not so bad. Life on the road, I mean. And once a year, right around the holidays, I go back." Bo passed a hand over an ear. "I get spruced up a bit, and I hitch my way to where they live now. First time, Adele got flustered, introduced me to the girls as a friend of their dad's from the old school. They were so little when I went away, and I'd changed enough in the years since, they didn't recognize me at all. They ask me questions about what their dad

170

was like when I taught with him, and I get to talk with them about me, sort of, only with no pressure, no . . . expectations."

"You never tried to . . ."

"What? Get back together again?"

"Yes."

"No. No, Adele and I knew that wouldn't work out. Only one thing worse than losing the people you love, John."

"What's that?"

"Losing them twice."

The eyes moved away to MIT, the right hand massaging the left wrist. "I'm sorry, John."

"About what?"

"About dragging my life into yours."

"Bo, that—"

"No. No, it was my deal, and here I've gone and broke it."

After a minute I said, "You know that Gore-Tex suit?"

Bo's face came back to me. "Huh?"

"Before you left. You said I'd be needing a Gore-Tex running suit."

"Oh. Oh, yeah, right."

"I got one for Christmas. Any suggestions on when and how to wear it?"

He let the wrist alone and, for a moment, seemed not to breathe. Then, "Well. Well, now, a couple of things . . ."

I spent most of the rest of that January day at the office, servicing some smaller cases and trying not to dwell on Bo. At home, I got a call from Inés Roja. She confirmed that there still had been no more notes. Roja also told me that Andrus and Tucker Hebert were back from the Caribbean and that the professor still wanted to meet me that next morning. At the Ritz-Carlton, no less. Inés sounded embarrassed saying that she thought the Ritz required a jacket and tie, even for bacon and eggs.

I followed the maître d' through the first-floor dining room. The high windows permitted only filtered light from Newbury Street to strike the crystal and silver spread before the men and women attending power breakfasts.

"We're targeting the ten highest risk companies in the . . ."

". . . course, five years down the pike, will I still be . . ."

"And our long-term resources just might be compatible with your short-term . . ."

". . . in which case, it would be mainly a northeast program with an acronym of its own."

Maisy Andrus treated me to a radiant smile over the rim of her china cup. She wore a white cotton turtleneck under an Icelandic sweater, the hair a shade lighter from the tropical sun. Her face was tanned, but without the worry lines or leathery look some women her age suffer.

The perfect example of the good life. Maybe an hour earlier, I'd left Bo, in rags on a cold bench.

Andrus suddenly appeared concerned. "John, is anything wrong?"

"No. Just thinking about something else."

The waiter came over with a cut-glass bucket of fresh juice and took our food orders.

I said to Andrus, "How was the trip?"

The blazing smile again. "Indescribable. I hadn't realized how much pressure I'd let build up inside, but Tuck was right. A vacation in the sun with him was all I really needed."

"Good weather, then?"

"Perfect. We stayed at a place called Little Bay Beach Hotel, around a point from the Dutch capital. Early mornings until the tournament started, we'd snorkel out to the point. Just light enough to see but before everyone else was up. Huge boulders covered with sea urchins, black pin cushions with glass spines you have to avoid. All kinds of other reef life: fish, stingrays, even what Tuck called a 'rogue barracuda.' My God, it must have been five feet long, hanging in the water, inches under the surface. Tuck said it was nothing to worry about, that it was just waiting for us to kill something it could share."

Andrus shivered, rubbing the back of her neck through the cotton. "Most days, we stretched out on lounge chairs, sometimes in the sunshine, sometimes back under thatched roofs on poles. I drank when I wanted and devoured twenty thick paperbacks just for fun. We wandered all over the island. The French side is more pastoral, with sort of country restaurants, the Dutch side more glitzy, with casinos and discothèques. I'd never go dancing at one of those in Boston, my students would be all over it. But down there we partied till sunrise, especially with the tournament people. Tuck and his partner finished third in the Celebrity Doubles part, and I ate the most spectacular things, including roast shank of ostrich at a restaurant Tuck scouted out for our last dinner."

Andrus was gushing a little, but I didn't want to interrupt with business until she turned to it herself. The waiter provided a convenient break by bringing our meals.

In between bites of an omelette, she said, "Any progress on my case?"

I condensed what I'd learned since the drive to the airport, including Gunther Yary. I came down hard on the last note at the law school and Hebert's dismissal on the phone.

"I'm sorry about Tuck, John, but he was doing only what he thought was best, and he was right. Inés showed me that note when I got back, and you know what? It didn't shake me. Not in the least. I feel recharged, reborn."

Andrus rubbed the back of her neck again.

I said, "Sunburn?"

"No. No, some damned insect got me in bed, our last night on the island. I can't even see the infection without being a contortionist. Inés scraped it and applied some Bacitracin." Andrus shivered again. "I hate that stuff, like somebody's spit on you. Plus it itches like poison ivy."

"Probably a sign it's healing."

"That's what Enrique used to say." Andrus left her neck alone, a bittersweet smile crossing her face. "You know, I've been quite lucky that way, really. The two men I've been with the most have been the best men I've known."

Her eyes refocused, and I think Andrus suddenly realized I was still a widower.

Brusquely, she said, "So, we'll be leaving in a day or two for California. I'll be back in mid-February for a lecture, but only briefly. What, if anything, do you think you need to do in the interim?"

"That depends. Who's going with you?"

"Tuck, of course. Inés is staying here. I'll be mostly speaking and networking out there, not writing."

"Manolo?"

Andrus sighed. "He was terribly moody when we got back. Like a neglected cat, if that doesn't sound inhumane. I think we'll have

173

to bring him with us, but more for his sake than as a bodyguard."

"That last note. It went through the school's interoffice mail."

"Yes?"

"It's possible that some of the outsiders, like Louis Doleman—"

"Who?"

"The man whose daughter took her life after reading your book."

"Oh. Yes, sorry. Go on."

"It's possible that someone like Doleman or Gunther Yary could have figured out how that works, but more likely it's somebody closer."

Andrus waved impatiently. "And therefore?"

"Something a cop said that I've been thinking about. People who get their kicks scaring other people like to use the phone for threats."

"Why?"

"It's more direct. More personal."

"But this one sends notes."

"Yeah. Why?"

"Why notes, you mean?"

"Uh-huh."

Andrus caught the waiter's eye and placed her utensils at two o'clock on the plate. "I have no idea."

"Maybe it's because you'd know his voice on the phone."

"A possibility, to be sure."

"Professor, be sure of another thing, okay?"

"What's that?"

"Maybe our boy doesn't use the phone because he doesn't have any voice at all."

Andrus looked at me strangely, then brayed a laugh loud enough to turn heads.

Walking from the Ritz in a snow flurry toward my office, I realized that neither Maisy Andrus nor I had mentioned Alec Bacall. At Charles Street I turned right instead of continuing through the Common. I couldn't remember hearing Bacall's address, so I had to check three lobby directories on Boylston before finding his building. Prewar (almost any war), it was opposite one of the oldest burying grounds in Boston, a fenced square of gravestones dating from colonial times.

Taking the elevator to the fourth floor, I knocked on the door marked BACALL OFFICE HELP. Del Wonsley's voice sang out.

Wonsley was sitting at the reception desk in a tasteful waiting area, holding a telephone receiver to his sweatered chest. "Hello, John Cuddy."

"How are you?"

"Fine, fine."

"Is Alec in?"

Wonsley's tongue made a pass between his lips. "Just a second." Into the receiver he said, "Kyle? Kyle, I'm going to have to put you on hold for just a moment. Okay." Pushing one button, then another, Wonsley took a breath and said, "Alec, John Cuddy's here. Do you . . . right. Right, I will."

Wonsley pushed only one button this time and didn't muffle the receiver. "Go ahead. And try to be . . . up, okay?"

I said, "Okay."

Opening the inner door, I could see Bacall rising behind a magnificent cherry desk. The flakes fell lightly outside a tall bay window framing the Common across the street. There was a large Kurdistan rug on the floor, a smaller one hanging on a wall.

Even though the room was very warm, Bacall wore a cable sweater and his trademark double-pleated slacks. From a distance of twenty feet, he looked stooped still but boyish, with color in his cheeks and no bags under his eyes.

He said, "John. Good to see you."

Wonsley's comment about "being up" kept me to "Same here" instead of a relieved "You're looking well." Fortunately, too, because at close range the illusion became transparent. The handshake was still like steel, but awfully dry and almost brittle. And the face . . .

"Is there some development regarding Maisy's case?"

We took our seats, and I filled him in. Four times in five minutes Bacall coughed deeply into a handkerchief.

After I finished, he said, "It sounds as if you've worked diligently without flushing anything to wing."

"That's about right."

Bacall coughed again, harder and longer than before. He tossed the handkerchief into the wastebasket and took another from a side drawer of the desk. "Kleenex would be more sensible, but I've always preferred cloth." He pursed his lips. "Did Del say anything to you?"

"No."

A wry smile. "Oh, my, John, I do hope you lie better to those who don't know you. After we saw you and . . . Nancy?"

"Right."

"After we saw you and Nancy at First Night, I had a series of tests. They came back positive."

"Positive."

"Yes. The clinic was very good about it. They've had a lot of practice in being very good. They should do something about using the word 'positive' though, don't you think? I mean, 'positive' really shouldn't mean what they use it to mean, if you'll forgive the redundancy."

"When you say the tests came back . . ."

"The tests showed AIDS, John. Not just exposure, not just AIDS-Related Complex."

"Alec, I'm sorry."

"John, I'm sorry to spring this on you. But I couldn't believe you hadn't noticed anything New Year's Eve, and I wanted you to hear it, or most of it, from me."

"Does Andrus know?"

"Not yet. I left a message at the school for her to call."

"Tommy Kramer?"

"Yes. He's reviewing my will and . . . oh, I'm sounding pessimistic, aren't I?"

When I didn't reply, Bacall went on. "There will be good days and bad days. This is one of the good ones, I'm pleased to tell you. And Del's been able to keep me from looking ghastly by the judicious application of makeup. He's a marvel at it, used to work backstage in summer stock here and there. I must admit, though, it makes me feel just a bit like a drag queen to doll up this way."

"What about those new drugs?"

"My doctor—or doctors, one of the problems with the disease is that you suddenly have more *médicos* on you than a star halfback with a bruised toe. My doctors are not optimistic about them because of the diabetes. But they're thoughtful, caring people, and they're working on it."

I nodded.

"There's something else I want you to know, too, John. My condition doesn't affect my concern for Maisy and her situation. Not one iota. Whatever you need from me, you'll have. Del and I will be winding down the business to manageable proportions. If worse

176

comes to worst, he can decide whether to revive it or instead sell it for the good will and leasehold value." Bacall gestured at the window. "It is a hell of a view."

"Alec, I won't—"

"Forgive me for interrupting, John, but I want this understood. Winding down the business means Del and I will have more time for each other, but it also means that, good day or bad, I'll have time for Maisy and the cause. More time, ironically enough, than I've ever been able to devote before. I intend to stay active for a long, long time. If you need energy, resources, just plain legwork or telephoning, you let us know, and it's yours."

"I understand. Thank you."

Bacall swiveled his chair gently toward the window, so that he could appreciate the view without turning his back on me. "When I took these offices, I arranged the furniture this way because I was afraid the scenery would be a distraction." Keeping the chair stationary, he brought his head around to me. "The last few days, I find I look out often, probably more than I have the last few years. I look out on that graveyard, men and women who died before I was born. Before AIDS was born. And I realize that people have always died from something, and most before their time."

"Cemeteries can do that for you."

Bacall began to rock slowly in the chair. "As a boy, with all the doubts and conflicts I felt, there was one thing of which I was absolutely certain. I would live forever. I might never feel completely at ease with myself, but there would never be a time when there wouldn't be a me. Then I learned that forever has just one rule."

"What's that, Alec?"

"Forever's rule is that nothing is forever." Turning his face to the window, Bacall seemed to sit straighter in the chair. He kept rocking, but his speech became as clipped as his beard. "Sometime, if we could, I'd like you to tell me more about life, John."

"I doubt I know more to tell you."

"Sometime we might try. But just now, I'm afraid this good day is tripping into bad. On your way out, could you ask Del to come in, please?"

I got up quickly and left him, rocking and watching his view.

23

"Now that we're halfway through February, John, you've got to start thinking specifics, not just general stuff anymore. The distances are coming along fine, and you're running on the packed snow like it was a groomed, gravel track. But it's time to start planning the race in your mind. Go out and drive the course, all the way from Hopkinton into Boston. But drive her like a runner, not a driver. You're gonna notice something. Except for some miles in the middle, you've got rolling hills. That means you have to run a little different. On the way up, keep your knees high to synchronize the arm and leg motion. Don't look down at the ground unless you've got paper cups and orange peels to step around. Keep your eyes on the horizon. That way, you don't get discouraged by glancing up and seeing how far you still have to climb. The idea is to run up the hill, not into the hill. So lean forward on that incline, like you're riding a horse and coming forward in the saddle for him. On the decline, lean back, like you're still on that horse and laying back in the saddle to balance him. Don't let gravity help defeat you.

"People talk a lot about Heartbreak Hill. Fact is, Heartbreak isn't just one hill, it's a series of them, with plateaus in between. From mile seventeen to mile twenty-one. That's the firehouse at the intersection of Route 16 and Commonwealth all the way to the top of Chestnut Hill at Boston College. The inclines are bad, but the plateaus

178

are worse. The plateaus, they remind your legs of how much nicer it is to run on a flat surface. Remind you just enough to take the starch out of those legs for the next incline. Then you think, 'Well, at least I get to go downhill too,' but the decline is the worst of all, because it stretches the wrong muscles at the wrong time.

"Yes, you've got to respect Heartbreak, John, respect it and learn it. Go out to the firehouse and run just Heartbreak, when you're good and fresh. Run it nice and easy. See how it feels, how long it really is. Spot some landmarks and memorize them. Marathon day, it's the landmarks that'll tell your mind how much farther you've got to go after you can't depend on your legs for messages no more. Yes, once you train a little on Heartbreak, you'll know you have to ease off earlier in the race.

"What I'm saying is, save some for Heartbreak, John. Save a lot."

Absolute temperature, five above. With the wind chill along the frozen river, nearly thirty below. Doing eight miles instead of ten, a concession to the February weather. Thanking God and Nancy for the Gore-Tex suit, I wore longjohns underneath it, wool mittens and ski mask over it. I even stuck the temples of a pair of sunglasses through the edges of the eye slits on the mask, the lenses reducing both the glare and the bite of the wind. If you're not too cold, you're not too old, right?

The temperature made the running paths icy. By the time I'd turned for home at the four-mile point, my stride and my breathing were on automatic pilot, my mind drifting to the Andrus case.

It had been a month since I'd seen the professor at the Ritz for breakfast, and she was due back in Boston that day to deliver a lecture. In the interim I'd helped a defense attorney on a questionable manslaughter charge. I'd also called Inés Roja three times: no more notes at the school or house, Andrus telling Inés the same thing from San Diego.

The notes. Our boy sends one when Andrus leaves for Sint Maarten, but none when she comes back. And none when she leaves for San Diego. Does that mean he knew about the Caribbean trip but not the California one? Walter Strock, Tucker Hebert, and Manolo obviously knew about both junkets, Louis Doleman probably neither. Ray Cuervo and Gunther Yary each were sharp enough to find out where Andrus was at any time.

Another thing. The mode of delivery varies: U.S. mail, by-hand delivery, pasted label, intraschool system. Why be erratic in both when and how the notes are sent? To throw Andrus even more off balance?

My frustration level was lowered by Andrus being three thousand miles away as her case went nowhere. Passing the Hyatt Regency, however, I decided to burn off the frustration I did feel by upping my pace a little, the wind flapping the Gore-Tex jacket against my shoulders as I ran before it.

At the office that day, Inés Roja called. The professor had arrived from the coast for her lecture that night. If possible, Andrus wanted me to come to the town house by five P.M. and ride with her to the site. I said I'd be there.

After spending the afternoon on the manslaughter case, I walked through the cold to the mansion, the sidewalks nearly as glazed as the running paths had been. It was just getting dark as Manolo opened the door for me. If he'd been out in the sun of San Diego much, he didn't show it. He was sweating heavily, the foyer like an oven. I took off my coat, Inés coming downstairs in a short-sleeved blouse and dark skirt.

"John, it is so good to see you."

"Same here. Have you had your furnace adjusted recently?"

"I am sorry?"

"It's pretty hot in here."

She smiled. "The professor is no longer used to the winter. It was eighty degrees Fahrenheit when she left California."

"She's upstairs?"

"Yes."

"Can I see her?"

"I will ask."

I watched Inés clop back up the stairs. Lithe and attractive when she didn't think about it.

I turned. Manolo, a long parka over his arm, was staring at me. He moved his mouth as if to spit, but just went out the front door, slamming it behind him.

"John, have you been sick?"

Andrus appeared weary, a pile of opened mail on the desk behind her.

"No, I've been running a little more. Probably dropped a few pounds."

"Good. For a . . . Alec told me that you and he talked."

"Last month, after I saw you at the Ritz. How is he?"

"I've spoken with him, and sometimes Del, from California. They seem buoyant. I'm going to see them after the lecture tonight."

Andrus massaged her eyes with the heels of her hands.

I said, "Would you like me to wait downstairs?"

"Oh, no. It was just the flight."

"Bad?"

"Bumpy. Storms everywhere east of the Mississippi. I must concede that San Diego offers considerable meteorological charm, if it weren't for the fact that I'd probably never get anything done out there."

"Tuck come back with you?"

"Yes. He's off running errands." She indicated the pile of correspondence. "I'm left to wade through all this."

"Any surprises?"

"Any . . . ? Oh, you mean notes. No, nothing."

"No incidents in San Diego either?"

"None. Tuck was with me most of the time, Manolo the balance. I must say, I believe my demented pen pal has lost interest."

"Yet you asked Inés to have me come over tonight."

"For two reasons. First, have you made any progress?"

I explained how I'd played out the string of people to see. "What's the second reason?"

Andrus frowned. "I'm mindful that the labeled book appeared after my last speaking appearance here."

I nodded. "What's your speech tonight?"

"The same one you heard at the Rabb debate, I'm afraid."

"Doesn't the audience notice that?"

Andrus shook her head. "Most of the people will be different. But even the faithful feel reinforced, hearing the same things."

"Where is the lecture?"

"Sanders Theater."

"In Cambridge?"

"Yes. Part of the Harvard Law School Forum."

"Harvard invites a professor from another law school to come talk?"

"Yes. Rather daring of them, but it's more a students' speaker series, really." She checked the digital clock on her desk. "Manolo ought to have gotten the Benz by now. Let me gather myself, and I'll see you downstairs."

"We going to wait for your husband?"

"No. Tuck said to go on without him."

In the foyer, Inés Roja and I made small talk until Maisy Andrus joined us. In a full-length fur with matching hat. Sensible against the cold, but I started to hope that there wouldn't be any animal rights folks at the speech.

I helped Roja into her coat, then pulled on mine. The secretary opened the front door, me moving across the threshold and out to the sidewalk. Cars were pushed up on the curb to park and yet allow a lane wide enough for traffic to pass. No sign of Manolo and the Mercedes.

As Roja closed the door behind the three of us, Andrus stepped by me, hugging herself against the night wind. Tugging on my gloves, I heard a flat crack and, just over my head, a sound like someone whistling in water.

Glass shattered as I tackled Andrus, shoving her behind the engine block of the closest car. Roja was already crawling behind me as another flat crack came from across the street and high. The mailbox next to the front door of the house clanged on its screws. The first bullet had gotten the imitation gas lamp over the doorway.

Andrus pushed herself to her knees and said, "What the hell is—"

"Shut up and stay down."

Roja said shakily, "We are being shot."

The rooflines across the street seemed even and empty. No silhouette, no muzzle flash.

I took a quick look at Roja, but didn't see any blood. "Inés, are you all right?"

She shifted her weight, one leg on a snowbank, the other on the icy cement. "Yes. Can you see anything?"

"No."

Andrus said very quietly, "Are you going to shoot back?"

Looking down at the revolver in my bare right hand, I couldn't recall taking off my glove or drawing the gun. "Not from this angle. I might go through a window or throw one high and over to another street or building."

Andrus faced her house. "Shouldn't we call the police?"

Eight feet separated us from the locked door. "Not till I'm sure we'd get to the phone."

Five or six minutes passed. I was thinking about the shooter's aim when a powerful engine approached, charging hard. Brakes squealed on the other side of the parked cars. A door was flung open, creaking on its hinges, and Manolo squeezed himself between two bumpers.

I motioned for him to get down, but he was signing frantically to Inés Roja. When there were no more shots, I let out a breath.

Manolo rushed over to Andrus, helped her up, and reverently brushed the snow off her coat.

Roja said to me, "Manolo was caught in traffic, behind a truck that stalled or something. He saw us from the corner"—she pointed behind her—"and was afraid for us."

I watched Manolo, who seemed awfully agitated. Almost theatrically so.

Then I moved toward the mailbox. My shoes crunched shards of glass from the light over the door. There was a perfectly round hole in the front of the box, off center but not by much. I put my right glove back on. Using a pen, I lifted the lid of the box and looked in.

Andrus said, "What are you doing?"

I coaxed out the folded white paper, undamaged from the shot. At the bottom of the box, bits of brick from the exit hole on the back wall lay around a flattened slug.

I unfolded the paper. Headline-sized words again, but twice as big as the snips from the earlier notes.

"ALL BAD THINGS COME TO AN END CU-NT."

I doubted Roja could read what it said, but she certainly could see what it was. The secretary began to cry.

24

"So what made you check the mailbox?"

Neely had a pad and pen on his lap, actually taking notes once in a while. Slouching on the parlor sofa of the Andrus mansion, he'd visited a new barber since I'd seen him last. The currycomb cut made him look like a lowland gorilla.

I said, "The shooter threw the second one high after the first slug already wrecked the lamp over the doorway. Seemed kind of co-incidental that he'd happen to hit the mailbox after my client had been getting threatening notes."

Neely used the pen to scratch behind his ear, then swung it in an abrupt arc toward the staircase. "How's this Andrus taking it?"

"Pretty well. She made calls to cancel things out for tonight. The secretary who came to see you is pretty shaken up."

"Minute ago, you said the shooter was a 'him'?"

"Just an assumption. We're figuring the shooter was the guy sending the notes."

"So you didn't make him on the roof there."

"No."

"You been looking into these threats for what, about a month now?"

"More than two."

"Anybody handy with guns?"

I'd been giving it some thought. "The Spanish son, Ray Cuervo, mentioned hunting with his father in the old country. Louis Doleman, the guy whose daughter committed suicide, talked a little about hunting too. And Walter Strock has a bunch of marksmanship trophies in his office."

"How about the other names I ran for you?"

"I don't see Steven O'Brien as a rifleman. And Gunther Yary of the Fourth Reich says he doesn't believe in guns."

"A Nazi who don't believe in guns?"

"He says freedom of speech will set us free."

"Christ on a crutch. The hell can you count on anymore?"

"One of Yary's storm troopers seemed a little more in the mold."

"Don't get you."

I laid it out, including the address of the storefront in Dorchester. Neely said, "How's about you leave the Nazis to us?"

"Fine."

He finished scribbling and lowered his voice. "That guy, the houseman. Manello?"

"Manolo. M-a-n-o-l-o."

"Right, right. Manolo. He was where when the shots were fired?"

"Getting the car. Supposed to have been stuck behind a truck."

"Supposed. Why 'supposed'?"

"Because I didn't hear any horns."

"Horns. Like you would if some truck was fucking up the traffic there."

"Right."

"Stupid thing for him not to think of."

"Yes and no. He's deaf. Might not have occurred to him."

Neely looked skeptical. "You really figure he could be the guy?"

"If so, I'm the only one who does."

"Let's hear it."

"One, Andrus pushed over the man who basically pulled Manolo back into life. Two, he's always around her for the notes except when she goes off to the Caribbean, and then a note appears at the law school when not many people know she's gone and nobody outside the school could easily access the internal mail system."

"Motive and opportunity for both the notes and the shooting. But why does he miss, then?"

"Don't know."

"Why does he wait—what, ten years?—to start at her?"

"Same answer."

Neely shook his head.

I said, "The husband's also not accounted for."

"The husband?"

"Tucker Hebert. Andrus says he was out running errands."

Neely plainly didn't like trying to keep track of all these people. "So opportunity. How about motive?"

"He gets most of the estate."

"If the professor there buys the big one."

"Right."

"Meantime?"

"Meantime, he's a former pro tennis player who gets sported like a trophy."

"What?"

I explained it to Neely.

He scratched behind his ear some more with the pen. "So we got a husband who's riding his wife's money either way."

"Except if Andrus were dead, he'd be enjoying it without her."

"Yeah, but if the perp is either Manolo or the husband, how come she's not getting notes out in California there?"

"I've thought about it."

"And?"

"If it's either Manolo or Hebert, hand-delivering a note out there points the finger."

"So the guy could use the post office."

"Without an accomplice to mail the notes from another city, the postmark would give the guy away."

Neely shook his head again.

I said, "You get anything from across the street?"

"From the roof, you mean?"

"Yeah."

"Nah. The techies went up. Easy to do, some kind of scaffolding on the far side. Too windy and cold for the roofers today, though. No shell casings, no footprints they could make out."

"How about the slugs?"

"They'll run them through ballistics, but don't wait by your phone, okay? The slugs, one splattered and the other got flattened by the professor's brickwork. I seen ones like that before they couldn't do much with."

186

I figured that gave me an opening. "Homicide going to be by?"

A grunt. "Nobody bleeds, they try not to bother those guys. Why?"

"Thought maybe there might be something we're missing."

Neely closed his pad. "Probably. There usually is. But then in the end you find out what it was and turns out it don't mean shit anyways."

"Even so, you mind if I keep looking into this?"

"Except for the Nazis, suit yourself. It's your time and her money, right? Lemme do the courtesy call on Andrus. I'll let you know about ballistics."

"I'd appreciate it."

Neely lurched to his feet. "Whew, tough day."

Uh-oh.

He patted his stomach. "Yeah, fact is, I been having the kind of day, if I was to break for dinner about now, I'd want somebody else to taste my food for me."

I got the hint and told Neely I'd wait for him.

"I was hoping you'd still be here."

Robert Murphy looked up from the wrappings of a submarine sandwich. The wax paper and a diet Coke nearly covered the one area of his desk not stacked high with files.

He said, "I can't even eat my dinner in peace?"

"Do me a favor, Lieutenant, don't talk about food. I broke bread with Beef Neely tonight."

Murphy set the sub down delicately and folded the paper over it. "Just ruined my appetite. Sit, but don't stay long."

"Thanks." I took one of the metal chairs.

"You okay, Cuddy?"

"Fine."

"You look, I don't know, kind of skinny."

"Been running, that's all. Listen, about that case back in December?"

"The one you had to see Neely on."

"Right."

"Now what?"

"Somebody missed my client and me with a couple of shots today."

"Probably forgot to allow for windage."

"Very funny, Lieutenant. Neely seems to think he's in charge because nobody got hit."

"Probably right."

"No chance you or Cross could come in on it?"

"We take the ones that bleed no more. Area cops draw the ones that never bleed. In between . . ." He shrugged.

"That's how Neely described it too."

"Besides, reason I'm still here is we're buried. Cross, she's out with the harbor boys, bobbing for what's left of some wiseguy."

"What's left?"

"His hands we found inside a Maserati over in Eastie. Nice Italian driving gloves."

"Back to my situation?"

"Two minutes worth."

"There were some slugs, Lieutenant, but no casings. I think it had to be a rifle. At least one of the slugs was intact, but flattened."

"What'd they hit?"

"Bricks."

"Don't—"

"—wait by my phone, I know. Can you do anything?"

Murphy sucked some diet Coke through a straw. "Not much. I can see the slugs get the full treatment, but that's about it."

"I appreciate it." I got up. "Since this isn't your case, I take it you have no objection to my staying on the investigation?"

"Your time."

I left wondering if all cops talked the same before they went to the academy too.

"How's Inés doing?"

Maisy Andrus set down the book she was reading. "Pretty well, I think. She's lying down, sleeping, I hope. The proximity of all this has hit her pretty hard. I think it reminds her of being . . . on that boat."

"Manolo let me in. Where's your husband?"

"Tuck hasn't gotten back yet."

I glanced at the clock on the desk behind her. Nine forty-five P.M. "I thought you said he was just running some errands?"

Andrus got huffy. "I in no way have to justify Tuck's activities to you, and neither does he."

"Professor, I'm tired too."

"I'm not tired."

I let it pass. "Whoever that was today is a reasonably good shot to have hit the mailbox nearly dead center."

"It's a large mailbox."

"On a downward angle from a rooftop on a cold and windy night. He wanted to miss you. Us. He's playing some kind of game, to get you rattled."

"He won't succeed."

"He is succeeding. You're upset—"

"I am not—"

"And you have every right to be. He's got some kind of private agenda planned for you, and I have to try to figure that out before he ups the ante much further."

Andrus heaved out a breath. "Understand this. I am upset only by your continuing to think that my husband could have anything to do with any of this. Or Manolo, as that ass Neely seemed to imply. Since I am not stupid, I recognize that whoever is doing this wants to keep me off balance, to discourage me from doing what I do. I am pained to admit that this evening he was successful. I canceled a speaking engagement which would have provided appropriate coverage to the issues I hold dear. I want you to continue your investigation on my behalf, but I do not, I repeat, I do *not* want you harassing my husband in any way. Now, is that clear?"

"Crystalline."

"I'm sorry." She leaned her head back. "You're not stupid either. I know that. Will the police be much help?"

"You've met Neely."

"Yes, but aren't there any other police?"

"Bluntly, not until our friend comes closer."

"As he suggested in the note."

"Yes."

"Well, it will be a while before he has another chance."

"What do you mean?"

"We'll be going to New York tomorrow. I'm conferring with the new National Council on Death and Dying."

"Professor—"

"That's the successor organization to Concern for Dying and the Society for the Right to Die. Then it's on to D.C. for a few days of lobbying before we fly back to the coast."

"When you say 'we' . . . ?"

Andrus set her expression firmly. "Tuck, Manolo, and I."

"Professor—"

"Please stay in touch with Inés." She softened just a little. "I had to cancel Alec tonight, too, though I'm going to try to see him early tomorrow. Please do whatever you can to help."

I said, "I will," no longer knowing who Andrus meant for me to help. Or how.

"Hey, John! John-boy, how you doing?"

I was almost at the corner of Charles and Beacon. Tucker Hebert waved to me from half a block away. He tried to pick up his pace, skittering down the sidewalk with mincing steps, like a hockey coach in street shoes crossing the rink.

Despite the crisp wind, a heavy dose of eau de Dewar's rolled toward me. "I never will get the hang of skating around up here. Didn't get this ice stuff more than once a decade where I come from."

Hebert must have seen something in my face. "John, I hope you're not still put out about that phone call thing, but like I said back then, Maisy needed the rest more—"

"I'm not upset about the phone call."

The eyes swam in a glassy sea. "What's in your craw, then?"

"Somebody shot at us tonight."

Hebert tipped forward on his toes and lost his footing. Going down, he grabbed for my arm just as I grabbed for his and steadied him.

"Shots? At the lecture?"

I would have asked first if anybody was hurt. "We never got that far. It happened in front of the house."

"God almighty! I never would have—Lordy! Maisy, John." Hebert's fingers nearly pierced my coat sleeve. "Maisy, is she okay?"

"Yes. Nobody was hit."

"Oh, God. Thank—"

"Of course, the shooter wasn't trying to hit us."

Hebert opened his mouth, but no words came out.

I said, "The slugs went way high. Just a warning."

"Warning?"

"Yeah."

"Of what?"

"Good question. You finish your errands?"

"Huh?"

"Your errands. Maisy said you were doing errands."

"Oh. Oh, yeah. Well, truth is, I was just out having a few snorts. All this time in San Diego, I've been kind of missing some of the places around here."

"Any places in particular?"

"No. No, just here and there. You know how it is."

"The police may be calling you on that."

"On what?"

"On where you were this afternoon and tonight."

"The police? Lordy. Maisy, she's . . . at the house?"

"Right."

Hebert let go of my arm and took off for the mews. He slipped three times and went down once before making the corner.

25

I SKIPPED RUNNING THE MORNING AFTER THE SHOTS WERE FIRED, instead calling Inés Roja, who said she was feeling much better. Andrus, Hebert, and Manolo had left the house and the city safe and sound. It took Roja just a few minutes to dig up the only home address I didn't already have, although I decided to save that one for last.

The condominium complex abutted the sea, a cluster of structures four stories high with weathered shingles. I found a parking spot on the street, not even diehard sailors thinking about braving the waters off Marblehead in February.

I went through the foyers in five buildings before I found "Cuervo, R." on a mailbox behind an unlocked entry door. I climbed two flights to the third floor, Cuervo seeming to have a duplex condo that included the fourth.

I could hear a stereo set low on a jazz tape. I knocked, got nothing, knocked again, and heard the slap of shower thongs on a hard surface. The door opened, and Cuervo, barechested in tennis shorts, looked out at me.

"What are you doing here?"

"I'd like to talk with you, Mr. Cuervo."

"Ray, please. I thought we had a talk already?"

"Something else came up."

"I'm, uh, entertaining." He sent his eyebrows toward the interior staircase behind him. "Can't it wait?"

"I'm afraid not. Somebody took a shot at your stepmother yesterday."

"Somebody . . . you mean with a gun?"

"That's right."

"*Dios mío!* Come in, come in."

Cuervo's living room had a view of the harbor through a glass wall, French doors leading to a wooden deck. He waved at the sectional furniture around an elaborate home entertainment center that dominated one of the other walls. "Sit down. I'll be right back."

Cuervo took the stairs two at a time. I heard just vague voices, then a door opening and closing. Cuervo came back down, pulling a rugby shirt over his head, the collar of the shirt uneven.

I said, "I'm sorry to be interrupting anything."

"That's okay. Her night was just about up anyway."

A shoe hit the floor upstairs, and Cuervo got serious. "So what's this about Maisy?"

I went through it for him.

Cuervo raked his hair with his left hand. "Unbelievable. I can't believe none of you got hurt."

"The shooter wasn't trying to hit us."

"How do you know?"

"I know. The question is, do you have any idea who it could have been?"

"Me? How would I know anything about it?"

"You told me you and your father used to go hunting."

"Sure, we . . . Oh, come on, man. You're thinking I had something to do with this?"

"That's right."

"Hey, lots of kids go hunting with their fathers. Doesn't mean I'd—look, I don't have any reason to shoot Maisy."

"Any reason to scare her?"

"I don't know what you're talking about."

"You said last time that you didn't care about the split on your father's estate."

"That's right. She got the house in Candás, I got the liquid stuff."

"Any nonfinancial reason for getting back at her?"

"Like what?"

"Like sexual?"

Cuervo hurled himself from the sectional piece. I rolled to the left, felt him land, then rolled back, clamping my arms around his. I pushed his face into the cushion for about ten seconds, then let up enough to hear him say "Okay, okay. Let me go."

I stood up and over Cuervo as he turned back to me. He kneaded his left bicep with his right hand, then switched off to the other arm.

I said, "Just what exactly happened between you and Maisy Andrus?"

Cuervo cocked an ear toward upstairs before speaking in a low voice. "I was maybe fourteen, fifteen. After my mother died, I was pretty used to having the run of the house in Candás, you know? I mean, it was just my father, Manolo, and me when I was home from school. Well, one day I was coming back after going to the beach, and I was dripping wet on the tile floor near the staircase. So I stripped down as I was climbing the steps, hurrying so the water wouldn't get all over the rugs upstairs.

"I kind of burst into the bathroom, naked, and there's . . . there's Maisy. Naked, too, just stepping out of a bath. I was stunned, I guess. Then Maisy looked down at me"—Cuervo dropped his eyes to the crotch of his tennis shorts—"and she said, 'Ramón, you're your father's son,' and smiled. Looking back on it, I guess she meant it to cut the embarrassment, but at the time I took it . . . I took it for my father's marrying a whore, okay? A whore who'd make a play for her new husband's son."

"You ever talk it out with her?"

"No."

"Why not?"

Cuervo blushed for the first time. "We don't do things that way."

" 'We'?"

"In Spain. We don't do that kind of thing. It's just . . . different over there. You wouldn't understand."

"This scene with Andrus in the bathroom. Is that why you were so long coming home to see your father?"

"Probably. It was all a long time ago, all right? Not a real happy time to remember either."

"Where were you yesterday?"

"Yesterday?"

"Right."

"At the plant."

"In New Hampshire."

"Yeah. Where you saw me before."

"When did you leave?"

"I don't know. I headed back here around four, four-thirty. What difference—oh. Look, I told you, I don't know anything about the shooting. I don't even own a gun anymore, okay?"

"You said Maisy Andrus got the house. What about the hunting rifles you and your father used?"

"I don't know what happened to them. I was thinking about college, man. I didn't care about guns."

"I'll let you get back to your day."

Cuervo glanced upstairs, then at the clock on his VCR. "Hope she isn't expecting breakfast."

I followed Louis Doleman and his teddy-bear hair through the second door of the spacelock.

He said, "Marpessa? Company's here."

I let Doleman take his seat before I took one opposite him. The same cardigan sweater and slacks as in December. The same worn copy of *The Right to Die* open, facedown, on the TV tray. I gave him the benefit of the doubt on the cupcakes. The macaw perched on the arm of his chair, giving me a revolving-eye once-over as I leaned forward, elbows on my knees.

"Mr. Doleman, I wonder if you can help me here."

"I'll sure try, Mister . . . ?"

I'd said my name for him thirty seconds before. "Cuddy, John Cuddy."

"Sure, sure. Cuddy. What can I do for you?"

"I'm thinking of doing some hunting this week."

"Hunting? Hunting? My boy, you can't go hunting this time of year."

"Not here. Overseas."

"It's winter in Europe too."

"Not Europe. Below the equator. It's just turning fall there."

"Ah. Ah, yes, I remember that. What . . . what is it you want again?"

"I'm trying to decide what firearms to bring with me. I wonder if I could see some of yours."

"Mine? Mine, they're awful old, son."

"That's all right."

"Besides, I don't know, I don't think it's legal somehow for me to loan them to you."

Doleman seemed like that the last time too. Fading in and out, foolishly inviting a bigger, younger stranger into his house, then fixing on some detail. Loose to lucid. If it was an act, he was one of the all-time greats.

"No, Mr. Doleman. I don't want to borrow them. Just look at them toward deciding which kind I should buy."

"Oh. Oh, sure, sure. Come on." Doleman stood, waggling a finger at the bird. "Marpessa, you be a good girl now."

The macaw pecked his finger and made an atonal squawk, but stayed put.

I followed Doleman into his kitchen. The appliances all looked 1950s and crudded over.

He paused to move a case of generic soda cans away from a cellar door. "I keep them down in the basement, of course."

The stairs were steep, each step shallow enough for the ball of the foot to land just a little too far forward. Doleman almost pranced down them, an agile gnome at home in his cave.

"Over here."

He stopped in front of a padlocked steel cabinet mounted on the wall. The cellar was neglected, a strong, musty smell matching the dingy whitewash on the cement.

Doleman fished in his pocket for keys. Getting them out, he held each up three inches from his face before settling on one. "Here she is, here she is."

He inserted the key in the padlock, having to force the lock itself off the hasp. He pulled open the door, grating from rust. "Help yourself."

Three rifles and a shotgun, standing muzzles up. I worked the first one out. An M-1 with enough dust on it to have been there since Truman fired MacArthur. I looked into the bottom of the cabinet. The dust around the other butts seemed undisturbed.

"Been a while since you've had these out."

"Long while. Haven't taken a deer since . . . I don't know when. Still have to apply for some kind of goddamn permit though. Every birthday, seems like."

Probably every fifth. I tried the action of the M-1. The outside bolt you wedge back with the edge of your hand wouldn't move.

Doleman said, "That's a military weapon, son. The others are your sporting arms."

I put the M-1 back and tried the next, a lever-action Winchester. I sniffed the breech area. No smell of burnt powder or gun oil to have cleaned it. Same with the third, a Ruger. I left the shotgun where it was.

"These are your only firearms, Mr. Doleman?"

"What, four ain't enough?"

Smiling, I still let him precede me up the stairs.

Back in the living room, I said, "Thought I saw you over on Beacon Hill yesterday."

"Beacon Hill? Me? Not a chance. Don't go into the city these days."

Not counting his trip to the library for the debate, I guess. "Why is that?"

"Too dangerous. Besides, Marpessa there would miss me something fierce. Wouldn't you, Marpessa?"

The bird said, "Right you are, right you are."

Doleman beamed. "See that? See? Better than kin, better than a son or daugh—"

His face got doughy, the lips working at cross-purposes to each other. "What . . . what was it you wanted again?"

I could have asked him about his daughter's treatment, about his contacting the Mass General over it. About a lot of things. Instead, I said, "I'm all set, Mr. Doleman. Thanks for your time."

He nodded, but more as a good-bye as he retook his seat, flopping the opened book over into his lap and beginning to read. The macaw primped her feathers as I moved backward toward the spacelock.

The door to Walter Strock's house bowed open, Kimberly Weymond standing next to it. She was wearing a pink terry-cloth robe with a peekaboo front and a hood that rode down from the weight of her blond hair, recently washed. A floor lamp backlit the hood, making her look like a cobra. If you believed in omens, that is.

Weymond didn't have to be reminded of who I was. "Come in, Mr. Cuddy."

"Is Strock here?"

"No, but come in anyway."

I moved past her into the living room. A thick hardbound casebook and a nearly as thick paperback vied with peach five by eight cards atop a low, square cocktail table. In front of the table was a beautiful marble fireplace, a couple of logs crackling.

Weymond said, "I've always loved a fire after a long, slow bath."

I took a chair facing away from the fire and nodded toward the worktable. "I thought everybody used computers now."

Weymond glided to the table, nestling behind it Indian-style. "Some things are better the old-fashioned way, don't you think."

Great. "When do you expect Strock back?"

"Not for a while."

"Were you with him yesterday?"

"No. Walter and I see each other only a few nights a week." Weymond planted her elbows and made a pedestal of her palms, resting her chin in them and speaking through partially clenched teeth. "Walter's not exactly an everyday player anymore. He needs pumping up."

"You know where I might find his gun collection?"

"I might. What's in it for me?"

"The delight of betraying his confidence?"

Weymond laughed, the "I'm with it too, buddy" noise you hear in bars.

She said, "How about a trade, then?"

"What for what?"

"The carefully hidden location of Walter's gun collection in exchange for what you have on him."

"What I have on him?"

"In his office that day, when he asked me to leave. You've got something that gives you leverage over him, and I want to know what that something is."

I gestured around the room. "This isn't enough leverage for you?"

Weymond shook her head hard enough to free a swath of hair. She looked like a bad impersonation of a World War II pinup girl. "There's no such thing as enough leverage. I get the run of Walter's house because I pump him up, in a lot of ways."

"Isn't that kind of sexist?"

"Only if you take it out of context. This place is closer to school than my apartment, and I like nice surroundings. Walter's ego needs somebody young and attractive on his arm. That's some leverage. Young, attractive and smart, that's more leverage. See how it works?"

"Where're the guns?"

"We have a deal?"

"We have a deal."

Weymond bounded to her feet, the breasts jouncing in reaction to the rest of her body. "Come with me to the treasure trove."

I followed Kimberly up a flight of steps. She'd nicked herself behind the right knee shaving her legs. Under the circumstances, I wasn't about to mention it.

We went into what from dimensions must have been the master bedroom. Mahogany wainscoting applied halfway up the walls on all sides except for another fireplace. Velvet drapes, a Dhurrie rug, two easy chairs.

Weymond jumped into the bed as though it were a pool, an image of the athletic preteen she must have been not so long ago.

It was a pool, by the way. Sort of.

On her back, Kimberly laced fingers behind her head in a modified sit-up. "Walter must have read somewhere that water beds were 'where it's at.' " She gave me a sly smile. "Do I have that right?"

"What right?"

"The expression. 'Where it's at'?"

"As I recall. How about the guns?"

"Let's play a game."

"I don't like games, Kimberly."

"No. It makes sense. You'll see."

"Make it a short game."

"Okay. Now, move back toward the door like you're a burglar or something."

I sighed but retraced my steps to the threshold. "All right?"

Weymond hunched toward the headboard on her elbows. "One more step back."

I complied.

"Now come at me."

My eyes went around the room for a camera or even a lens, but there were enough furnishings to hide it.

"Come on, like you were going to attack me."

I started forward. On my second step Weymond hit a panel in the wainscoting behind her. A handgun shot out on an accordion device, like the boxing glove from a Three Stooges movie. She grabbed the weapon, an automatic, off what must have been a magnetic pad and leveled it at me.

Standing stock-still, I said, "Bad game, Kimberly."

Weymond kept the automatic at serious for a count of five, then let her arm weigh down with it to the comforter. "I don't think so. He calls it Walter's Walther. One of his brighter lights, to tell you the truth."

I walked toward her. She let me take the gun. A Walther PPK all right. I tested the action. Loaded, one shell jacked into the chamber. Safety off, ready for firing. Christ.

I made it safe. "Any more secret panels?"

Weymond swam out of bed, tapping a taller, recessed section of wainscoting on the other side of the bed. An AR-15, the civilian version of the Colt M-16 assault rifle, nosed out.

I moved to the Colt, bringing it to "present arms," and sniffing. Fired not too long ago, freshly cleaned and oiled. Locked and loaded, a slick weapon for home defense. But I'd heard M-16s often enough on city streets in Saigon. They make more of a popping noise than the flat crack of the day before.

I said, "Any others?"

"A shotgun in the hall closet downstairs. Not so melodramatic, though."

"No more rifles?"

"In the closet in the study. Walter's got a strongbox or something anchored below the floorboards. But they're a pain to get to, and anyway I don't have a key to that."

"Just to the front door."

The sly smile again. "And the back. Walter's at some conference. He won't be home for hours." Weymond casually showed a lot of leg. "Maybe you could use a little pumping up?"

"Thanks, but I'm afraid I'd keep reaching for my wallet, looking for a fifty to stuff somewhere."

The smile evaporated. "That's a sexist remark."

"Only if taken out of context."

I turned to go.

Weymond yelled after me. "Hey, what about our deal?"

"Should have gotten it in writing, counselor."

I went downstairs and out before she could pump up Walter's Walther.

26

"NOW WE'RE IN THE MIDDLE OF MARCH, YOU'RE PROBABLY THINK-ing you can shuck that Gore-Tex suit, start training in the kind of clothes you'll be wearing the day of the race. Forget it. Weather around here stays bad so long, it's better to keep warm when you run. Less chance of getting some kind of bug, knock you for a loop. Also more chance of losing a couple more pounds, which'll help your knees and ankles for the longer mileage this next month. So, stay with winter clothes for a while yet.

"Another thing. You've got to start focusing on your diet more. Backtrack from race day. Morning of the marathon, real early like six in the A.M., eat a banana for potassium. And toast, no butter, for carbohydrates. Some of the world-classers, they carbo-deprive from about race minus ten days to race minus three days, then carbo-load for seventy-two hours. They know what their bodies can take; you don't. So instead, eat maybe sixty percent carbohydrates for about a week before the marathon. Carbos give you energy, and they also store water a lot better than proteins or fats. Forget anything with alcohol or caffeine for that week. They're diuretics, and you'd be peeing away water that you'll be needing during the race.

"Running the marathon, whether she's a warm day or cold, be sure to start drinking water early, even before you're thirsty. The water you drink at mile two is the water your body's using at mile

201

twelve, and so on. Your system can't just absorb and benefit from water like a shot of adrenaline.

"One more thing for today. You'll be running as a bandit, not a qualifier. Since the officials'll force you to the back of the pack anyway, take my advice and go way to the back, like the last two or three rows. It'll be slower for you at first, but then as things start to open up, you'll be passing people instead of being passed. Sounds like a little thing now, but that'll psych you up, make you feel like you're winning rather than losing. Feeling like you're losing can sap you, wear you down mentally. And you just can't afford that over twenty-six miles, three hundred eighty-five yards."

You look like you did back in high school, John.

Smiling in becoming modesty, I laid Mrs. Feeney's St. Patrick's Day carnations crossways to her, the dipped-green flower heads slanting down toward the foggy harbor.

Well, maybe more like college.

"I have to admit, Beth, I feel pretty good physically. I thought I'd get rickety running almost every day, but I feel better, more relaxed even, than I have in years."

And Nancy. What does she think?

"She still thinks I'm stupid even to try it."

Really?

"That's what she says."

Oh, John. Always dense as a post that way.

"What do you mean?"

Don't you see that Nancy's opinion might be her way of supporting you?

"Frankly, no."

Then think about it some more. Are you still working on that case for the law professor?

"Not much in the month since the shooting. I talked with everybody who seemed connected with guns."

What about the police?

"Ballistics couldn't do a lot with the slugs. Based on the alloy, they think it was older ammunition, though."

Older?

"Yes."

Is that helpful?

"Depends. If we can come up with another slug, they might be able to tell they came from the same batch and maybe even the same weapon. On the other hand, there haven't been any more notes since the shots were fired."

What about the gay man who . . .

"He's been doing pretty well, I think. He left a message for me to call him early this week. I've tried three times since, but his answering service says he's out of the office for a few days. The professor isn't due back from the West Coast till April, so everything else is kind of on hold for another month."

Does that mean you and Nancy can enjoy the parade today at Chuck's house?

"I will. Nancy's working on a murder one, which means we're just going to have dinner together afterward at my place."

So you're going to the party stag?

"Not exactly."

Not exactly?

"There's somebody I think could use some cheering up."

Inés Roja tugged on the bottom of her green sweater. "I have never seen a St. Patrick's Day parade."

I inched the Prelude through the traffic just east of the veterinary clinic. "I thought New York staged a pretty big one?"

"I never knew anyone to go with before."

The last time I'd checked in with Roja about notes and Maisy Andrus, the secretary had apologized for not being more available. She'd been putting in extra time with the vet because another volunteer had been sick. I'd asked her if that included Sundays. Inés said yes, but just in the morning. Knowing Nancy couldn't make it, I'd insisted over Roja's protestations that I'd be over to get her. At noon, in green.

I said, "Nice sweater."

Inés looked at me solemnly, as if to see if I was kidding. Apparently satisfied, she said, "Filene's Basement. A wonderful place."

I persuaded two barricades of cops to let us through on the strength of the address printed on our invitation. Chuck was born into the Lithuanian enclave in South Boston, his dad a marine wounded on Guadalcanal. Chuck left the city, making his fortune by wise investments. He returned to buy a huge white house occupying one of the few large pieces of land in Southie. A piece of land at the intersection where the parade wheels ninety degrees.

A big Irish flag in green, white, and orange rippled in the breeze over Chuck's front door. I parked the Prelude in his long driveway.

As I killed the engine, Roja said, "Please don't leave me alone with people."

"I won't."

As it turned out, Inés was the hit of the party, a mixture of fifty or sixty people, only half of whom were descended from the Emerald Isle. We ate superb corned beef, drank enough Harp to float a PT boat, and got tours of the renovated house from Chuck himself, a rangy guy in a chartreuse shirt and cowboy hat. I took some good-natured ribbing about Nancy and heard Inés laugh for the first time, a merry, musical sound.

A whoop spread through the first floor, a lead element of the parade just reaching our corner. We joined the others carrying green beer and stronger spirits into the cold. Standing on the lawn, everyone applauded the bands and toasted the heroes and jeered the politicians. In between targets there were good stories and silly jokes and painful attempts to affect a brogue.

Back inside, folks opted for coffee and soft drinks to dilute the alcohol. As the party broke up around five, Inés and I said good-bye to Chuck, she helping me jockey the Prelude around the couple of cars that were staying later.

Stopping for a traffic light on Summer Street, Inés made a purring noise, then gave a tempered version of the merry laugh. "That was a wonderful party, John."

"It's a good time."

"The parade. You went to it every year?"

"When I was in the city. Even during Vietnam, when there wasn't much support for things military, the parade was a big thing because every block in the neighborhood had somebody in the service, many of them overseas."

"Tell me, from when you were a little boy, do you remember the parade the same way?"

"No, not really. I remember it being bigger and sharper and better. But I think that's just a function of growing up."

"Yes. Yes, you are right. We remember as better the things from when we were young."

I was about to keep the conversation going when I noticed a tear running down Roja's left cheek. I turned back to the windshield and watched the traffic instead.

At the Andrus house I pulled onto the sidewalk and came around to open the passenger door.

Inés got out and stood tall, still blinking away tears. Looking up into my eyes, she said, "That was the best time I have had in many years, John. If only . . ."

At which point Roja shook her head and pushed past me, fumbling out a key to open and close the front door as fast as she could.

"You didn't have enough at Chuck's?"

I took the wineglass from Nancy's hand. "Just carbos so far today."

" 'Carbos'?"

"Bread and beer."

"I hope you're learning more about running than you have about nutrition." She pushed the sleeves of a cowl-necked sweater up to her elbows. Topping off her glass, she raised it. "To St. Patrick?"

"Not after work kept you from the party. How about 'To forever'?"

Nancy clinked her glass against mine with that half smile that makes a little ping in my chest. "To forever."

A minute later I had two hands on the steak tray, aiming it for the oven, when the phone rang in the living room.

"Nance, can you get that?"

"Sure."

I centered the steaks and flipped the dial to Broil. I was just setting the timer when Nancy's head came around the corner, minus the smile.

"It's Del Wonsley."

27

THE MEDICAL FACILITY WAS ONE I'D NEVER HEARD OF, TUCKED away in the Longwood Avenue area near Brigham's and Women's Hospital. I found the right floor and suite, but the door was closed.

"John."

I turned around as Del Wonsley got up from a tub chair. Closing the current *Newsweek,* he looked bushed. "Thank you for coming. It'll only be a minute. They're . . . treating just now."

"What happened?"

Wonsley dropped the magazine onto the seat behind him. "AIDS leaves you open for a lot of complications. The diabetes is playing yo-yo with his waking hours. Usually these things are pretty predictable, but this episode is lasting longer than the others. So, Alec wanted to be sure to see you."

Wonsley read my face and managed a smile. "No, no. I think he's going to pull through this time. Weaker, but he'll make it. It's just that in seeing you now, Alec is playing the percentages."

"Is there anything I can do?"

"Be straight with him. No hearts and flowers. Just talk business or whatever, like he was laid up with a broken leg and had to meet people here as an inconvenience."

The suite door opened. A black female nurse with a round face came out. She held a metal pan, discreetly shrouded by a towel to conceal the contents. An East Indian female doctor followed the nurse and beckoned to Wonsley. They moved off to talk, Wonsley coming back as the doctor continued briskly on her way.

"You can go in now, John. But only a few minutes, all right?"

"Come get me if I overstay my welcome."

Wonsley went back to the chair.

I knocked, heard something, and went in.

They would have to invent a new kind of bleach to make the sheets whiter than his face.

Alec Bacall nodded to me, one fist compressing a little sponge ball. The arm had a clear plastic tube in it, some not-so-clear liquid pulsing downward and into him. I moved closer.

His eyes strained from the sockets, sunken and shriveled. The flesh sagged at his jawline, bruises of purple and blue providing the only color on the bed. I'd seen Bacall at his office in January, eight weeks before. Given the changes, it could have been eight years.

"Alec."

He nodded again. "I'd say sit, but Del probably told you not to stay that long."

"Just as well. I've been tossing down booze all day at a St. Pat's party."

The eyes went left-right-left. "God, I've lost track of that sort of thing. You and Nancy went to the parade?"

I told him about Inés.

"Good, good. She needs that, and more." Something moved inside Bacall, a brief spasm traversing his face as well as his body. Then, "About Maisy?"

"She's back in San Diego. No notes since February. No progress, either, I'm afraid."

"What do you make of the notes starting and stopping like that?"

"I don't know, Alec. It must be that the guy knows her movements, including major events like arriving in and leaving Boston. It could be that she's carrying her trouble with her."

"I don't understand."

I explained my views on Tucker Hebert and Manolo.

Bacall lolled his head from side to side on the linen. "I don't know much about investigating people, but I think I do know something about judging them. It just can't be Manolo or Tuck, John."

"I don't see many other prospects right now."

"Will you stay with it?"

207

"As long as I'm needed. Or wanted."

"Thank you." Bacall's pupils wandered, and his eyes closed. I'd almost turned to go when the lids rose. "John?"

"Yes?"

"I said I was a good judge of people, but sometimes being too close blurs the vision. How do you think Del is doing?"

"He's still smiling."

A forced laugh. "Do you know, do you know what is really unfair about his generation?"

"No."

"The smiles. Or, more precisely, the teeth themselves. Like half the kids his age, Del's never had a cavity."

"You're kidding?"

"Not kidding. Never, not one. The fluoridation came a little late for you and me, but he's never even *heard* a dentist's drill up close."

"Doesn't seem fair."

"No." Bacall hesitated. "No, it doesn't seem fair at all." Another hesitation. "I'm feeling pretty sleepy, John." He released the ball, and it sought the depression his hip made in the bed. "See you soon, eh?"

I took his hand the way he offered it, like a black solidarity shake. "Take care, Alec."

Closing the door behind me, I watched Wonsley get up. "Alec said he was getting sleepy."

"They keep him pretty well sedated. That's one of the problems, balancing all the different dosages."

"I have kind of a hard question."

Wonsley's tongue darted between his teeth and back again. "Ask it."

"He looks so much worse than the last time I saw him. Should I be—"

"Trying to visit him more often?"

"That's not how I wanted to sound, but basically, yes, that's my question."

"Like I said, I think Alec will come around from this bout. But he's not responding well to the drugs, and if that doesn't—well, it's no secret from you what we'll do then."

I dropped my voice. "The hospital will go along with that?"

"The only way it can. The doctor will let me sign Alec out for a home visit while he's back on an upswing so we don't need all those tubes and shit. Then Alec and I will enjoy the upswing as long as it lasts. When it's downhill again, I'll do for him."

Without my saying anything, Wonsley continued. "I grew up in Chicago, John, South Side. My daddy, he'd take me to the lake, Lake Michigan. We'd go down to a la-de-dah yacht club like Columbia, by where Monroe hits Lakeshore, and we'd fish from the concrete walls. Back then it was lamprey time. Not much salmon, but plenty of perch and other runts for me. Man, that water was blue. Like a glacier melting into a stream, blue like it would hurt your eyes. You don't expect that.

"Well, after my daddy died, I tried going to the lake alone. I found out something real important. I could still fish, because he'd taught me how to do it right. It wasn't as much fun without him, but it was still good.

"I'm going to lose Alec, John. I know roughly when, and I'm going to see to it that I know exactly when. And after I lose him, life won't be so good for a while. But Alec's helped teach me how to live, and it'll get better. I can't stop AIDS from taking him, but I can stop it from taking me too."

Wonsley drew in a breath. "So, if you need anything else, you give us a call."

"I will. But if I don't, let me know when he's coming home the last time?"

The tongue darting again, Wonsley nodded quickly and entered Bacall's room.

28

FROM A TRAINING STANDPOINT, THE LAST HALF OF MARCH AND the first half of April were the worst. Wild changes in the weather. Teens one morning, forties the next. Blizzard snow to blinding sun. As the longer distances in Bo's program climbed past fourteen miles, I learned where the working water fountains were. The second floor of the Harvard Boathouse. The rest room of the MDC rink on Nonantum Road. I carried change in my pocket for sugar drinks at convenience stores in Newton and Watertown.

Medically, I stayed healthy, but my knees and hips began to hurt after ten miles each time. I started to wonder if legs were like tires, only so many miles in them before they blew. But hurting or not, I finished each run, gaining confidence that I could go as far as I had to, maybe even twenty-six miles.

The Andrus case, however, stayed dead while she completed her visitorship in San Diego. Juggling an arson investigation and a missing person matter, I couldn't understand it. Sending notes only sporadically might avoid diluting their effect, but there hadn't been any activity since the sniping incident in February. Granted, Andrus hadn't been back in Boston, either, but Hebert or Manolo, or whoever, must have had some kind of timetable, some overall strategy. I just wasn't seeing it.

* * *

"I've taken you about as far as I can, John."

I stopped stretching against a tree. The Wednesday before the marathon, I'd just finished a tapering run of six miles. The April sun was warm, so I was wearing only shorts and a long-sleeved T-shirt.

"Less than a week left, Bo."

Sitting on his bench, the man moved a shoulder inside the two sweaters he still wore. Tied around his waist were two other layers and the sport jacket, a green carnation from the holiday wilted in its lapel. "What I mean is, there's nothing left to tell you."

"How about hanging around anyway, see if I finish on Monday?"

"No need. I know you'll finish. Besides, the race herself is part of your life, John, not mine."

"I'd still like you to be there."

"No. No, I think maybe I'll go somewheres else. This climate, it doesn't have much of a springtime. Hell of a winter, but no spring." He fingered the carnation. "I think I'd like to be someplace I'll see live flowers this side of June."

Bo stood, wiping his right hand elaborately on a sweater, then extending the hand to me. "Good luck, eh?"

I took it. "Thank you, Coach."

He shook his hand loose from mine and pulled the Redskins cap down tighter with it. "Remember to do that last tune-up distance on Friday, now."

"I will."

Turning away, Bo stuck both hands in his pants pockets and began to walk upriver. He paused once, taking the left hand out to remove his glasses and pass a sleeve over his eyes.

When I got home from the office that evening, there was a message on the tape machine from Inés Roja. Maisy Andrus, Tucker Hebert, and Manolo had flown in from the coast a day early because Hebert was leaving that afternoon for a tennis exhibition in Europe. Trying the number at the town house, I got a busy signal.

I showered and pulled on some clean sweat clothes. As I tied the drawstrings to the pants, the telephone rang in the living room.

"John Cuddy."

"John, John! It is Inés, Inés Roja."

"What's—"

"The note, John! There was just now another note in our mailbox here!"

"At the house?"

"It says 'TONIGHT YOU DIE BITCH.' "

"Call the police. Nine one one. I'm on my way."

I put on my training shoes and took the four-inch Combat Masterpiece from the closet. Due to the one-wayness of the streets, it was literally faster to run the seven blocks than to drive them.

Reaching the front door of the Andrus house, I couldn't hear any sirens, but the cops might be coming with just flashers. Somebody was shouting inside. I grabbed the door handle to crash it, but the handle turned in my hand, opening the door. Going through it into the foyer, I could hear Inés Roja clearly.

From somewhere above, she was crying out, "He is going to shoot the professor! He is going to shoot the professor!"

I started up the staircase.

Suddenly Roja appeared at the top. "Oh, John, he is going to shoot the professor!"

I got out "Where—" when Manolo barreled into Inés, pushing her off balance. He fired at me before I saw the rifle clear the balustrade. Something tore at the waist of the sweatshirt, a searing sensation in my left side. Reflexively, I pulled the trigger, rocking Manolo at the left shoulder but not putting him down.

I dropped back a step to steady my weapon as he worked the bolt on the rifle. My foot slipped a little on the stair, my second shot missing as Manolo raised the rifle as high as his shoulder would allow. Inés lunged at him, cuffing his arm as he fired and sending his next bullet wild. Manolo bellowed as he pushed her off, the first sound I'd ever heard him make.

Steadied, I fired three more times, each slug punching Manolo in the chest, the rifle dropping from his hands. He bucked off the wall, his palms coming together and twisting on the wrists, like a shortstop handcuffed by a bad hop. Staggering forward, Manolo pitched through the balustrade, the staircase quaking as he struck the Oriental rug on the first floor.

As I moved toward her, Inés Roja was sobbing in two languages at once.

29

NEELY SAID, "CHRIST, MY WATCH STOPPED. IS IT WEDNESDAY OR Thursday?"

Patiently, Murphy said, "Thursday, twelve-fifteen A.M."

Neely spoke to himself as he wrote. "Mass General, Room 309."

Murphy said to me, "The Roja woman didn't tell us anything at the scene about saving your life."

Three pillows propped me up in bed. I shifted my rump to the left, the drain in my side starting to burn as badly as the bullet had. "She was pretty shook up, Lieutenant. Might not even remember hitting his arm. How is she now?"

"Zonked. The M.E. gave her something just after he pronounced Manolo."

Neely looked up from his pad. "M.E. had to say it three times, the way you aced him there."

I turned back to Murphy. "How about Andrus herself?"

"She went back to sleep. The woman gets home from the coast, all 'jet-lagged,' she said. When she wasn't bitching at us about messing up her house. Said she took some pills, went to bed, slept through the whole thing, firefight and all."

"Nobody else in the house, right?"

"You got there before we did. Roja never called it in. Said she was about to when she heard Manolo heading toward the professor's bedroom."

Neely was doodling. Murphy was biding his time.

I said, "There are some things wrong here, Lieutenant."

"Like what?"

"Manolo had plenty of motive and opportunity on the notes. Even on the sniping incident last month."

"I'm goosing ballistics to give us a quick read on whether the slugs from tonight match those. The weapon Manolo used was a Remington."

"You might check with Ray Cuervo, the son from Spain. He said his father had one of those as a hunting arm."

Neely stopped doodling. "So what doesn't add up, Cuddy?"

"First, Manolo's supposed to be doing this for revenge, right?"

Murphy said, "Go ahead."

"Wouldn't you think he'd wait till she was awake?"

"Again?"

"Manolo wants to avenge the killing of his father figure. Pass for now that it takes him over ten years to work up to it. He decides to bust Andrus with a hunting rifle that maybe belonged to the old doctor. Poetic justice. But wouldn't you think Manolo would wait till she was awake?"

Murphy thought about it. Neely looked lost.

Murphy said, "You mean because of the notes."

"Right. Guy intends to scare her with the notes, especially that last one tonight, wouldn't you think he'd be sure she was awake enough to read the last one and be in terror? And wouldn't you think he'd hold off shooting her till she was looking at him, eyes open?"

Neely said, "So maybe the Roja woman surprised him. Who knows?"

Murphy said, "Anything else?"

"Yeah. Manolo seemed to think of himself as being in charge of the house security. Even if he's going to kill Andrus, maybe especially if he's going to kill her after she reads tonight's note, wouldn't you think he'd have made sure the front door was locked?"

"Was the front door ever unlocked?"

"Not that I know of."

"So it's more like he must have unlocked it on purpose before he started after the professor."

"And why would he do that?"

Murphy rubbed his chin. "Expecting somebody."

"And probably not me."

Neely said, "I don't get it."

Murphy said, "It's thin, but this Manolo leaves the front door open, maybe he expected a guest for the execution."

Neely looked from Murphy to me to Murphy. "Aw, fuck. You mean this ain't the end of it?"

The next time I opened my eyes, Dr. Paul Eisenberg and Nancy Meagher were standing over me. "Don't tell me I slept until visiting hours?"

Nancy shook her head. "Ever the adolescent."

Eisenberg said, "I was coming up to check on you anyway. I heard Ms. Meagher threatening the nurses' station with dire legal consequences if she wasn't permitted to see you, so I included her on my rounds."

I said, "How did I draw you, Doctor?"

"I was on duty last night. Heard about a private investigator shooting someone, getting shot himself, and being rushed here as the closest facility. A nice change of pace from the ordinary, if you'll forgive my saying so."

"So you're not on the case as my specialist for internal medicine."

"Oh, no. No problems that way."

"The slug missed all the vital stuff?"

"Completely. Just gouged a wormtrail through the bit of fat you've got over that left hip. You're in pretty good shape."

Nancy said, "He was training for the marathon."

"Am training for the marathon."

Nancy said, "No."

I said, "Yes."

Eisenberg said, "You mean, to run the Boston Marathon this Monday?"

"Any reason I can't?"

Nancy turned away and began pacing. "I can't be hearing this right."

The doctor combed his beard. "It's not my call medically, but physically, it's certainly not a good idea."

Nancy said, "Listen to the man."

"I didn't even take any stitches."

Eisenberg came over, lifted my johnny coat. "We let a gunshot heal from below. If we closed it over with sutures, an abscess might form." He dropped my coat.

"So it's not that bad, right?"

"A bullet makes a dirty wound, Mr. Cuddy. The slug itself, fibers it introduces from your clothes."

"But you washed all that out."

"We used a saline solution to irrigate the area, yes."

I said, "If I run, what's the worst that can happen?"

Nancy said, "John, you're a dunce."

Eisenberg looked skeptical. "The wound could weep through the dressing, perhaps even break open. You'd lose some blood and risk an infection."

"So if I run and the worst happens, I won't die before I finish the race, right?"

"Right. But you could be very sick thereafter."

"Which means I might be on antibiotics and maybe in bed for a while?"

"Probably."

"If the wound breaks open."

"Yes, but you'll also be rather weak to start with."

"Any weaker than if I'd had a bout of the flu?"

Eisenberg said, "Honestly? Probably not as weak as the flu would make you."

I looked at Nancy and shrugged. She crossed her arms and stalked out.

I was saying good-bye to Room 309 when I heard a knock. "Come in."

Inés Roja opened the door a little. "You are all right?"

"Come on in, Inés."

She closed it behind her. "I wanted to thank you."

"I'm the one who should thank *you*."

When Roja looked puzzled, I described her hitting Manolo's arm and throwing off his aim.

A shake of the head. "I do not remember doing that."

"Things were happening pretty fast."

"After I called you, I heard a noise downstairs. I searched for something, anything, as a weapon, but there was nothing I could see. Then Manolo was coming up the stairs with a rifle. I tried to talk to him, to sign to him, but he kept moving toward the professor's room, pushing me away. I didn't know what to do. I was shouting, but she wouldn't wake up. Then I heard you and . . . and the rest you saw."

"Are you all right?"

"Yes." Roja lowered her eyes. "No. No, I am not. I cannot seem to do anything to please the professor."

"She's probably upset too."

"No, no. She was like this before . . . Manolo. From the time she came in the door from the plane. Nothing can please her, everything makes her angry. I think the reason Tuck left so soon for the tournament is because even he cannot stand to be around her."

"She'll ride it out."

Roja bit her lip. "Today the professor said she would not need me for a while. That I could just as well leave."

"What are you going to do?"

"I don't want her to be alone in that house, but that is what she wants."

"Can't Hebert come home early from the tournament?"

"The professor says she does not want him either. I could use a vacation from all that has happened, but I want to tell you something first. So that you will still watch over her."

"What is it?"

"I helped Manolo with his English since I worked for the professor."

"Yes?"

Roja bit her lip again, facing the floor. "I saw all the notes. I do not think Manolo could write . . . could compose them alone."

She looked up, tears brimming. "I think someone else must have helped him, John."

30

THE VIETNAMESE DOCTOR WHO DISCHARGED ME THURSDAY morning insisted that I ride a wheelchair and elevator to the public entrance. It was a blue-skied sixty degrees, and my body was balky from the hospital bed. I decided to walk off my stay before going to see Maisy Andrus.

Winding down Cambridge Street, I took Charles to the Public Garden, my side feeling a little tight but not hurting. In the garden, the curly-haired man who oversees the flower beds was directing a couple of helpers with wheelbarrows containing clumps of pansies and other more exotic bloomers. A big van with R. B. COOKE & SON, INC./PACKERS AND MOVERS was backed down to the Swan Pond. The workers were unloading detached shells of white swans. Already on the lawn were red and green benches. A couple of other guys were lashing green pontoons to the dock.

I sat for an hour or so, watching the flowers get planted so that people could see and smell them. Watching the swans and benches get hoisted over the pontoons so mothers and fathers could bring little kids for their first rides on them. Everybody getting ready for spring. There are worse ways to come back to life.

I got up and walked west on the Commonwealth boulevard. Dogs were leaping for Frisbees, and college kids were playing hacky-sack.

A couple of yuppies in madras bermudas hosed the winter from their bay windows.

I reached Fairfield and went up to the condo. I tried Murphy, who wasn't in, then Neely, who was. I started to explain what Inés Roja had told me.

"Cuddy, Cuddy. Hold on a minute, okay?"

"Hold for what?"

"No, I mean just wait like, all right? Hear me out."

"Go ahead."

"Murphy calls me this morning, he's got the ballistics report already. The flattened slug from the mailbox is a match for the ones we dug out of the plaster from where Manolo tried to whack you."

"So the slugs match."

"So what does that tell you?"

"That the same rifle probably was used in both the sniping at us and the shooting at me."

"Tells me more than that, pal. Tells me that Manolo was the shooter, both times."

"Maybe he was. That—"

"We found a rag there, closet of his room at the manse. Oil on the rag's same as the oil on the rifle."

"Neely, just because—"

"What I'm saying here is, you got the right guy, okay?"

"Neely, what I'm saying is that there might be another guy involved. Somebody to help Manolo write the notes, maybe get him stirred up about the professor injecting her husband way back when. Get it?"

"That's the line you were pushing at the hospital. Just what do you got besides Manolo of the Morgue there?"

I repeated what Roja said about the notes and suggested police protection for Maisy Andrus.

"Cuddy, I got to tell you, I don't see it that way. We got a sniping, we got a match on the slugs, we got the gun, we got the dead guy with the gun. You got smoke and mirrors."

"What will it take, Neely?"

"To put a uniform on her door?"

"Yes. Round the clock."

"Never happen. She's got the money, she can hire somebody. Like you, for instance."

* * *

219

From inside the town house came "Go away."

I leaned my forehead against her unopened front door and spoke louder. "Professor, we have to talk."

"I see no need for that. Please just go away."

"Not until I've finished what I started for you. It won't take long."

I heard a sound of exasperation as Andrus yanked open the door.

The eyes burned out from a taut face. Her hair was tousled here and matted there, as though she hadn't brushed it since sleeping on it. A breath of warm air from behind me rustled some of the loose strands. Andrus shuddered violently and moved behind the door.

I barely got in before she closed it.

Andrus shook again. "Can't stand drafts."

"Are you all right?"

Her head ratcheted up. "I'm fine! Or I would be if I weren't being interrupted every five minutes. What is it, Mr. Cuddy?"

Wondering what happened to "John," I gestured toward the parlor.

Andrus made a noise that actually sounded like "harrumph" as she strode in ahead of me and sat rigidly on a wing chair. "What?"

"First, I'm sorry about Manolo."

"Manolo? A traitor! Do you realize what my husband *did* for him? What *I* did for him? He deserved what happened."

I had the sensation of speaking to a different person, another member of a family whose personality diverged one hundred eighty degrees from the rest.

"Does your husband know?"

"Sir, my husband is d— Oh. Oh, you mean Tuck, don't you? I've left messages for him, but we keep missing each other."

"You mean, he doesn't know about all this?"

"It is not the sort of thing one can synopsize for a Parisian hotel operator."

"Don't you think he ought to come home for you?"

"No. No, I don't, not that it's any of your business. I am hardly the damsel in distress here. This is my home, and I am perfectly capable of living in it alone for as long as I desire."

"Inés Roja said you—"

"Mr. Cuddy. I prefer to be alone right now. Alone means no Tuck, no Inés, and no you."

"Professor, Inés thinks Manolo may have had help."

"What on earth are you talking about?"

220

I started in about the notes.

Andrus threw up her hands. "Out, Mr. Cuddy! I have been betrayed, betrayed by a man I thought loyal to me and to my family. That will take some getting over, and I would prefer to do so on my own, without your irrelevant inquiries and whether that meets with your approval or not."

She got up, but I didn't turn to go.

"Professor, have you seen a doctor?"

"I was not injured last night. Thanks to you, I'm told. Don't worry. You will be compensated for that, and I'll cover any medical bills."

Andrus went to push me toward the door. I hit her at each shoulder with the heels of my hands, sending her reeling back two steps.

The eyes burned again. "How dare you!"

"Can't you see yourself? Your appearance, your attitude."

"What I see, sir, is a trespasser and a batterer who used to work for me. Are you leaving?"

"Yes."

Staying out of the warm breeze, she slammed the door behind me.

On Friday morning I decided to spare my side the warm-up run but walk over to the river anyway. Bo wasn't there, but hundreds of obvious marathoners were, just jogging loosely for a few miles, getting the kinks out toward the race three days later.

By Saturday I figured Nancy might have cooled off enough to talk with me. The A.D.A. who answered at the courthouse said no one had seen her, and there was no answer at her apartment. When I tried Maisy Andrus, I had to wait fifteen rings before she picked up. Her voice was hoarse, like she'd been using it to yell. Telling me "positively for the last time" to butt out, she hung up.

By Sunday I was feeling restless and a little lonely. I walked over to the Hynes Convention Center for the Marathon Expo.

The building was filled with everything that ever had to do with running and a lot that didn't. Displays of the old-time shoes and shorts and singlets. Clips of Jesse Owens humbling Hitler in the thirties and Roger Bannister breaking the four-minute mile in the fifties. Longer pieces on Bill Rodgers in the seventies edging into Joan Benoit in the eighties. All watched reverently by probably the biggest, slimmest crowd the Hynes had ever hosted.

But after a while, being jostled this way and that, I felt nostalgia yielding to commercialism. How-to books and exercise videos, health foods and vitamin supplements, rowing machines and stationary treadmills. Uncountable cross-sectioned shoes in front of as many sales reps trumpeting arch support and heel stability. College kids working for restaurants and handing out discount flyers for beer and pasta "last suppers." I'd been trained by a pro, but I was basically an amateur, a little overwhelmed by the breadth of a sport in which I knew I just dabbled.

At a pay phone I tried Nancy at her apartment again. No answer. Maisy Andrus at the mansion. Busy signal.

I recovered my quarter and walked home.

Coming into the condo, I heard a movement near the kitchen. All I had were my keys and the chance of making the bedroom for a weapon.

"John?" said Nancy's voice from the kitchen.

I exhaled and moved around the corner into the living room. "How did you know it was me?"

She came out of the kitchen. "I could hear your ankles grinding."

Nancy was wearing jeans and one of my old chamois shirts.

I said, "After the session with Eisenberg, I didn't expect to see you for a while."

Her face was flushed, and she used the back of her wrist to wipe away the perspiration. "I thought I'd try to cook you something."

"Unfortunately, I'm down to just pasta for the race."

"I heard that's what they push, so we're having spinach linguini, nonalcoholic beer, and whole-grain crisp-crust bread for your—what is it, your 'carbos'?"

"My carbos."

About midway through the meal and a particularly good hunk of bread, I said, "This mean you don't still think I'm stupid about running the marathon?"

"No. This means I think you are so incredibly *more* stupid for even considering doing it after getting shot that I realized I had to do what I could by way of damage control."

"Nance?"

"What?"

"How long you been working on that line?"

"All afternoon."

"Should have been more concise."

222

"I tried it a lot of different ways. That was the best."

I munched my crisp crust and shut up.

After a moment Nancy said, "So, I'll drive you out there and then come back here."

I put down the bread. "You'll be at the finish line?"

"Reluctantly. But I've got a trial first thing Tuesday, so I can't stay over."

"For once in your life, call in sick."

"Can't. But that reminds me. You should phone Del Wonsley."

"Wonsley?"

"Yes. I heard his voice on your tape machine as I was coming in."

"Did you catch any of the message?"

"Yes." Nancy used a soup spoon to twirl some pasta onto her fork. "Good news, I think. He said Alec Bacall is coming home tomorrow."

31

"IF I HADN'T SEEN IT."

Nancy wagged her head, watching perhaps thirty other people dressed just like me standing in an auxiliary parking lot off Route 495 in Hopkinton. In a rain shower, temperature in the high forties.

I said, "These conditions are supposed to be good for the race."

Nancy made an indescribable noise.

Getting out of her car, I fiddled with the green garbage bag I was wearing, my head through the hole I'd made on top. My fiddling had to be from the inside, because I hadn't cut any arm holes.

"John, please be careful."

"You'll be at the finish line, in the archway of the bank?"

"With the stretcher bearers. Good luck, you jerk."

I closed the passenger door, and she drove off.

A yellow shuttle bus arrived. We trash bags filled it front to back. Inefficient, should have been back to front. Nobody was carrying much, just wearing extra layers against the wind, rain, and cold. Nervous banter, the laughter too hearty.

It was a few miles to a school building. From a van in the circular driveway a kid read incomprehensible instructions over a loudspeaker, presumably for the registered runners. Hundreds of us bandits stood under eaves and overhangs, dodging the raindrops and trying to sound modest about what time we'd finish. A lot of the folks were my age or older, and no one mentioned not finishing.

At eleven-thirty people began moving in throngs toward the street. I followed, the throngs swelling to form their own little parade. We were pointed toward the village green and past the yellow ropes that corralled the sixty-four hundred registered runners, in numerical order, white cardboards with red numerals flapping against breast plates and spinal columns.

At the back of the pack I stripped down to shorts, a cotton turtleneck and the BODY BY NAUTILUS, BRAIN BY MATTEL T-shirt Nancy had given me for Christmas. Balling up my outer clothes, I added them to one of the ragged heaps on the sidewalk.

The crowd buzzed, and the report of the starter's pistol provoked a loud, long cheer. Nobody in my part of the pack moved for a good six minutes. Beginning slowly, I finally crossed the start line at eight minutes after noon, jogging downhill lightly and freely. There was more spring in my step than I expected, and no pain at all from the closing wound in my side.

A remarkable number of people flanked the road despite suburban, even rural, countryside and lousy weather for spectating. The elderly in lawn chairs, holding umbrellas in gnarled hands. Kids in slickers with peaked fronts like the beaks of ducks, splashing both feet in rain puddles. Middle-aged men in Windbreakers and baseball caps, John Deere or Boston Bruin logos, applauding stoically.

An oompah band had fun in a supermarket lot. A country and western group strummed from a truck dealership. Under a carport, a souped-up Dodge Charger idled, trunk lid up and facing the street, two stereo speakers booming out the theme from *Chariots of Fire*.

A younger woman running my pace paired up with me, and we talked in brief, grunted sentences. At one point we had to veer around a video crew in street clothes, gamely jogging beside a TV reporter who was doing her first marathon and providing the station with a "running" commentary.

There were other funny things early in the race, so many I missed a few of the mile markers as I got caught up in the atmosphere. A guy in a Viking helmet. Two women in tuxedos and top hats. A brawny gray-head in a strappy undershirt wearing a coat-hanger crown, the hook dangling an empty Budweiser can a foot in front of his mouth.

And the T-shirts. Every conceivable college and university, but also some with legends. LES MISERABLES. SAY NO TO DRUGS. NOT

225

TILL YOU CRY, TRAIN TILL YOU DIE. One man's front read CELIBATE SINCE CHRISTMAS, the back, WATCH THE KICK.

By mile ten, however, the initial adrenaline was gone. Age ache returned to my knees and hips, and my side at the wound began to burn every other step. I found I had to concentrate. Breathe rhythmically. Maintain the stride. Drink lots of liquids. I also found I had to come to a stop to take the water, otherwise I knocked the cup from the offerer's hand and couldn't swallow properly.

My partner pulled up lame at mile eleven. I said I'd wait for her, but dejectedly she said no, it had happened before and wouldn't get better.

After that the images are a little hazy, just kind of strung together.

Passing Boston's Mayor Flynn, a former basketball star at Providence College a couple of academic generations before I hit Holy Cross. I thought back to the tree-lighting ceremony and his short speech, when Nancy almost said the "O" word. Then I looked at Flynn. Hizzoner's face was red as a beet but the legs still churned, what looked like two well-conditioned cops on either side of him. If he could do it, so could I.

The rain perfect for what we were doing, neither too hot nor too cold. My clothing felt like just a particularly moist outer layer of skin.

A blind man and a sighted woman, him jogging her pace, his hand resting lightly on her forearm. Each smiled a lot, but for each other, not the crowd.

The sweet but refreshing tang of Exceed, the orange drink restoring lost chemicals. Just as Bo said it would.

Runners with numbers at the side of the road in agony, clasping blown-out knees or torn Achilles tendons. Members of the crowd put sacrificed jackets around the runners' shoulders as race officials with walkie-talkies tried to raise the sweep bus.

Wellesley College, roughly the midpoint of the race. The young women stood four deep, cheering so wildly I heard them for half a mile before the crest of their hill. Some offered liquids, others paper towels to wipe off the salt caking our legs.

On the downslope, passing a woman in her forties. Cellulite jiggled over the backs of her thighs as she muttered her way through a downpour.

Mile fifteen. The legs no worse, but my left side really throbbing now, no matter which foot was striking the ground. I probed it once with my index finger. Just a little blood seeping through the dressing.

Orange rinds, scattered over the road like autumn leaves, slippery as banana peels. After nearly going down once, I began picking my way around them.

Johnny A. Kelley, eighty years young, exulting in his fifty-seventh marathon. A painter's hat worn backward on his head, he blew kisses to the increased roar he received as each section of the crowd recognized him.

Mile seventeen. Column right onto Commonwealth at the firehouse to begin Heartbreak Hill. Counting the inclines and plateaus to stay oriented, I remembered Bo's advice and kept my eyes on the horizon. Four-fifths of the field were walking, the other twenty percent of us still running, my knees feeling like I was climbing a rope ladder.

Gaining on a father propelling his son in a wheelchair. I realized the man got no rest at all, having to push on the upslopes and then drag on the downslopes. A few of us offered to spell him. The father smiled and shook a drenched head.

Mile twenty-one. Boston College and the top of Heartbreak. Exhilaration, then the incredible bunching pain in the backs of the legs from going downhill. My calves went mushy, and my feet kept tangling. My left side felt like somebody was plowing it with baling hooks.

No functioning water stations for two miles until just below Coolidge Corner, where a guy my age and his kids braved the rain outside a majestic synagogue. They poured from Belmont Springs bottles as fast as they could, all of us thanking them. I remember the daughter saying she thought I was her five thousandth cup that day, my legs warning me not to stop for too long.

The marker said "25" at Kenmore Square. Every joint below my waist had tossed in the towel, the bones sawing and grating against each other. The crowd chanted a single phrase. One more mile, one more mile.

At Hereford Street we made a right toward Boylston. The first ninety-degree turn for a while, I found I had to consciously plan how to do it. An older man in front of me took the corner too fast. His hamstring snapped like a dry branch, and he went down. Several people from the crowd pushed through police barriers to aid him.

I eased left onto Boylston Street, three hundred yards to go. The crowd was still enormous, easily two hours after the technical winners had passed. They screamed, clapped, and whistled, most of us summoning a little extra to acknowledge the encouragement.

The finish line itself was under a viewing stand. Yellow and white awning, beneath it bunting in orange, blue, and white, the colors so vivid through the rain. Crossing the line, I thought I heard Nancy calling my name, the official clock glowing 4:11:31. Not counting water stations, I stopped running for the first time in over four hours.

Hands on hips, I kept walking to postpone the cramping. Scanning the crowd, I looked for an old Redskins cap and taped glasses. Not there. Other runners slumped on the sidewalk or trundled with tiny steps, wrapped in foil-like Mylar blankets to ward off hypothermia.

Under the archway of the bank, Nancy waved to me, holding a little camera high with her left hand, as though she were taking a photo over the heads of people in front of her. "I got you crossing the finish line!"

In yellow foul-weather gear, the peak riding down almost to her nose, she'd never looked more beautiful to me.

I stopped and posed in right profile. Nancy brought the camera to her eye, clicked a button, and put the camera in a coat pocket.

I said, "I heard you yell to me."

"I couldn't believe I could finally go inside."

"I want a hug."

"Not on your life. You're the most disgusting creature I've ever seen."

"What happened to the stretcher bearers?"

"Unionized. They went home at four."

I tried taking another step, cramped, and had to grab a signpost to keep from falling. My hand away from the hip, Nancy got a look at my left side.

She hurried over and steadied me. "John, your shirt's soaked with blood!"

"That's not the problem."

"Then what is?"

"My legs hurt."

"Revelation. Your legs should hurt after you *drive* twenty-six miles."

"Maybe at your age."

That brought a smile. "You're a dunce, John."

"If I can just rest my arm on you . . ."

Nancy took my hand and drew my arm around her shoulder. "That's Dunce, capital D, and I'm worse for loving you."

We moved off like that, medic and soldier, through the crowd still cheering for the people still coming in.

32

BACK AT THE CONDO I TOOK A LONG, SLOW BATH, MY REOPENED side and a blackened toenail the only visible damage. Pride made me crawl over the side of the tub rather than call out to Nancy for help. After I toweled off, I taped a new dressing on my side and got into some clean clothes.

Nancy and I celebrated with pizza delivered by Domino's and ale chilled by refrigerator. The six o'clock news gave extended coverage to the race. It was an out-of-body experience, seeing the start better from a helicopter's point of view than I had at the back of the pack, the winners crossing the finish line in half the time I took.

By eight o'clock I was walking well enough for Nancy to head home and prepare for her trial. Just after she left I thought about trying to see Alec Bacall, which made me think about Maisy Andrus. Fired or not, I couldn't seem to let go.

I picked up the receiver and punched in the number of the Andrus town house. The voice we all recognize said, "I'm sorry, the number you have dialed is not in service at this time. Please—"

Depressing the plunger, I tried again. Same message.

I thought back to Saturday, the hoarse voice. To Sunday, busy, like maybe she'd taken the phone off the hook. Now Monday, not in service, like maybe she'd left it off the hook.

I got the snub-nosed Chief's Special from the bedroom. What was seven blocks after twenty-six miles?

This time, though, I didn't run it.

It was a moonless night, not much activity on the holiday now that the marathon crowd had dispersed. As I turned onto the little mews, there was no one in sight.

I hobbled to the front steps and used the knocker. Nothing. I waited, tried again. Still nothing. Then I heard it.

The sound of glass breaking, followed by a strangled cry.

The door was locked. My legs didn't want to work, but I finally braced a shoulder against the hinge jamb and generated enough force to smash my right foot through the wood at the lock.

Inside the foyer, weapon in hand, I could hear the sounds of a struggle from the kitchen. I crossed to the swinging door, hitting it and diving onto the linoleum.

I slid to a stop three feet from Maisy Andrus, thrashing around on the floor.

Arms outstretched, back arched, her legs pistoned like a brat throwing a tantrum. Her eyes and throat bulged, and her mouth was locked half open, saliva cascading down her chin and cheeks. One leg kicked out, toppling a breakfast stool.

I realized that she was alone. A windowpane over the sink was broken, but only as if something had been thrown through it from the inside. Water drummed from the faucet.

Then Andrus began to choke, and I got on the phone for 911 and the closest hospital I knew before trying to help her.

Dr. Paul Eisenberg came around the corner, a chart in his hand.

I worked my way up from the cheap plastic chair in the waiting room. "How is she?"

The skin on his forehead wrinkled toward the baldness above it. "Not good. Coma, signs very low. Where's her husband?"

"Europe. Tennis tournament in Paris, I think she said."

"He should be notified."

"What the hell is wrong with her?"

Eisenberg consulted the chart. "You told the EMTs that Andrus was choking when you got there?"

"She was having a fit of some kind when I got there. The choking started after that."

"How long before you got to her did the fit start?"

"I don't know for sure. I heard glass breaking, turned out to be a window in the kitchen. I was to her within two, three minutes after that."

"In the kitchen, you say?"

"Yes. I thought it was somebody trying to get at her, but maybe it was her trying to signal for help with the fit."

Eisenberg sighed. "Probably not. Not consciously, I mean. Was there any water near her?"

"Water?"

"Yes."

"Doc, she was writhing on the floor like she'd been gutshot. The only water was the faucet running in the sink."

"And which window was broken?"

"The one over the sink. Why?"

"Have you seen her much the last few weeks?"

"Yes. Well, no, just a couple of times."

"How did she seem to you?"

"Pretty tired. Haggard, even."

"Irritable?"

"Yes. Much more than before she went out to San Diego."

"Sensitive to breezes or drafts?"

I stared at him. "Yes."

"Has she been in any wilderness in the last six months?"

"Wilderness? Not that I know of."

"Camping? Or maybe on a farm?"

"No."

"Out of the continental U.S. at all?"

"No. Wait, yes, down to Sint Maarten."

"Caribbean?"

"Right."

"When?"

"December into January."

Eisenberg jotted something on the chart. "Incubation period is within the brackets. That's a possible, but not likely."

"What's a possible?"

"Sorry. A possible source of the infection."

"What infection?"

"You have to understand, we don't see this anymore, not in cities. I saw it only twice in Brazil, and I don't think there have been six deaths in the whole U.S. over the last—"

232

"Dr. Eisenberg, what the hell is wrong with her?"

He told me.

"Sweet Jesus of God."

I lay awake until after midnight Monday, when the effects of the marathon finally overcame everything else. Tuesday morning I got on the phone. First, I called in a favor from a friend at an airline. He patched his computer into four other carriers before finding what I needed to know and making reservations for me too. By Tuesday afternoon my legs were recovered enough to drive south to Providence. I hand-carried Steven O'Brien from counting beans at work to leafing through old clippings at home. Just to be certain.

When I got back to Boston, I dialed Mass General. Paul Eisenberg's voice told me Maisy Andrus had died two hours earlier.

That left only one stop more.

"Oh. John."

Del Wonsley's voice and face both showed surprise in seeing me. "I was afraid you might not have gotten my message."

A polite way to ask what the hell had taken me so long.

"Can I come in?"

"Oh, sure. Sorry."

I stepped over the threshold into a first-level entry, the walls lined with tapestries.

Wonsley said, "Please, come up."

We climbed the stairs of the Bay Village town house to a second, living room floor. Two men I'd never seen were there, chatting quietly over cheese and crackers and fruit. The men looked surprised, too, as if they had been expecting Wonsley to bring up someone they knew.

Wonsley introduced us, then said, "Would you like to see Alec?"

"If I can."

"I think he'd like that."

Wonsley led me up another flight to a door off the corridor, then whispered so no one below us or behind the door could hear him.

"Try not to stay too long."

"How strong is he?"

Wonsley's tongue darted out and back. "As strong as he'll ever be. Why?"

"I should ask him some things and tell him some things."

"John, it . . . it won't matter soon."

"Tomorrow?"

"I think so. He's asked me to be ready then."

Wonsley went downstairs, and I opened the door.

The bedroom was dark, just some muted track lighting near the four-poster. Alec's head was framed by the pillows under and behind it. The covers were pulled up close to his chin, the left arm out but with no tubes in it. There was a lot of medicinal stuff on the night table beside him. Small bottles of pills and tablets, the leather case holding some ampules of insulin, a couple of syringes in cellophane blister packs arrayed around it. From two corners I could hear solo piano, a stereo secreted somewhere.

I got close enough to Alec for him to become aware of me.

"John? John, good to see you."

Much of the hair was gone. Deep pouches under the eyes shaded his cheekbones like a charcoal sketch.

"Alec."

His hand came up from the comforter a few inches. I took it, felt him squeeze. I squeezed back with a little less pressure.

"Del called you?"

"Yes."

The wry smile. "I'm afraid the time for makeup has passed. Something about Maisy?"

He hadn't heard. I thought about what I'd gone there to tell him, thought about how I'd want to spend the time if I were Bacall. Thought about Beth.

I said, "No, Alec. I came to have that talk."

His eyes asked the question.

"About life," I said.

After a short while he drifted off in mid-sentence, breathing pretty steadily. I squeezed his hand one more time and said good-bye.

33

FROM BEHIND THE WHEEL, ANGEL SAID, "YOU SEE, ESPAÑA IS not a morning country."

I nodded at him as we bounced around another bright but unpopulated corner in Gijón, a picturesque city that reminded me of New Orleans. My passenger seat was black leatherette with no headrest, an after-market chrome stickshift rising from a rubber nipple on the floor. The speedometer optimistically suggested that Angel's SEAT 600 was capable of hitting 120 kilometers per hour, or about seventy-two mph. I decided the plastic Virgin Mary on the dashboard couldn't hurt.

The flight that was supposed to leave Kennedy at eight-thirty P.M. didn't actually take off until ten-thirty. I cadged a nap during the six and a half hours in the air, but with an additional time difference of six hours, it was 11:00 A.M. Spain time before the plane landed in Madrid. At customs, the officer in a tan shirt and black epaulets checked only my passport, not the small duffel bag.

In Madrid, a cab took me to the *Estación del norte,* a magnificent marble building with an orange tile roof and an elaborate, platformed interior. Unfortunately, the next train to Gijón wasn't until ten P.M. My own body clock was so screwed up that I was more hungry than sleepy. For lunch, I had a *menu de día* that turned out to be four courses, wine included. The weather was pleasant, and my joints were still sore from the marathon, so to loosen up I walked around Madrid for a few hours. Grand public buildings and banks, ornate gold work bordering the doors and windows, blackened statues on the parapets. Food stores with hams and legs of lamb hanging in the windows, large whole fish staring blankly from beds of cracked ice. Men and women with lottery tickets attached by clothespins to strings around their necks, crying out extended syllables like 1930s newsboys hawking an extra edition. The entrance line for the Prado Museum, a clever entrepreneur plying the captive parents by block-printing the names of sons or daughters in the matador-of-the-day space on bullfighting posters.

I slept a little during the train ride north to Gijón. A taxi strike was in progress when we arrived at six A.M. I wasted another couple of hours before Angel, a scholarly looking guy of thirty, befriended me. I'd had the foresight to cash two hundred dollars into pesetas before I'd boarded the plane in New York, and we agreed on a fair price for driving me where I wanted to go. Now, in the car, I found I had to focus on what Angel was saying to follow him at all.

"You see, the Alcalde, how you say it, the major of the city?"

"Mayor."

"*Sí, sí,* the mayor. He want to make the taxis to forty more, but the drivers, they say no. They have the *huelga,* the strike, *sí?*"

"Right."

"Like from the *beisbol?*"

"Same word, different meaning."

"*Sí, sí.*" Angel swerved around a piece of lumber in the road. "You will stay in Gijón when we get back?"

"I'm not sure."

"You should stay in our city. Gijón is a better city from Madrid. No much expensive, good food, less persons. No crimes, you don't lock the doors in the night. Most days, we have the rain, but for you, the sunshine."

We left Gijón behind and began winding through the countryside. Full morning light lifted the dew from green hills, occasional glimpses of the ocean to our right. Except for the curvature of the earth, I could have seen the south of England.

We'd been paralleling the coast for a few miles when Angel pointed. "The *corrida* of Candás you ask me for."

A line of stone cabanas overlooked a jettied beach. Some small fishing boats were grounded on the sand, mooring lines swaying up to the cabanas. Part of the jetty curved around, creating an enclosure that might be dry at low tide.

I said, "Slow down a little, please."

Angel did. A ritzy outdoor café was opening on the town side of the bullring, white tables and chairs under red umbrellas.

"A man of great sculpture live here before they kill him. He was name Anton. There is a *museo* just for him. You have the time for it?"

"Maybe later." The cliff was rugged, dotted with gulls hovering and landing. The promontory rose about a hundred feet from jagged rocks poking through the surf. I didn't see what I was looking for. "Can we drive around a bit?"

"Around the town?"

"Yes."

"*Sí*. Candás is a nice town, you see."

We drove through narrow streets, cobblestoned walkways covered against the climate by the overhang of buildings. Little cottages of beige stucco under orange roofs, flower boxes and pots in the windows. A carefully restored theater commanded the main drag.

"Can we drive up, Angel?"

"Up? *Sí*, up."

We ascended and rounded a curve, and there it was. I let him go past, keeping track of where it was as we continued on.

After a few blocks I said, "I'd like to walk for a while. Choose a bar to sit in, drinks on me."

"I can walk you, tell you some things."

"I'd rather try it on my own. Can I leave the duffel bag here in the car?"

Angel shrugged and parked under a sign that said *Cerveza*.

I approached the house, catching just the perspective in the photo on Ray Cuervo's bookshelf at the veal plant. Peeking through blinds, I couldn't see anyone. I tried the front door. Unlocked.

I entered the house of the late Dr. Enrique Cuervo Duran. A lot of dark beams contrasted with rough plaster on ceilings and some walls. Beneath my feet the reddish tile on the floor was set in black grout, the staircase Ray Cuervo had described stretching upward in front of me. I stood still long enough to be sure no one was moving in the house. Beyond the staircase I came into a room with a view of both the ocean and the bullring below, some gulls hanging and wheeling in the air currents above the cliff.

On the lawn, Inés Roja lounged in one of two chairs, perhaps twenty feet from the edge of the drop-off. A small wicker table sat between her and the empty chair. On the table stood a dark green wine bottle and a single, clear glass, like an iced tea tumbler. Roja's hands were folded in her lap, chin tilted into the sun, eyes closed.

I walked outside, the breeze freshening as I reached her. Resplendent in a long-sleeved dress over sandals, she turned her head slowly to me. The black hair was slicked back, held in place by dainty silver combs. As her eyes opened, a lazy smile crossed her face.

"Not surprised, Inés?"

"I was expecting you." She motioned at the other chair. "You will have some cider?"

"No thanks."

"A pity. It is new *sidra,* just opened. It will be very sweet."

"No."

When I stayed standing, Roja got to her feet, picking up the bottle in one hand, the glass in the other. She held the bottle high over her head and the tumbler at waist level.

Pouring three inches of cloudy yellow liquid in an exaggerated arc into the tumbler, Roja said, "To carbonate the *sidra.*" She held the glass up to the sunlight and spoke to it. "The professor is dead, then?"

I waited a beat. "Yes."

A dreamy smile this time. "And you have come to kill me."

"No, Inés."

"Then to . . . arrest me."

I didn't say anything to that.

Roja shook her head. After drinking the cider down, she poured another few ounces. Back in her chair, Roja set the bottle on the table and sipped from the glass. "Sit, John."

I couldn't see any weapons. Angling the empty chair away from the cliff, I sank into it. "You seem awfully at home here for a refugee from Cuba."

Roja closed her eyes. "If you have come this far, that tragic tale no longer persuades you."

"It doesn't. Still, the *Marielito* story was clever: nobody would inquire too much about a Cuba you never knew. Of course, your father didn't die on a boat at sea."

A small grimace.

"Your father committed suicide, here in Candás. Just after his cover-up came to light."

"Does it amuse you to hurt me, John?"

Roja's tone was flat, emotionless.

I short-formed Steven O'Brien's clippings in Providence. "Your father was Luis Loredo Mendez, basically the local prosecutor. His old friend Dr. Enrique was dying. The doctor had saved the life of the prosecutor's young wife, Monica Roja Berrocal, in childbirth. Your mother, Inés, having you. Your father looked the other way when Maisy Andrus helped the doctor along. When everything came out, your father was disgraced."

Tears began to gather next to the nose under each lid.

"He killed himself, you and your mother leaving Spain for New York. Eventually, you found out that Andrus was still rich and famous, while you and your mother—"

"Lived in a rathole, John." Same flat tone, no trace of rancor. "A vile, crumbling tenement in the Bronx. I spent years thinking about Maisy Andrus, about what she had done to my family. While my mother died slowly, cleaning for other people of means like the good professor."

I lowered my voice. "So you got the job as her secretary in Boston."

"Yes."

"How?"

Roja finished her glass and poured some more, minus the exaggerated arc. "It was easy. Growing up in New York, I read the newspapers, articles about the great Maisy Andrus. Giant of the law, champion of those without hope. But I never forgot what she did to us. Last year, the week my mother died, I saw such an article. It was . . . intolerable. I took the train to Boston. I went to the law school, to see Andrus. To think out a proper way to kill her.

"But the great professor was interviewing for a new secretary that day. She came from her office, hardly glancing at me. 'Are you my next interview?' she said. Realizing she did not recognize me, I said yes. In her office, Andrus said, 'What is your name?' I replied in the American fashion, 'Inés L. Roja.' I was thinking to add 'The L is for Loredo,' my father's surname, when she said, 'I have property

239

in Spain. If you speak Spanish, it would be a great help to me.' If Andrus had not done that, I don't know how I would have dealt with her."

"But she did."

"So poor with the memory of names, so ignorant of our language and culture. She did not recognize even my mother's surname."

"And that gave you the idea."

"Yes." The dreamy smile again. "Manolo had never met me here, and her stepson Ramón never visited the law school or her home in Boston. I decided it would be better to stay close to her for a time. To make her die slowly, like those she had hurt."

"The reason you volunteered for the AIDS clinic."

A shiver. "It was horrible. But I learned. I learned that the AIDS was a fitting death for the good professor. However, it was uncertain and could take years in the coming. That was too long."

"So you went to the veterinary clinic instead."

"I read first. I researched and studied until I found what I wanted. Then I went to the clinic. A doctor there was beginning a new project. He needed help. It took me only a short time to gain his confidence."

"And then it wasn't so hard to get what you needed."

"I knew the incubation period could vary, so I had to be careful." Roja took more cider. "But when she comes back from her rich-lady vacation in the Caribbean, she has a little problem from a mosquito bite. It is nothing, but it is enough."

Andrus had said that it was like someone's spit on her neck. "So that's how you administered the rabies."

The voice of a teacher, explaining the instructions to a test. "I scrape the skin. I watch the little points of blood come up. I have the saliva specimen on a gauze pad, and I spread it on her. Later she tells me how much her neck itches. I know from then that I have done it, that I now can just wait and enjoy it."

There was something very wrong. Roja was too calm, feeding it to me too freely. "The notes, Inés. Why the notes?"

"To bring on her worry. To ruin her peace of mind even before I have the chance to give her the rabies. Do you see? To make her think about dying, like my father, my mother. And me."

"The notes were risky."

"Yes, but I researched them as well. I read the files of hate letters she received. I made certain that my notes sounded as though a man had sent them."

"Why did you come to me?"

Roja frowned. "The notes in the mail were not working on Andrus, John. Not even the one I put in the mailbox of the house. I got Alec concerned about them, but he could not cause the great professor to worry either. Even when I went to the police, the idiot Neely I know will never think of me. No, even then she is not upset enough."

"So you bring me in, to make it seem like something she should be worrying about."

"Yes."

"That was taking a bigger risk, wasn't it?"

The dreamy smile was making me chilly. "You flatter yourself, John. It was *some* risk. But I needed you for another reason also."

I said, "Manolo."

A gentle tipping of the head. "Manolo fired the shots at us. Outside the house, to make the good professor more scared, but also to keep everyone thinking it is a man behind the notes. A rifle is a man's weapon."

I didn't bother to debate her. "How did you get Manolo to do that?"

Roja poured more cider. "I explained to him that a bad man was trying to scare the great professor with the notes, that she had to take the threat more seriously. That he had to help me persuade her."

"So Manolo shoots to miss."

"But to hit the mailbox, to lead you to the new note in it."

"Why didn't you send any notes to San Diego?"

A shrug. "The one at the school had no effect on Andrus when she came back from Sint Maarten. Also, I found the notes were not . . . satisfying unless I was near her, to see her reaction to them as they arrive."

"And last Wednesday night, at the house?"

"Simple. I tell Manolo, 'The professor is in danger, go get your rifle!' Then, downstairs, I unlock the door for you. When Manolo comes back from his room, I sign to him about you. I tell him, 'Cuddy. Cuddy is the bad one.' "

I said, " 'He is going to shoot the professor.' "

Now a wicked smile. "I tell him the same thing I can yell at you when I hear your voice downstairs."

"You hit Manolo's arm, threw off his aim."

"I can't let him kill you." A condescending glance. "I thought you were a professional, that you would shoot him with ease. Then you stumble on the stairs, and I realize that he will kill you. That is not sure enough."

"Not sure enough of Manolo being out of the picture."

"Exactly."

"And you couldn't let him live because—"

"Because he would discover that I killed the woman he took an oath to the old doctor to protect. Manolo would not rest until he found me." The wicked smile again. "That is the other reason I needed you, John. I did not want to die the way Manolo would avenge Andrus's murder."

I kept my voice as neutral as possible. "After that, in the hospital, why did you tell me you thought somebody else was helping Manolo?"

"Because I thought you would see it anyway. Also, I cannot dare being there as she suffers the seizures, so I wanted to be sure you are bothering her with questions. Questions that she would have no patience for as the disease grew within her."

"Why come back here, Inés?"

"To live in this house as my home! Andrus destroyed my family, took my father from my mother and me. We left in shame for what she did. Now the great professor repays her debt."

The pupils danced in Roja's head. "The irony, John, do you see the . . . exquisite irony? Andrus could not live here, not even for a day, because she killed her husband. I will live here, for the rest of my life, because *I* have killed *her*."

"Inés, the Spanish authorities aren't going to allow that."

"You know them so well?"

"I know the police in Boston. And the prosecutors. They'll pursue you through the government here."

"Extradition?" She slurred the word.

I said, "Yes."

"Do you really believe I will let that happen, John?"

"You confessed to me. No compulsion, no threats. The scientific evidence from the autopsy will establish Andrus was killed by rabies."

"Only three persons ever lived once the rabies fit comes. I know, I did my research well." Roja blinked, shifting clumsily in her chair. "Andrus always . . . spouted her message, John, that it is right to die. Now she has become her message. It was right for her to die."

"Inés, I'm going to the police here. They'll hold you for the authorities in the States. The law will catch up to you."

"The law?" Roja laughed, that merry sound from the St. Patrick's Day party. "John, John. The great professor had such faith in the law. So much faith. Well, I do not. When my father was disgraced and Andrus went unpunished, I lost my . . . taste for the law."

Melodramatically, Roja swung her gaze around us. I looked quickly, but saw only a gull, landing at the edge of the cliff.

"This is where I should have spent my life, John. I may have lost my taste for the law, but I have found revenge to be quite sweet." She lifted the tumbler, a little unsteadily. "Like new *sidra* on the tongue."

I was about to tell her she'd had enough when the glass slipped from her hand and thumped onto the grass. Roja's eyes rolled up into her head as she slid down and out of her chair, hitting the ground before I could catch her. The impact knocked loose one of her silver combs.

On my knees, I cradled Roja's head in my right palm. "What did you take?"

Her lips barely moved. "It is too late."

"Inés, what did you put in the cider?"

The eyes came back, but unfocused. "I did all my research well. See, I even cheat the hangman."

"Inés—"

"Tell me, John. Do you really believe in the law?"

The wind whipped a hank of hair across her face. I brushed it away from her mouth. "Like you once said, Inés, I'd rather put my faith in people."

The merry laugh spooked the gull. Its shadow passed over us as Inés Loredo Roja went slack against my hand.